The Shepherd

A Bronze Age Tale

Tristan Nettles

The Shepherd

A Bronze Age Tale

Addison & Highsmith

Addison & Highsmith Publishers

Las Vegas ◊ Chicago ◊ Palm Beach

Published in the United States of America by
Histria Books
7181 N. Hualapai Way, Ste. 130-86
Las Vegas, NV 89166 USA
HistriaBooks.com

Addison & Highsmith is an imprint of Histria Books. Titles published under the imprints of Histria Books are distributed worldwide.

Library of Congress Control Number: 2023948275

ISBN 978-1-59211-384-2 (hardcover)
ISBN 978-1-59211-405-4 (eBook)

This book is dedicated to Ashley,
whose debt I can never repay.

Prelude

"Come on, Ralla, hurry up!" exhorted the younger brother, impatience and excitement each vying for supremacy within his little person who stood off center of the footpath outside their home, looking back expectantly. Twilight would settle into darkness soon. The short chirps of crickets could be heard all around, which seemed to provide the music in which a myriad of fireflies danced along on their curvy courses. "Ra-lla!" the young boy whined out once more just as his sister's frame entered into the yellow light emanating outwards from their front door.

She came out at a run, looking towards him with a mooning smile as she quite quickly covered the ground between them. His little body turned, at first very slowly and then at a faster pace as she passed right by him without even slowing down, giving him a playful bopping on the head as she did so. "Better hurry up, Agarus!" she called back over her shoulder tauntingly. "You don't want to be late!"

Throughout the nearby woods similar scenes played out as one's, two's, three's and sometimes even in four's did the village's children come, meandering their way towards its center in a fast-rising tide. Through the unmarked but intimately well-known trails they came forward out of the growing darkness, carried both by laughter and the pitter-patter of little feet against the well-worn ground.

Ralla and her brother, Agarus, were amongst the very last to spill forth from the many earthen tributaries which emptied into the sudden clearing at the village center. Ralla suddenly stopped upon entering the circle, seeing that most of the others had already arrived. Agarus, running up from behind her only a moment later, did not expect the opening to be thus blocked and so collided into his sister from behind causing them both to tumble out into the silver lit sand. A few of the other children nearest to them who saw the pair's inglorious entrance let out a quick guffaw as Ralla ignominiously began to brush the sand off herself, standing back up as she did so. Agarus, no worse for wear but also suffering from the same sandy coating himself, imitated his sister's response, though without any of the felt embarrassment. He was still too young to suffer from that emotion yet.

"Where are we going to sit, Ralla?" questioned Agarus sincerely, looking up into his sister's face with an adorably bedraggled expression. His imitation had not been very efficient.

"Mm," she started to hum as her head tossed back and forth in search of an answer to his very pertinently pressing question.

"Ralla! Ralla!" a friendly voice called out from nearby, gesticulating with one arm in a happily frantic waving motion. As Ralla looked over to see from whom the voice had called, she recognized Bodi sitting amongst a group of the others, gesturing for her to come over.

"Right over there!" she answered back to her brother triumphantly, taking hold of his hand and leading him across with her.

"I didn't think you'd make it!" cheered Bodi as Ralla and Agarus arrived to sit down and join them.

"I told her to hurry up," Agarus whined out accusingly while directing a stinky eye over towards his older sister. "Then she left me behind in the woods alone and told me to keep up!" His last imputation had kicked up a bit of steam within the youngster who, despite not yet having ever felt shame before, had no such ignorance regarding anger or frustration. It was hard being a little brother sometimes.

"Oh, be quiet, Agarus!" snapped back Ralla with a mix of both scorn and the well-worn haughtiness of an older sister. "I didn't leave you behind!" She paused for a moment in quick recollection. "In fact," she went on, "you pushed me down into the sand when we got here!"

Bodi laughed as some of the others there began to turn and offer up their smiles and hellos.

"No, I didn't!" cried out Agarus with all the indignation that a four-year-old could possibly muster. "I didn't see her, Bodi," he defended himself emphatically. "I just ran into her is all," he finished in simple innocence.

"Hush now I said," quipped Ralla. "Can't you see that it's about to start?"

"Shhhhs," commenced passing up from amongst the throng of little heads throughout the crowd, beginning first with the eldest one's and then quickly cascading down the ages. The smallest amongst them had to be gently prodded into silence a few moments later as they had simply begun to imitate and repeat back the "Shhhhs" that they had heard and seen from everyone else.

"Well now," entered in the comforting and familiar voice of the old patriarch as silence got itself underway. He sat there perched upon a rock beneath the night sky like some antiquated owl. "Let's see here," he paused in brief rumination before continuing. "Have I ever told you children the story about the shepherd?" he asked them, swinging his loving gaze from left to right towards the gaggle of little ones who had so recently gathered about his feet.

"No, Grandpa!" shouted out the youngest one, followed by two and then three littlest ones in rapid succession.

"Only the one time," answered another who was a few years older.

"We want to hear it again!" came the same reply in unison from the oldest pair who, together with all the rest, were spread lying and sitting about on the ground in front of him in eager anticipation. Sparks crackled and shot upwards from the embering campfire, sporadically illuminating the enveloping darkness as the storyteller thus prepared himself to speak.

"Alright then," he let out with customary ease. "Listen to me now then, my children," his regalement started. "This tale I tell you now must be well remembered, for everything in it is as true as each of you is alive right now." He paused for effect, looking about them as the silence lingered on for another moment. "And even more miraculous than that truth," he began anew, "is that it was all brought about by a mere shepherd, just a boy, no older than you are now, Bodi," finished the elder, looking out towards the middling child as he concluded speaking thus. The others all passed quick glances towards him, including Ralla, who gave him a little nudging on the side as well.

"Mm-hmph," sounded the old one, clearing his throat to begin as the littlest ones once more jostled and jumbled themselves closer together for a better position.

"It was during the time of great war," he started out serious and morose, looking about his audience, the youngest of which were already lost by captivation. "There was a terrible suffering of the people throughout the land," he continued, eyes widened and with arms spreading out. "Armies with their soldiers ravaged and ransacked freely, afflicting everyone, man and beast alike with their violent and savage destructions," the wizened old elder brooded ominously. "The gods, it seemed, had abandoned our people for a time, children." He drew off once more, gazing into the flickering flames of the nearby fire before adding ponderously, "Or perhaps, it was we who had abandoned them."

Chapter 1

Wooden wagon wheels creaked and groaned beneath their heavy loads as the dust-filled road filled with the clanging and clattering sounds of marching soldiers. The afternoon sun loomed high in an otherwise cloudless azure sky, bellowing down a fiery heat like the breath of some great dragon. Slow and steady thus did the immensely armored serpent slide as it traversed itself across the land in pursuit of its own head.

"Bollocks it's bloody hot t'day idden it?" jettisoned out one of the helmeted mercenaries to the comrade trudging alongside himself halfway down the line.

"Hmph?" grumbled back the other soldier stiffly, looking up one-eyed and half-cocked, as one who is walking under a heavy burden is apt to do.

"Eye said it's right bloody hot t'day idn't?" the first man reiterated more loudly, looking sideways towards the other as he did so. "Like Persipinese cunt I'd say," he finished with a restrained laugh as he shifted the heavy kit worn about his back.

"Aye, strenuous day it is," replied the other soldier laconically, turning his gaze back down towards the Earth as one step followed the other in a ceaseless repetition. Somewhere off in the distant front could be heard the low thumps of the war drums keeping a cadence.

"I'd give ten sequesties to be back in Pharsalus right now," carried on the first man with unprovoked fondness. "The women, the weather, the food, ah ..." He let go a sigh of happy remembrance before continuing. "It's enough to make a man want to put down roots and raise a flock I'd say," he concluded in earnest, keeping his face turned towards the other while he did so.

"It shan't be too many hours longer," spoke back the second of the two, more out of cordiality than a willingness to speak.

"I had a missus there, you know," told the first and much larger of the two men. He was a lumbering sort of fellow, both uncannily tall and full of girth. "My missus there," he continued on unabatedly, "she told me I'd regret leaving her pretty person to go off marching with you lot." He finished with a laugh, shaking his head in hindsight.

"Humph," came the short reply with just enough hint of amusement for the first to continue talking.

"Well, she was right I'd say, gold and plunder be damned," he lamented. "All it's been since signing on is march, march, march—always just march but never no rhyme or reason to it all. Titan's balls it's hot out!" he complained loudly in exaggerated exasperation, wiping away the sweat from his own brow.

"They'll be gold and plunder a plenty," retorted the second soldier back knowingly. "After the fighting's done."

"You've been with this outfit before then 'av ya?" returned the living giant out of curiosity.

"Aye," answered back the second. He himself was a shorter, humorless type of man. Both squat, as well as brutish, with thick forearms and an intemperate demeanor. A perpetual half scowl seemed dressed to his countenance, even when not marching with a full load under the hot summer sun.

"This is my third campaign with the general," he stated flatly. "I've land and a farm back East from the first two," he told prior to carrying on. "And after this last one, Gods be praised, I'll have enough to live out the remainder of my days in peace, with my family," he ended with a heavy emphasis.

"Land and a farm back East he says," whistled back the first of the two men with a good-natured approbation, as if to say, 'well look at this high and mighty fellow!' "Alright then," he stated. "I'm happy to hear that, I am," continued the friendly stranger with a ready smile.

"Wife and little ones too then?" questioned the huge man further.

"Indeed," replied the scowler who was becoming more willing to engage as familiarity increased.

"I've a wife as well as two daughters." He paused in a moment of fond recollection. "My wife was pregnant with our third when last I left out," his story continued. "She will have been with child by now," figured the father, a hint of worry and concern creeping into his otherwise stern voice. "A boy I hope," he finished stoutly, looking up and over full for the first time at the person marching next to him, a slight smile creeping into the corners of his square mouth.

"No worries, friend!" comforted the first back cheerfully. "She'll be right as rain she will," he reasoned convincingly. "You made all the proper prayers and sacrifices, did you not?"

"Yes, yes of course I did," flew back the quick and obvious answer.

"Well see there?" replied the first with a confident ease, his assuredness rubbing off onto the other. "You've got nothing to worry about then!"

The morose soldier's smile widened.

"The gods clearly favor you, my friend. My friend …?" he let the inflection hang.

"Yusri," answered back the shorter of the two men.

"Yusri, is it? Right fine name I'd say," complimented back the first with niceness. "They call me Grieves myself."

"Grieves?" Yusri reiterated.

"Aye, that's the one," he confirmed. "I never did really care for it myself, on account of its much too easy to pick a pun." He gave examples. "Always it's, 'what's it grieving you today, Grieves?' Or, 'sorry to Grieves you but—"

Yusri chuckled slightly.

"Why then did your people name you thus?" he questioned a little curiously.

"Not rightly sure I suppose," came the shrugging reply. "Perhaps it was that they wasn't too pleased by my person!" he finished, letting out an uproarious laugh as he admired his own perceived wit.

Yusri shook his head in amusement as the two marched on, both squeezed between the mass of men and beasts to their front and the other similar mass that was constantly pushing up from the rear. Clouds of dust hung about them like fog on a windless morning. The piles of excrement from all the pack animals had to be near constantly stepped over and avoided.

"Third campaign tho is it?" asked Grieves nonchalantly after a few moments had passed. "You mustuv been in some real right uns then," he questioned further. "Eye'v urd stories eye av."

A glint of soldier's pride gleamed from the eyes of Yusri as he replied in the affirmative that it was so.

"There were some red days," he began. "That's why I don't so much mind the marching." He shifted back to his front before adding gloomily, "The marching's the easy part."

Grieves searched the man next to him under an inquisitive stare.

"Were you at Aventum?" he decided to ask.

"I was," retorted Yusri.

"Gods alive!" exclaimed Grieves with unrestrained adulation. "Eye'v ear stumbled upon a lucky star eye av."

Yusri stayed silent while Grieve's prattled. "Was eye urd it that no great many made it out that day unscathed," recounted Grieves, recording what he had heard from others not there to one who actually was. "An yet ere yew are, a right champion e is!" congratulated Grieves with a jovial acclamation.

"It was a day of unrestrained slaughter and bloodshed," Yusri remonstrated back coldly, an involuntary angst taking sudden grip of his heart as he did so. "I was almost cut down more times than I can remember," he continued on through the intense trepidation. "Countless others fell in death and agony all around me." His chest space tightened even further as memory flashed back that day's horrid abyss of deadly mayhem into the forefront of his mind. "We held the line," was all that he ended with after a moment's silence in which he breathed out heavily, shaking free the foul remembrance by force.

"My apologies, friend Yusri," soothed Grieves gingerly. "I meant no harm by it."

Quiet reigned supreme as the previous instant's severity lingered in advance of passing.

"Is it true that the general's never lost a battle?" Grieves asked out next, switching the topic of conversation.

"Aye, it's true," Yusri answered back plainly enough, his usual laconic manner restored.

"Long may it continue," responded Grieves solemnly as he made a sign to the Gods.

"Long may it continue," repeated Yusri with an equal reverence, imitating the same sign.

"Any idea where we're headed to now, then?" Grieves inquired after with sore shoulders and pair of burning feet.

"Over there." Yusri pointed off into the distance close to where the plain ended near the mouth of a deep mountain valley. A fat river ran lazily along the backside, cutting its course down towards the lowlands from whence they'd come. Already could be seen the column's front breaking off from the road and beginning to spread out into the grassy plain to set up camp.

"Thank the Gods," answered Grieves in happy relief. "Eye think my feet woulda worn down to nubs if we kept going much farther."

Chapter 2

A pack of mounted scouts galloped wildly across the outcropped terrain, hair and manes both pulled taut by the winds' swift passing. Their horses' hooves made fly rock, turf, and gravel with one fell swoop as the black riders rode in reckless abandon enroute to the far side of the mountain's valley where the great army had not yet penetrated. Last year they had come to observe, now they were back to invade.

The patrol spotted something. It was a most curious sight to behold and one which appeared all the stranger as distance decreased. Yet from the time they had first laid eyes upon the apparent enigma and subsequently began their approach, it had made no attempt to neither hide nor flee.

As they reached the wall of white wool, which formed the outskirts of the kernel, they checked their horses' speed into a canter before forcing themselves onto a path through the cacophony of baas and alarmed bleats. It was a flock of hundreds, and yet when they finally reared up and pulled harshly their stallions to a still, it was but a mere boy who wore the cloak of shepherd. A very strange scene to behold indeed.

"You, boy!" called down the group's captain harshly from atop his slickened steed, next near to shouting. "What is the meaning of this foolish madness?"

"The old ones must have seen us coming and run off," one of his men answered him, looking about as he did so. "They didn't want to lose the flock so they forced the boy to stay."

"They would have known that it was lost already," countered another. "Why lose the boy too?"

Such was all that occurred within the same few moments of the horsemen stopping next to the Juniper tree in whose shade the boy was bathing. He seemed oblivious to their arrival as he stood up, blinking on account of the sun's brightness.

"Hullo there," he greeted them openly in a rustic dialect through squinted eyes that were further sheltered by a small hand outstretched above both his brow. His tilted head shone up without guile into the faces of both men and mount alike, the latter of which were still foaming at the mouth and impatiently pawing their restless hooves upon the dry earth.

The angry, astonished captain gripped his horse's whip before lashing it down upon the impertinent youth who gave a cry of pain and reflexive leap backwards. The other's input was ignored as the captain maintained his fierce vigil over the freshly terrified child. "Where are your people thus, and why have they left you alone here?" he barked again with temper flaring.

The young shepherd boy remained with his hand held fast to the spot of stinging impact. The corners of both his eyes had already sprang forth small streams which ran in dirty trails down the cheeks of his dusty face. "I have no people, sir, and I am not alone here," he sniveled back, full of fright and demure.

"Speak sense boy!" roared the captain, raising his hand and whip once more in preparation to strike.

"I have no people, sir, and I am not alone here!" the sheep herder cried out again despairingly, cowering like trapped prey before the baying hounds.

"The boy is a fool," commented the rider nearest to the captain.

"I say we kill the boy and send the sheep back into camp," chimed in another with lackadaisical indifference.

"Aye," agreed a third. "We still have to clear the mountain pass before nightfall," he said, looking up towards the unchecked approaches. "We've no time to waste on a peasant with no breasts," he concluded, grinning round to the others.

"Now, now, don't be so quick to judge, Finnigan," jested another of the scouts to the group at idle. "We all know Simon fancies a good buggering of the youth every now and again," he finished, looking over expectantly at the butt of the joke's witticism.

"Yeah, yeah," came the accented rebuttal on que. "That's very funny coming from the man who learned to fuck by using goats." The rest, aside from the captain and the boy, laughed heartily.

At the onset of laughter, the captain broke free his ire-filled glare and turned himself back around to face the others.

"And which one of you rapacious and rapining fools is going to lead these many sheep back into the camp that's so many leagues away?" he interrogated. "You, Rickimer?"

Another rider, who was drawing wine from out of his goatskin, burst into fresh mirth, spewing purple mist through the air. He was not the only one to be tickled by such a fancy.

"Silence!" the captain interjected loudly to his men. "Damn children," he scolded them, taking command. "Matrius," he looked over to whom he spoke, "you will take the shepherd with his flock back into camp."

"The rest of us," he turned back to the others, "will continue on to reconnoiter the forward passes as ordered."

"Yes, Captain," submitted the chosen man to his dictated task, looking across towards his new charge as he did so. "And what of the boy once camp is reached?"

"Do as you like," retorted the captain flippantly, not even deigning to look over. "Only be sure to give my compliments to the general for all the fresh mutton," he directed with a final glance.

"Yes, Captain," affirmed Matrius. "Your compliments to the general, will do sir."

"Alright then, the rest of you villainous bastards," rallied the captain to his remaining troops.

"Try not to let any wander away on the way back now, shepherd Matrius," Finnigan playfully derided as he and his mount prepared to make haste.

"Try not to bugger n'e of'm either!" added another cheekily, and for good measure.

"Leave off!" the captain shouted, slapping down the whip onto his charger's rear to restart the hunt. The other riders quickly circled and then dug their horses' hindquarters deep into the ground ahead of pushing off in pursuit, up towards the mountain passes. Matrius sat atop his own steed and watched them go a little distance before he turned and gave consideration to his own assignment in detail for the first time.

The little shepherd boy was sitting crouched beneath the same Juniper tree whose shade he had been caught resting, silently watching the retreating horsemen go.

"Gather your flock, shepherd," spoke Matrius calmly after a few moments ponderance. "Some've begun to run astray."

A small bunch of the animals had in fact been scared away by the recent commotion and were now loitering about the nearby hill which formed a base to the mountain slope.

"Did you hear what I said?" the horseman asked, growing slightly vexed.

The youth turned his attention to the lone scout remaining with a wary perplexity. "Yessir," he answered plainly with an adjoining nod of deference.

"Off with you then," commanded Matrius. "And be quick about it," he bespoke in mild threat. "Or you will find my whip to be as thick as the captain's, and no less studded," he finished, flashing the same type of whip as had been used to injure him previous.

The young sprout sprung up quickly from his stance and immediately set about regathering the flock without a sound, swiftly scurrying about in order to bring his large collection back into a single muster.

Matrius retrieved from his pouch a cuff of bread and proceeded to eat and drink in observant silence until the boy's task was complete.

"Come here, shepherd," Matrius instructed him after the herd was corralled.

The boy did as he was told, approaching with cautious apprehension, keeping a firm eye on the rider's whip as he did so. Matrius, noticing the cause for concern, provided some small reassurance. "Don't worry," he calmed like a crooked priest. "I'll not beat you without a reason."

Thus did the youth slowly shirk alongside the horseman's mount, looking both downcast and depressed. "Take this," Matrius ordered him as he handed off his remaining chunk of loaf.

"It will be a long walk back to camp," he informed him as the latter began to eat in hunger. "You must take in enough food and drink now to keep your strength up." He watched him as he spoke. "I'll not play the part of shepherd should you decide to fall out halfway," informed the scout with sour haughtiness while peering at the herd.

The subject of regard ate quickly and quietly beneath the scout's steady gaze until Matrius handed over his goatskin as well. "Now drink," he ordered him, "and then we'll make ready."

The skin was dutifully accepted, and the shepherd did as he was told, drinking to quench his thirst. "Careful, boy," Matrius chided him crossly after many chugs. "That's wine, not water."

Hearing this, the sheep herder ceased his suckling and politely handed back up the leather pouch before wiping an arm across his mouth and belching loudly.

Matrius spied the youth curiously while resecuring the wineskin back onto his mount. "Enough waiting then," he started abruptly. "You're going to bring your flock with me back into camp; is that understood?" inquired the horseman directly.

"Yessir," the shepherd boy repeated once more in simple compliance.

"Good then, let's go," Matrius began, nudging his mount into walking.

"Hulloo!" called out the shepherd boy unexpectedly, taking Matrius slightly off guard. It sounded almost like an owl trying to say hello. "Hulloo!" he repeated again to the flock at large, whose ears at once pricked up to the apparently familiar wailing.

Matrius watched while the boy repeated his words. To his surprise, a part of the circular gathering which was closest to the camp began to break free from their orbital animus and peel off in that direction.

Once underway, Matrius made his way to the back of the herd from where the shepherd boy led them and began to walk his horse beside him.

"What did you mean when you told the captain earlier that you weren't alone here?" he scrutinized.

"The sheep," the boy answered plainly.

"The sheep?" Matrius questioned back, not fully comprehending.

"Yessir," the young lad confirmed. "The sheep are with me."

"So, you really are a fool then?" Matrius said to him, staring low as he did so.

"All things are possible," the shepherd boy replied after a few moments' pause.

"Hulloo," he then called out again. Its use seemed to bring the flock back on center whenever parts of the wings began to spread.

"What's your name?" probed Matrius further with a mild interest.

"My name is Pan, Pan Shepherd," he answered, looking up and over whilst still walking alongside.

"Pan?" Matrius queried. "What peculiar names you bumpkins have," he said out loud, though mostly to himself.

"What about your parents? Your family?" He paused before proceeding, "Who looks after you?"

"Looks after me?" copied Pan back with strangeness. He was starting to look around with a sort of dimmed confusion on his face.

"Yes, boy," Matrius stoked hotly. "Where are your people thus?" he reiterated again for the second time.

Immediately Pan responded by proclaiming rather louder than the situation warranted, "I have no people, sir, and I am not alone here!"

"You make jest with me, peasant?" Matrius checked him angrily.

"Hulloo!" the shepherd suddenly cried out, his shout mingling with the added sound of humor as it carried towards the flock. "Hulloo!" he repeated a second time just a moment later, this rendition being even louder than the first and with an accompanying saunter to boot.

At this fresh outrage, Matrius reached out his leg and kicked Pan hard, directly in the shoulder, causing him to fall down. It did not, however, have the desired effect.

"Hulloo!" he garbled out once more from his prone position on the ground, resulting in himself getting all the more lost into laughter.

The furiously stunned scout required a few more seconds of perturbed thought to figure out the youth's sudden caprice until it finally dawned on him. The little shepherd boy was drunk.

"Gods alive," Matrius derided, scoldingly under his breath.

"You've never drank wine before?" he called down incredulously from atop his horse, the tone gone from that of threatening to that of surprised disappointment.

"No sir!" came the cackled response as the boy's giggling continued, unabated, while he stumbled side to side, trying to regain himself back on solid ground. "Hulloo!" he called again on still shaky legs between the near ceaseless cascades of laughter.

"Pan!" the horseman shouted from above as the young shepherd boy continued to wave and wobble unsteadily. He had gone from being loud and animated to right after becoming still and silent.

"Get co—" just as Matrius started again to speak, Pan opened up his mouth and let fly a stream of purple vomit that fell into the middle of the trail. The sickly child stood there for an instant longer and then opened up his oral cavity for a second time to let loose another gastric river that was sent splashing down into the first before his eyes glazed over and he fell to the ground sideways, moaning incoherently.

"Sons of Hades!" Matrius cursed aloud once more, unable to yet accept his rotten luck. Why does everything have to be so damned difficult? he thought to himself in upset exasperation whilst looking low at the incapacitated youth who was now wallowing pathetically in the dirt.

Matrius jumped off his horse and yanked the young shepherd up by his woolen garment.

"Look at me!" he shouted, attempting the use of noise to force his way through the intoxicated inebriation. The boy's body responded more like that of a rag doll than a person, being unable to hold neither firm nor form.

The flock meanwhile continued on its way and was fast dispersing without the constant attention and shepherding of the now hammered Pan.

"Look at me I said!" Matrius yelled again, slapping the boy across his face hard enough to awaken a flash of dazed eyes which lost their luster almost as soon as the focus was gained.

Matrius let the lifeless body fall back into the dust with disgust. How ridiculous, he thought to himself. Now what's to be done?

As he looked through his mind in search of an answer, one became readily apparent.

"Come here, you little bastard," spoke Matrius roughly as he pulled up young Pan like one does a pup by its collar.

He next climbed back aboard his mount and stuck the sauced-up shepherd between his own legs, propped up against himself.

The boy slept heavily as his sheep increasingly became a gaggle instead of a flock with each passing second.

"Haa!" Matrius called out when he kicked his horse into gear and began moving at a trot back towards the mutinous herd. Something had to be done soon in order to induce all the animals back together again.

Matrius looked down at the passed-out Pan to make sure that he was really a slumber before he cleared his throat and attempted with much embarrassment to imitate what he had previously seen and heard.

"Huhlew!" he called out awkwardly with a faulty tone. Not a single lamb responded in the slightest.

"Furies slay me!" Matrius swore under his breath, the warmth of shame creeping up from his core and causing him to feel even more heat than what nature was already providing in abundance.

He sighed heavily and then prepared himself to try again. "Hullew!" he countered, different from the first. It wasn't correct, but it was coming closer. "Hullew, hulloo, hulloo," whispered the horseman repeatedly as minutes passed by, trying desperately to get the sound just right ahead of making another go towards the flock at large.

"Hulloo!" Matrius then let fly without restraint and was at once rewarded by the sight of innumerous ears pricking up from the call. "That's more like it," he said aloud as his calm and confidence, both so recently on the ebb tide, now began to flood back in.

"Hulloo!" he repeated, each effort becoming more and more natural until eventually the sheep could not tell any difference between them. "Hulloo!" he continued on until the flock was once again just as it had been until the little shepherd boy had gotten himself lost into drink. Little wretch, Matrius thought to himself, though without much of the earlier conviction he had once felt. Now with an even keel restored, his feelings of scorn and frustration had dissipated quickly so that he was soon returned to his naturally neutral demeanor.

Thus did Matrius continue to accompany the large flock in a slow but steady movement back down towards the camp below. The caravan traveled for some hours like that as it descended its way out of the mountains and into the valley. Eventually, when the sprawling encampment was well within sight and the sun low amongst the clouds, Pan Shepherd himself began to rouse once more.

"Oh," he groaned piteously in his place, still leaning back against the rock that was Matrius' chest.

"Is that you, shepherd?" the horseman poked with some amusement once he heard the mewing start. "Now you wish to rejoin us a?" Matrius interrogated with an easy spite. "Lazy dog," he saddled on lightheartedly.

The boy made no attempt to answer. He was feeling crippled by the splitting headache of alcohol-induced dehydration.

Matrius, knowing all too well the effects in which the young youth suffered, patted his back heavily and told him, "The pain in your head will soon cease once water is taken."

"Do you have any?" croaked Pan with hopefulness.

"I do not," the scout disappointed him mightily.

"I—" Pan's voice broke and then cracked from the dryness of his own mouth before he began anew. "I do not remember how I got here," he said through squinted eyes and thick saliva.

"You had your first drink today at my expense," Matrius reminded him without much kindness. "Then you became ill and lost all manner of sense so that I was forced to carry you."

"Why?" asked the sheep herder blankly.

"Why what?" questioned Matrius back the same.

"Why did you carry me?" doubled down Pan.

The bemused Matrius was at first taken aback but by-and-by he told him.

"What?" he first queried. "You wanted that I leave a perfectly good boy like you to the buzzards?" He paused in wait. "Pah," he continued after no remark was made. "I think not," he said in conclusion. "You'll fetch a fair price at the meat market anyhow."

Pan did not understand the connotation.

"I do not remem—" as Pan began to speak, he suddenly became like the small green island lizards that lived off the coast, and which can be put to sleep by gently covering their eyes and then pushing in lightly on their bellies. They always awaken a short time after being lain on their backs, and when they do find themselves awake it is quite unnaturally upside down! So like the lizard, Pan almost leapt from his half-conscious position, opening his eyes at once fully to the waning sun whilst at the same time crying out, "My she—" but even before he had finished the words, his sight had shown him clear as day that there was indeed no mystery. His sheep were right there where they were supposed to be, casually strolling closer to the enlarging camp.

"What has happened?" Pan asked again with growing alarm and unease, trying to slip himself out of his seat atop Matrius's horse.

Matrius let him slide off whence he stumbled back to his feet and began glancing around like a cat searching for mice. "Don't be stupid," he said, looking down sharply. "You drank too much wine and became unconscious," charged the horseman with mid-ranged accusation. "Now that you're awake again, however, you will finish leading these sheep back into camp for me," he ordered, gesturing across in that direction.

Looking around, Pan Shepherd could see clearly that he was now far away from either home or choice. Thus, he was forced into meekly surrendering to Matrius's will, so he once more took to the position of walking in line behind his bleating herd, feeling miserable.

"How did you keep them all together?" Pan asked Matrius after a few minutes spent traveling with no speech.

"I copied you," he told him, looking over with a grin.

Pan nodded in acknowledgement ahead of speaking further. "What will happen to them now?" he next wanted to know.

"We will eat them of course," Matrius answered obviously.

"Eat them?" Pan bewailed loudly and in a panic. "But who?"

Matrius pondered the boy curiously once more prior to making up his final mind and rebutting him sharply, "The army, you little fool."

Chapter 3

Dusk was onsetting when Matrius's caravan of meat and wool finally arrived at the camp's front entrance. The little sheep herder who walked alongside them had by now been dragged for hours under the crushing weight of fatiguing despair. "Hulloo," he still crooned dryly whenever necessary, though only sporadically and with a halfhearted conviction. Matrius, by comparison, was in very high spirits indeed after having almost completed his orders and would soon be set to collect his rewards by way of both the cooks and the slavers.

As the flock, with its escorts, reached the newly built wooden palisades right outside the main entranceway, a scribe who was on assigned duty there took quick notice of their approach.

"Well now." He whistled impressively, catching the attention of some others nearby. "It looks like fresh meat's what's on for supper tonight then boys!" he called back over his shoulder, well pleased, as the first lamb in the flock of hundreds reached him.

"Fine work by your lot today it seems, scout," complimented the one who had started scribbling, keeping tally of each passing sheep. "What troop are you with?" he next asked without taking sight off his records.

"Captain Faroh's squadron," Matrius responded with the correct esteem from atop his well-worn stallion.

"Captain Faroh," the scribe repeated whilst still looking down at his work of pressing marks and notches into the soft clay tablet. "And where are they now may I ask?" inquired the same writer who now gazed up for a moment in order to better hear his reply.

"They continued reconnoitering the forward passes," informed Matrius. "Captain Faroh charged me with bringing in these provisions while they continued making their runs."

"Very good," replied the scribe whilst staring down in fixation upon his earthen template and making fresh impressions upon it. "Very good indeed," he reiterated, no doubt made happy by the sheer amount of unexpected supplies that were being delivered on his watch.

As this interaction proceeded, Pan Shepherd could only stand there mutely, being both too despondent and weak to speak.

"Okay," the record keeper piped in once more. "Actually sorry, my apologies," he corrected himself. "May I ask you for your name?" he probed further, "for the accounting purposes."

"My name is Matrius," the scout spoke freely but with the first few flurries of impatience blowing in.

"Matrius," the scribe repeated without facing up though still nodding his head in the affirmative. "I've got it all now," he told him. "You're free to go," waved on the bureaucrat with a bookworm's authority. "These men will take it all from here," he ended, giving a last thankful look to the scout before turning away and calling over to some of his associates on hand.

"Let's go," Matrius directed curtly towards Pan, who himself was in the midst of a profound melancholy watching his entire life being taken away from him without so much as a word. He could hardly contain the anguish that boiled up, even in his weakened state.

"I said move," Matrius broke in forcefully a second time, flashing a grim countenance and his horse's whip as a sign of what was to come should the young Pan Shepherd continue with any further disregard.

Pan accepted his admonishment with a bowed head and obedience. Large tears swelled both eyes before he wiped a hand across them and walked quietly over.

"Give me your hands," Matrius next ordered him upon his arrival, forcing Pan into blind submission.

Matrius then took hold of his request and tied them each together with a length of slackened rope so that soon he wound up tethered to both man and beast alike.

"Wouldn't want to lose you now," he accentuated with mocking humor whilst clapping on the last knot.

Pan could only watch in tearful silence as he was being held fast. After the restraint was completed, he was then dutifully informed by pleased demeanor to, "Follow me." With that cryptic expression alone leading the way, Matrius then urged his horse back into a walk so that both he and his new bound prize quickly swelled into the now swollen complex.

The young prisoner was thus forced to keep up or else be dragged, and despite his enfeebled condition, he continued to walk forward one foot after the other towards a destination unknown.

He walked atop planks of bare wood laid over skinny rails of ground which on either side had already become deep and sticky with the gunk and grime of ten thousand men and animals. He saw women with flamboyantly colored garments and bright hair sitting and standing outside of various cloth-built establishments wearing broken smiles that were supposed to appear pretty to all those who passed them by. Pan had never seen so many people in that crowded and confined a space before, and for a little while, he completely forgot about his ill health and total loss. His fresh mind had completely escaped into the dizzying array of wondrous new sights and sounds that were abounding all around him.

On their way, they passed through narrow alleys of tents and ramshackle workshops that were propped up with loose wood and spare parts. Each one was jampacked full of bronzed-clad men who both looked and smelled atrocious to the little shepherd boy who was only used to fresh air and open spaces. Everywhere he looked were cooking pots, stacked weapons, and large groups of horridly barbarous men babbling, laughing, and sometimes even fighting with one another. The smells of shit, mud, and food were almost too overpowering for the light-headed, famished, and exhausted young shepherd to stand.

As the pair were making their way through a clearing in the encampment, which had a great white and splotched gray tabernacle with soldiers standing guard outside around its front, Matrius stopped his horse abruptly, causing Pan to awaken from his daze. He saw his captor give salute to a group of importantly dressed horsemen who were just then entering in from the other side of the bounds.

"General!" Matrius snapped to with obvious deference towards the leader of the bunch after the latter had taken his notice. First, he flew up his right knuckle to forehead and then bent his neck deep in homage.

"Ah," came the deeply taut voice from that who was formed finest of all figures there atop his resplendently red stallion. "You are one of Faroh's men," he said approvingly and with confidence. "Where is your captain now?" asked the general, looking around searchingly. "I have still not received any word or reports from his quarter."

Matrius looked to Pan as though he had just been transfixed from a man into some sort of talking statue while he answered with his monotonous reply. "General," he stated formally and with immense respect. "My captain sent me along with this shepherd boy and his flock back into the encampment." He paused for a small period before carrying on, "The rest of the men continued up to reconnoiter the forward passes and should be returned back here by nightfall." He then relayed the message that he was instructed to pass along earlier as well. "I was charged in addition by Captain Faroh to give his compliments to you, sir, on account of all the mutton," Matrius loyally reported.

"Did he now?" replied back the piqued general with a freshly purchased good-will. "And how much did the good captain send us?" fished the commander pryingly.

Matrius looked across to Pan for the first time during this brief encounter and saw that he too was staring intently right back at him. "I—" Matrius started and then broke off under the commanders piercing gaze to begin anew. "Er," he stuttered quickly but continued on, catching himself timely enough. "There were too many to count general," was the firmly forced reply finally proffered. "Hundreds though, I'm sure," pinned the scout on further, gratuitously.

The general's eyes seemed to shine right through them both as he conspicuously looked from one and then to the other. "Hundreds you say?" he questioned deeper, seeking for an exaggeration.

"Yes, General," Matrius confirmed with wide-eyed affirmation. "Without a doubt."

The general looked again to the destitute young boy made captive at the back of Matrius's mount. "With only this single boy as guard?" he interrogated deeper, directing a suspiciously uncertain brow outwards in Pan's direction.

"Yes, General," Matrius confirmed once again with the highest esteem.

"Explain how," dictated the general with supreme authority, like a tiger's growl. "Quickly."

Matrius immediately and obediently obeyed, recounting the trip in its entirety to the general with his attending staff present. As the expounding wound further the story of Pan's drinking wine and then getting drunk was told, even the general himself simpered slightly above imperceptive at its telling.

After Matrius had finished giving his recounting, the general turned his eyes back onto young Pan. "You, shepherd," his iron voice followed right after, "how could you keep so many sheep by yourself?"

Pan stared back thoughtfully while his ruminating mind searched for an answer. "I don't rightly know, sir," came the worn-down and parched response handed out a few seconds later. "I kept them, and they kept me I suppose," ended the rustics tale sadly.

"You couldn't have watched over so many sheep alone," the keen-eyed general accused him. "So who helped you?" he demanded to know. "Where are your people?" scented the commander ravenously like how a zealot hunts rats.

Upon the last inquisition, Pan Shepherd instinctively replied, "I have no people, sir, and I am not alone here."

"What do you mean that you are not alone here?" shot back the general with his penetrating curiosity directly across Pan's bows.

"The boy is a fool," broke in Matrius swiftly, who already knew well what the upcoming answer would be. "He has a special way with the sheep, your grace, but in all else is as simple as a mule," Faroh's horseman blurted out.

The general stared at Pan for a short while longer in advance of turning away back to Matrius and speaking with him directly.

"Be sure to give my compliments to your captain as well," the general honored, tipping his head slightly after the fact. "We never do fail to find satisfaction in his dealings," he stringed along the comment further as both he and his entourage made a move to end their impromptu rendezvous and head back towards the tabernacle.

Before the general broke his heavy gaze from them completely however, young Pan Shepherd erupted into a passionate cry and fell down onto his knees in the sticky black mud to begin wringing his tied hands in fervent plea.

"Please, sir!" he cried over to the commander and chief with a pitiful wailing and the gnashing of teeth. "Do not let them take my sheep away from me!"

Matrius flew back a withering stare at the now groveling Pan Shepherd and immediately jerked the leather binding hard so that the boy was flung over sideways with half his face landing in the mud. Still, he begged on.

"Please, sir, please!" Pan cried hopelessly. "Do not let my lambs be eaten!" It was a deplorable scene, and one in which the general did not at all appear eager to acquiesce to.

"The boy really is a fool," smarted the general aloud to some rattling laughter outside of his cabal. He gave another look back towards Matrius in acknowledgement to the apparent fact proved.

Matrius moved to kick the boy hard. "Tell me," the general broke in ahead of the strike, his resonant voice cutting seamlessly through all of the shepherd boy's lamentations, "where are you taking him?"

"To the slavers general," recorded Matrius, bowing his head, with one hand still on the jerkin.

"He's unlikely to fetch a very high price now," lessoned the commander knowingly. "Not in his condition."

Matrius looked back to the broken down, exhausted, and mud-soaked youth with some consideration of that fact before the general again opened his mouth to speak.

"Since you wish to sell him anyway," he said with a well-seasoned nonchalance, "then one of my officers here will accord you the proper sum for his worth."

"General?" double checked the flabbergasted Matrius incredulously.

"He will make a very fine slave, no doubt," elucidated the towering warlord assuredly. "The simple ones always do."

Chapter 4

Having thus been unexpectedly freed from one master, the young Pan Shepherd was then immediately yoked onto another. The boy's lips still quivered like a bowstring as he was being led away by the two footbound attendants that were duly assigned with having his vile filth removed.

"Move faster, dog," the first escort sneered venomously, leading the group's way through a maze of men, carts, and animals. He wedged open the crowd by his passing, and it stayed that way because of the reeking, crusty youth following closely behind who none would dare touch with anything more than just their eyes. Upon the third man's clearance, however, the trio's wake was immediately made buried back into the endless sea of movement which ceaselessly churned about them on all sides.

"I can smell the foul wretch from here," opined the rear guard disdainfully. "He's burning my nostrils."

Pointed as their barbs may be, however, the insults only echoed past harmlessly. The fatigue and dehydration, coupled with his abject loss, had left young Pan in a state of almost total discombobulation.

"The river will help to wash off some of his stink," joked back the wedge jarringly as he continued to unceremoniously push and shove his way between the thickened masses. "It will do nothing for his looks though!" He laughed insultingly.

As they left the densely packed center area towards a more sparsely filled outskirts, the jostling and jumbling gradually decreased. A few minutes more saw them reach the rear of the camp that was nestled along a soft crook in the wide channel that flowed by, ever peaceful, like a brook. In the water, all manner of persons could be seen bathing, washing, or simply fetching it for their own needs.

The young shepherd was himself led to a spot on the riverbank near many of the others and ordered to disrobe by his two guards in preparation of being forced to bathe, despite his nakedness.

"Hurry up!" one berated unkindly towards the tepidly moving Pan, who still had enough sense left to feel ashamed at his own exposure.

While slowly entering the river, he at first felt apprehensive and disliked how its silty bottom pushed up goo between his toes wherever he stepped. Then, however, his overwhelming thirst soon took over so that in another moment he had submerged himself completely and began to drink deep gulps till satiation. The water was cold but completely fresh having only just recently descended from the mountain highlands in whose entrance an army now sat encamped.

"Hurry up, you louse!" shouted out one of the two escorts who had accompanied him for his cleansing from the shore after a few minutes had passed. "Can't you see it's almost dark?"

Pan heard their growing exasperations loudly enough, so he dunked himself once more in final rejuvenation before heading back unto the riverbank to where his embittered chaperones were impatiently awaiting his arrival.

"Took you long enough!" scoffed down the wedge with a cockamaimie hands-on-hips stance as Pan came out of the water, wet and naked, reaching instinctively for his muddily heaped clothes in which to cover himself.

"No, you fool!" shouted out the other man, who had clasped a linen garment in his hand that he'd been carrying with him. "Let those rags alone and put this on," he commanded, rudely handing over a blue tunic made of good quality.

Pan decidedly let his mud-soaked, filthy, wet ensemble lie, opting instead to put on the freshly proffered tunic which fitted him more like a vestment than anything else. The material was like nothing he'd ever felt before. Once redressed, he then scurried along hurriedly for a second time back in the direction in which they'd come. On this trip, however, young Pan was made to push and prod his way through the crowds like everyone else after having lost his natural repellant of stink and filth from inside the river's bottom.

Those three traversed themselves along that way for some time, enroute to the great hive's busy center. Everywhere they passed along their trail small fires were being started and attended to combat the swallowing darkness. A communal glow soon permeated the city of tents as shadows flickered and danced anew with every wind-blown wisp. Eventually they reached a sort of shallow den which was rowed off with long wooden tables that were propped up by pitch poles held firmly down in the dirt by wooden stakes.

Here the smells of hot food in the air were almost too overpowering for the young shepherd to stand. He at once felt his famished state more acutely than anything else surrounding him.

"Gods, I'm starved," commented the first man hungrily to the other, stating Pan's sentiments exactly.

"And I," the latter agreed wholeheartedly.

"You keep eyes on the welp then while I fetch us some food," minded the one attendant to his partner.

"I'll do it," confirmed the half-distracted watchman who was already looking around for their refreshments. "I'll see to the drinks as well."

Both nodded in accord before pulling apart to set about retrieving their specified procurements. One of the two men disappeared into the mass of moving people nearby while the other remaining instructed Pan to sit down and stay there. Stay for how long, Pan didn't know, he only knew that his stomach would continue devouring itself further without any food. Still, they waited there by the half-filled tables being served by young tavern wenches and old whores. Bitter drinks arrived, and more, until Pan Shepherd finally recognized a man coming back through the crowd carrying three bowls in his hands and a loaf of bread tucked under one arm.

"Long lines tonight?" questioned the fellow that stayed behind to the one who had gone, upon his return.

"Backed up all the way to the shit houses," came his acknowledgement. "Must mean the food's good tho," he finished with a surmising smile before looking down at the young shepherd.

"Here you go, worm," he lambasted provokingly, plopping a wooden bowl onto the table in front of him that was filled almost to the brim with some sort of meaty brown stew. Lamb no doubt. "Take it."

Pan did not wait for additional instructions or confirmations before engaging straight away in the devourment of his dish after having been made ravenous by hunger. The possible sources for the meal were pushed far from his mind.

"Hungry dog he is," ridiculed the drinks man who was already on his second tankard while watching him eat. "Smells decent enough though," he observed for himself while receiving his own portions worth and a rip of bread.

"Aye," the stew bringer confirmed with a glance prior to drinking. "And I'm hungry as a wolf!" he jokingly exclaimed before howling aloud in imitation and immediately commenced to eat upon his own victuals.

"I've been thinking," illuminated the companion sitting nearest to Pan, after the pair had spent a few minutes ingesting greedily without any words.

"God's have mercy," poked back the other with a benign smirk on his face between bites.

"I'm serious, Tarwin," came the defensive parry with a drunkard's vigil.

"Alright," Tarwin bit down while chewing, "thinking about what then?"

The freshly minted and presented caricature of moroseness started breaking up before his mouth propped itself open to speak. "Whores mostly," he jestingly guffawed, displaying meat gristle between his teeth.

"I figured as much," Tarwin depreciated with mild mannered disapproval, shaking his head sideways and spitting out the hook. "What else is new?" he asked rhetorically, returning back to eating.

"Do you remember that raven-haired beauty that I told you about from last night?" followed up the libertine to his comrade full of conviction, zeal, and another overturned cup.

"I could hardly forget her if I tried," Tarwin responded back dully, tearing off another piece of bread and scooping it down into his last remaining stew as he did so. "You've barely stopped mentioning her."

"Tits out to here," the whoremonger recalled again fondly, holding his arms up and out in front of his chest as an example. "What was her name again, though?" he pondered in remembrance but was still unable to grasp it. "Ah it's no matter," the addled purveyor relented after a shortened spell. "She was delicious though, I'll say that," his blissful memory enchanted once more.

"So you keep saying," Tarwin remonstrated back, grinning. He was well-informed and hearing déjà vu for the umpteenth time.

"I know," his counterpart abruptly let on after having just surmised an obvious stratagem. "Why don't you come out with me tonight and meet her for yourself?" He pushed over half-drunkenly across the table, looking slightly belligerent. "I could introduce you!" plied the merchant with vigor, continuing his daily trade.

"You know, Korballa," Tarwin humorously tried to edify, "if you keep spending all your money on whores, you'll never save enough for a horse." He poked some fun while making his point. "You're getting all the wrong mounts," punned along the impromptu instructor, smiling. "And they're not even yours after you pay for them!" he launched even more of his derisive ridicule. "Only rented by the hour or the ride," Tarwin's flourish of joke-filled criticisms ended and he pushed away his empty bowl atop the table and enjoyed another libation.

"I don't see you prancing around on the backs of any mounts yet either, Tarwin," Korballa threw back, slightly stung, his wits still clearly about him.

"Only because I too often let myself get talked into going out whoring with you!" exclaimed the falsely sanctimonious Tarwin, gleefully.

Korballa laughed, regaining his ease. "Ah, I see," entered the friendly rejoinder. "Blame me, will you?" he accused amusingly. "I don't remember ever putting a blade to your neck though," the pupil now preached.

"A blade, no, but a cock? Maybe," Tarwin ruefully refuted.

"Those whores' tents are too small," the lecherous vagabond knowingly reasoned.

"Too small by far," his licentious counterpart agreed, who, despite feigning an earlier coyness, was well acquainted with the tent's dimensions.

"Still though," Korballa reminded him with a grin, "we've never crossed swords yet!"

Pan sat there, mute and unmoved after having finished with his supper, listening intently to the two men speak. Try as he might, however, since his thirst and hunger had both now been sated, an overwhelming tiredness was fast taking over.

"Besides," Korballa announced further, prolonging his discord. "There's nothing else to do in this camp besides eat or fuck anyway," the issue was stated plaintively enough. "This whole campaign hasn't seen my sword leave its scabbard one time in fighting," the sodden soldier truthfully revealed as he patted down his weapon's scabbard.

"That's your cock," Tarwin reported in response to Korballa's purposefully misplaced hand.

The apt identified culprit fell into a fit of laughter. "My other sword I mean!" he corrected himself with a wide grin.

Bellows ensued while Pan's confusion only widened.

"There's not that many people left to conquer I suppose," Tarwin shrugged off disappointingly after the two inebriates had regained their composure. "Just look at where we've come to now," he lamented, waving an arm around to make his point. "It's the edge of the damned world," the critic impugned. "Nothing left out here but savages and dung heaps most likely."

"Some men tell tales about humongous hordes of barbarians and evil spirits living beyond these mountains," Korballa warned warily in their direction, making a cautionary sign to the gods as an assurance.

"Aren't you a little old to be believing in ghost tales?" Tarwin loosely chided. "And besides," he went on, "we'll find out soon enough." The gossiper let it be known, "The general's sending a division through the passes tomorrow."

"Tomorrow?" Korballa repeated with a raised interest.

"Those were the orders passed along this afternoon," Tarwin dug his heels in. He had heard the issuance himself. "That must be why the general was questioning captain Faroh's scout earlier," he conjectured. "To make sure the routes were all cleared beforehand."

"Makes sense to me," acknowledged Korballa with an over pronounced nod that betrayed his high degree of inebriation. "Well I hope there are a great many hordes of them," he challenged boldly, mired deep in liquid courage. "Big wealthy hordes, so I can grow rich and fat off all the plunder," the soaked sod boasted about his dreams greedily.

"Assuming you lived, of course," interloped Tarwin, with a sober-minded snideness into Korballa's self-indulgent pleasantries.

Pan Shepherd heard all this and more until fatigue finally won over and he fell asleep there with his head laid flat upon the table.

"Wake up!" pierced the loud and obnoxious shout after some time had passed. "Wake up I said," the drunkard reiterated more loudly less than a second later, slapping Pan's head stingingly with the reverse side of his hand.

Young Pan was thus yanked out from his slumber once more and made to again regain his feet and follow blindly. His two guides made a noisy way through the encampment, which was by now riddled by mostly sleep and silence. Pan could hear them both talking plainly enough, but he was too exhausted and sleep ridden to care. Instead, he only looked up, observing for himself the crescent moon and the endless heavens which radiated outward in all directions like a million diamonds inside of a black lit canopy.

"Here it is," informed Korballa to the accompanying pair once some indiscriminate spot had been reached inside of the sprawling grounds.

"Go inside and sleep there," Tarwin commanded, pointing to one of the tents nearby.

Pan looked to where he was directed but didn't yet move, having felt a natural disinclination about entering such an unknown space in the darkness.

"Hurry up, boy!" Korballa snarled threateningly, ready to be done with this unwanted nuisance once and for all.

Pan briskly moved away from the dangerous man, glancing back just once more before bending himself low enough to enter the lightless domain. Once inside, however, he began carefully feeling his way around the blackness before quickly making the discovery that many other people were sleeping there as well.

"Let's go," Pan heard Korballa dictate as the two friends prepared themselves to leave.

"This is the last time I go out with you again like this," he heard Tarwin give notice as they started to depart. "So do not ask me again."

"Sure, brother," the intoxicated Korballa replied in good faith. "But that's what you said the last time!"

Each man thus laughed and made his merry on the way to their sordid destination leaving behind young Pan Shepherd to fall swiftly back into the realm of dreams.

Chapter 5

"Hey," a faint whisper arrived sweetly into the dreamscape. "Hey you," rang in softly once more. "It's time to wake up now," the voice told him, its owner tugging gently on his blue tunic.

Pan's mind creaked and groaned like a wooden ship at sea as it brought itself back slowly into the light of day. Once come about, however, the newly awakened Pan found himself unexpectant company to a small girl even younger than he was. She was standing in front of him, staring conspicuously with radiant orbs of emerald whilst possessing yellowed hair that shone like gold's reflection. He sat up as though still dreaming, wiping away the excess sleep from his eyes. The tent was now empty except for them.

"Who are you?" Pan questioned her, blinking, his wits still not yet fully intact.

"I'm Beocca," she innocently introduced herself.

"Well, what are you doing here?" followed up the shepherd boy with keenness.

Beocca giggled. "I'm here to wake you up, silly."

"Wake me up for what?" Pan dove deeper still.

The little messenger was for a short time confounded by this last response. "For work, of course," she stated obviously, hesitating for a moment until curiosity got the better of her. "Say, are you really stupid or something?" the young girl prodded without any scorn or malice, prior to explaining her notion's meaning. "The ones who sent me to fetch you said that you were."

Pan searched over her countenance thoroughly but found nothing in it to incite alarm. "All things are possible," came his ambiguous reply, shaded with a natural smile.

"I guess," Beocca figured with uncertainty, not being either convinced or satisfied by his puzzling innuendo. "Well then," challenged the youthful maiden towards her wayward errand. "So are you going to get up now or aren't you?" she directed to know until his noncommittal response drove her into submitting further, "you'll get in trouble if you—"

"Listen," Pan interrupted her, standing abruptly. "Do you know who is in charge here?" he asked curiously.

"Here?" Beocca misunderstood him, looking around the tent with incomprehension.

"Not here," Pan reorganized her thinking. "Inside the camp," the shepherd boy clarified with outstretched arms to show his meaning.

"Hm," the small girl pondered in thought with a hand on her chin whilst still looking down until she placed it. "His name is General Ballista," Beocca helpfully enriched him.

"General Ballista," Pan repeated aloud, storing the name in value. "Could you please take me to see him?" he next wondered at her.

Beocca's expression turned grave as she informed the shepherd with much alarm, "But you're not allowed to see him," she reasoned to herself assuredly, even appending on as extra, "and neither am I!"

"It's okay," Pan reassured her nimbly. "Just tell them that I forced you."

This rebuttal almost stunned Beocca into silence, and she now really did feel as though she must be dealing with a fool.

"What are you talking about?" inflamed the shocked victim of this obscene antagonism back with an unruly passion.

"I have something very important to tell him," Pan persuaded on further, despite her mounted opposition. "You must take me to see him."

Little Beocca was very much disturbed at this most recent course of events which carried her far out and beyond the bounds of anything aforementioned in her earlier instructions of waking up the slave boy. Barring a more developed judgment, however, and under his directing pressure as well, she finally relented and so agreed to take him.

"What do you need to tell him about so badly anyways?" Beocca requested to know while they were still coursing their way through the burgeoning encampment on that very warm summer morning.

"That he's putting his army into danger," opined the sheep herder knowingly with a convincing conviction.

"Danger?" Beocca's ears shot up at the news. "But how do you know?" she interested concerningly, looking back over towards him.

"My sheep," Pan returned her answer simple enough, returning a glance as they stepped further along the board bound trail.

"Your sheep?" Beocca repeated, clearly having misheard him.

"Yes," reiterated the shepherd boy, much to her confusion. "My sheep showed me, and then the two men from last night confirmed it."

He's as crazy as a loon, Beocca thought to herself whilst shaking her head in pity. Poor fool, she concluded inwardly after having decided to refrain from seeking any further particulars.

A few minutes more spent walking along their way saw that great and gray tabernacle from the previous day come into view.

"He lives in there," Beocca told him, stopping where she stood and pointing out and over towards the same spectacle that Pan was currently studying from across the yard.

The next moment his mind flashed lightning.

"What does General Ballista look like?" he angled at her, searching for an explanation.

"He looks big and scary to me," Beocca gestured at him with a spurned nose and upturned face, discerning clear disfavor.

Pan quickly cast aside that unhelpful news and sought for more. "Is his skin dark, with teeth like ivory?" he tried inquiring of her by using descriptive means.

"Hmm, I think so," the young girl proffered up after having been made ambivalent by the shepherd boy's capricious nature.

"And does he ride a red horse?" Pan followed up after.

"Yes," Beocca thought about it until remembering. "That's it over there," she directed his notice towards a groomsman who was brushing the same pedigreed stallion that Pan had seen the bespoken one mounted upon yesterday.

"I know this man," reported the shepherd to his overwhelmed guide. "I've spoken with him once before already."

Beocca found herself steadfastly dumbfounded by the unmitigated madness in which she now bore herself witness. Without knowing what to say next, but still desperately wanting to know more, the petite miss breathlessly imparted, "But what will you do now?"

Pan responded straight away. "I'll go see him again of course," he told her. "Thank you for bringing me by the way," he added sincerely, his friendly sentiments ensued with pupils staring. "My name's Pan."

With those thanks, introduction, and a quick smile as her only keepsake artifacts, Pan Shepherd turned hastily away and began making his direct approach towards the cloth rotunda as the stunned Beocca could only stand there watching in disconcerted disbelief.

The young shepherd thus began hurriedly scurrying his way across the muddy flats from where they had been situated enroute to where the main entrance way was now located. The two guards on watch there were entangled in speaking amongst themselves and so did not notice his quick approach coming up from their rear. Pan didn't even break stride as he streamlined past the first sentinel and carried himself to within just as the second one took any notice.

That surprised alarmist instantly broke off his conversing and snatched in earnest at the blue bound intruder who had just managed to slip inside his goal. Despite the change in light being sharp and contrasting, Pan was still able to make out a group of gentries who all stood standing around with their backs to him towards the enclosure's far end.

"General Ballista!" Pan Shepherd howled like a banshee while being accosted by the guard. "General Ballista, sir, I have something to tell you!" the rapscallion rebel proclaimed with much vigor and vim towards the shadowy group in meeting.

"You fucking sod," bitterly castigated the sentry who had taken his hold as he made way to injure him out of the tabernacle.

"Stop!" came a lion's roar from out of the pack of hyenas. A loud and forceful man stood up. He had been seated across from the rest at a heavy wooden table tucked out of view. Beocca was right, Pan's mind managed the thought. He is scary.

General Ballista stared odiously at the cause of commotion.

"You're the slave I purchased yesterday," the general recognized with a disgusted disdain. "Just how much of a gods damned fool are you?" he approbated with an appalled condemnation prior to looking at the one who held him there with an almost equal repugnance. He dictated directly, "Remove this boy from out of my tent at once and have him beaten severely."

Pan did not wait for those orders to be followed through, however, continuing instead to carry on with his yelling, unabated, even when the guardsman made moves to expel him. "My people!" the shepherd boy shouted out with a violent volition. "My people here!" he cried aloud once more in the last-ditch effort.

The general's eye's glared hard like the sun off new snow at the miniscule trespasser who was being dragged away from in front of his person. "Wait," he directed hostilely at that same lookout that had so recently failed in his own duty, causing him to immediately lose hold. "Now step back," moreover ordered the viciously incensed Ballista, who had himself been made violently vindictive at this unacceptable breach in process and decorum.

"Very well then," the general beckoned with a practiced grace like that of a wizened aristocrat after having resettled himself from his location opposite the slave boy. "Speak now then, little one, and hope that when you are done I do not have you castrated and made into a eunuch."

Pan Shepherd took stock of his situation, swallowing deeply as he readied himself to address the assembled council at large. "You should not send your soldiers through the passes sir," he started, prognosticating knowingly and in simple terms towards the general with his attending staff present. "Many men are lying in wait for you there on the other side."

The entire atmosphere changed in an instant. Heads looked peculiarly sideways, and a few whispers dropped low off the lips of some as well before the good general did re-intervene, his next words bathed in a sort of perplexed ferocity. "And how do you know what I am to do with my army boy?" he demanded reason.

"The men told me," informed the sheep herder with all due regard and humility, like a defendant does when facing their interrogator's scrutiny.

"Which men?" growled the white knuckled commander, holding back a full gale.

"The two men who took me away from here yesterday," Pan expounded as innocent as a lamb. "One of them gave me this tunic," he appended on helpfully for show whilst grabbing a handful of the blue cloth and presenting it out to him.

A pair of men who were just then standing towards the very back of the tabernacle with eyes half closed from nursing severe hangovers and a general lack of sleep almost fell over sideways when their ears caught wind of the news. They were simultaneously cured of their immediate ailment whilst at the same time being reinfected by another, fear. Each glanced at the other in silent horror while a few of their compatriots nearby who remembered that day's previous orders followed suit, putting increased distance between themselves to prevent any semblance of blame for the failure.

General Ballista nodded in assiduity ahead of challenging his interloper head on. "Those routes have all been cleared, boy," he retorted loudly and in open defiance. "My scouts have already confirmed it."

"Your scouts are wrong," Pan Shepherd shot back, throwing down the gauntlet boldly yet without ever having changed his simple veneer. It was dichotomous to a tee. "You'll lose many men if you go that way today general," foretold the sheep herder towards the surprised crowd of stunned onlookers. Such wanton insolence as was on display at present had been, up to this point, both undreamed and unheard of.

General Ballista resisted his immediate urge to strike Pan dead where he stood. "Tell me," he lured with a false politeness that hid a spider's web of malcontent. "How can you be so sure?"

"My sheep," Pan Shepherd conveyed without reluctance to the general's imposition, exciting even more attention from all those angry and bewildered spectators present. You could have heard a pin drop in so focused and palpable a scene.

"Your sheep?" came the general's own surprised and flummoxing search for clarity.

"Yes sir," settled the rustic's reply with certainty, his small voice bouncing around the shade-filled room towards those straining ears of the expectant throng. "My sheep showed me," he cemented firmly to an eruption of bedlam.

Chapter 6

"Cack," complained Grieves with a growing desperation that was bordering on despondence as he rapidly rummaged about his own kit. "Where's my helmet at?" he uttered to himself in worry-filled doubt prior to going public. "Where's my bloody helmet at?" chagrined again the big bull with a quick seeding frustration. "Has any of you lot seen it?" wondered around the peevish inquirer to his surrounding comrades in arms.

"You'd lose your damned head if it wasn't attached to you," came the increasingly familiar gruff of his new friend, Yusri, who was looking up and over as he continued to strap tight the leather bounds of his bronze shin guards in preparation for that day's ordered assembly.

"Might still lose it yet," opined another man, Bashar, unhelpfully, from one of the adjacent tents while slowly dragging a satiric thumb across his neck as an accompaniment.

"It's right beside you, you big oaf," scoffed down Bashar's rack mate, Sillius, towards the heavy shield on grass that was lying juxtaposed next to his helmet.

"Cyrinee's tits, Grieves," spit a different one of the surrounding soldiers by the name of Quiminax. "Sometimes you're simpler than an ox drawn mule," he teased, causing some of the others who were around and within earshot to make further merry at his expense.

A bit chastened by the gaffe but no worse for wear, Grieves's face brightened widely as he swooped down fast to recover his lost treasure, brushing off some of the dirt from around its rim as he did so. "There she is," he coddled it warmly. "Can't go off to fightin' without yew, darlin'," affectionately spit shined the freshly relieved Grieves ahead of continuing his dress directly.

"You've never fought with that helmet on before," automatically criticized Yusri upon his ears' reception of the endearment.

"Eye didn't say eye'd fought with it," Grieves challenged back with his usual stubbornness. "Eye said eye needed it to," he corrected, smiling and looking about for some approval from his companions, and finding none, he decided to martial on anyway. "An just 'ow come you've grown to know so much about it then, Yusri?" the crass accounter goaded past. "Riddle me that!"

"Your arms and armor are all too nice, for one," shot in Quiminax from nearby, who was almost himself fully mustered. "Just look at them," he decried whilst pointing downwards towards his equipment. "Even an untrained peasant could see as plain as Drako's stone, Grieves, that neither your sword, your shield, nor your helmet has ever gotten so much as a ding on 'em from out of danger."

"I maybe wouldn't go that far," joshed the freewheeling Sillius wryly, making a quip about Grieves during his own shield's retrieval. "Tripping over oneself can bring about its own set of dangers sometimes," joked the jolly jester. "Especially when you're as big an oaf as he is!"

"Quim's got you there, Grieves," piled on Bashar with relish. He was enjoying the good morning's ribbing.

"If there is any sort of trouble out there now, Grieves," Sillius drove in deeper, "you'd best to stay close to papa Yusri then alright?" He nodded with good humor towards his example. "You see here?" he reasoned with him. "It's easier to see than salt's white that Yusri's been through the ringer," the speaker praised his subject. "Why, just look at that helmet!" he appraised laughingly whilst picking it up as an example. "It's been all busted and bashed in to kraken and back," the orator high-lighted his conclusion, costing Yusri a grin.

As their group continued its spirited banter, each one of their battalions, and by the looks of it their entire division, was hurriedly preparing for the upcoming formation which had just been announced at dawn after revelry. All around that part of the camp, like ants in a pile, could be seen the moving bodies of soldiers reaching, grabbing, and putting on gear in preparation for that day's duties. A hot summer morning sun was already starting to radiate down an ever-growing heat onto the backs and heads of the assembling army. First one, and then all the metal bound warriors shone brightly from polished bronze after having finished armoring themselves with the equipment of war.

"What do you think the brass offal want with us today, friend Yusri?" asked Grieves to his closest companion, despite being so recently outsmarted. Grieves was just then himself securing the last ties to his short sword that he had been taught should be used for stabbing and thrusting with during close quarters combat.

"More hurry up and march I imagine," filled in Yusri with his perpetual half scowl. "Same as most days," he ended the insipid report while continuing to make ready.

"It doesn't look like anybody else is going, though," Bashar cut in as he observed around the rest of the camp on tippy toes. "Seems like it's just us."

"What's that?" whipped up Grieves again with another caper. "Just us?" he bemoaned. "but that ain't natural!"

"I don't see any of the other divisions forming up either," remarked Quiminax, who had also just started staring about, adding weight to what Bashar had just supposed.

"Nerva's cunt," Sillius cried afoul as well. "How come we're always the ones to get shafted with extra duties, huh?"

"Who knows?" struck in Bashar sarcastically. "Maybe they just want to march us to the gardens for a nice lunch," he added facetiously before gazing over towards second division and lampooning them with a jealous envy. "Those bitches aren't even dressed yet!"

"Something's not right." Grieves entered back into the fray. "I think our commander must not like us for some reason."

"He probably just doesn't like you, Grieves," the laconic Yusri pithily imparted like a Parthian shot, inviting boisterous laughter from the group.

"Still though," posed Quiminax once the moment had passed, adding in his rod to the fire as well. "If it is just us that's going, then it probably means we won't have to go very far," he carried through the thought to fruition. "Otherwise they'd just move the entire camp."

"It's easier to move a little than a lot," measured Yusri with experience. "Anyway I wouldn't get your hopes up," he padded on as extra upon standing, now fully prepared.

As if arriving right on cue, the army's adjuncts came rushing into the city of tent's thin promenades and packed alleyways, shouting out their cries. "Let's go! Time to move!" they screamed, at first in unison, then breaking off into pieces and making their way towards the many groups at large that altogether made up the whole. One such adjunct eventually filed his way into the area containing Grieve's and Yusri's squadron where he kept up the pace of moving through, hard and fast.

"Grab your gear and go into the staging area!" he barked loudly, looking right and left at each man in turn as he stepped past. "Now!" he reiterated shrilly and in rapid succession while continuing his rounds. "Move it, move it!" They heard him and the others maintain as their volume gradually dropped with distance like the wailing of an enchanting siren.

"Looks like it's time to go then," Sillius posited obviously.

"Seems that way," built on Quiminax with a hopeless resignation.

"Let's go, you ladies!" insulted one of the minder's nearby, targeting Yusri's group and pushing them to begin squirming themselves through the ruckus like everyone else enroute to their appointed destination.

"It's hotter than blazes out," grumbled Grieves over to Yusri as they each took their positions shoulder to shoulder to one another inside of the formation shortly thereafter. The cries and shouts of their superiors caterwauling and haranguing all those still not in place or else coming together too slowly filled the air.

In a brief a time, however, the 2,000 armored and assembled hoplites of fourth division were all standing at attention within the parade grounds awaiting further orders. It was an impressive sight to see.

"Urry up and wait more like it," Grieves condescended towards Yusri in another low whisper without turning his head. "Eye'm already sweating my arse off," he deplored bitterly, seeking company to his misery.

Yusri remained silent without looking over.

Rigid as a stalk, that one, thought Grieves to himself before shrugging it off and losing his mind to its wanderings.

After a few minutes spent frustratedly baking in nature's oven, Grieves noticed the battalion commanders returning back from a meeting with their divisional commanding officer. He stood there, still and gazing, as he watched the battalion commanders call each of the brigade commanders together into a semicircle before delivering their instructions to them. A short time later, the brigade commanders were dismissed and returned to their men to brief them on the relevant information.

"Alright, soldiers, listen up!" their brigade commander eventually shouted out, loud and clear, as does a practiced politician while at the podium. His nasally, mid-ranged tone carried well except to near the peripheries, where it increasingly meshed into a blend of competing echoes from all of the other commanders that were simultaneously dictating their company's orders up and down the line.

"Our task is to head up and take position just on the other side of those passes," he informed his men while pointing up towards the backdrop of picturesque mountains behind them. "We're to move in, settle down, and then hold tight just on the other side of that ridgeline until the rest of the army can move up and clear through," he continued his proclamation. "After that," he began, reaching his conclusion, "we'll follow up as rearguard and help to keep our boy's supply lines wide open."

"Looks like you were right, Yusri." Grieves glanced over in quick and quiet succession.

Yusri did not stir or reply once more, but Grieves felt sure that he was in agreement with him nonetheless.

Succeeding in his oration, their commander surveyed the men in detail prior to provoking them for a response.

"Now then," he pitched out to them expectantly. "Has all that been understood?"

The inflection of his question floated there like a small feather trapped inside of a light breeze before the anvil dropped.

"Sir, yes, sir!" thundered the soldiers unanimously and at the tops of their lungs, the force of which sent shockwaves through the air before his voice had finished trailing.

"Good," commended their commander with a pickled pride prior to taking his cue from further up the column. "Captains!" he next issued forth the call. "Have your men pick up their gear and then move 'em out!"

With their mission now known, the many individuals making up fourth division readied themselves to be synchronized for duty.

"For-ward!" enjoined the captains with their preliminary prescriptions to all of the echelons up and down the formation who were standing by. "Advance!" they shouted in concert, finally unleashing the lumbering beast into action.

The shoddy shuffling of two thousand pairs of soldiers' feet started interspersed and without melody for only a few steps. After that, every one of those hoplite's sandals contacted the earth in lock-step motion, creating a resounding reverberation with every other foot's planting.

Following not so great a duration, the marching soldiers, accompanied by their drums of war, cleared their encampment which sat in the increasing distance. Now there was only the winding river valley and approaching mountain passes to point their way. The day was hot, but there were clouds which would sometimes bring shady relief to those beneath like the thick boughs of a temporary tree. The grass on either side of the dusty dirt way in which they traveled was tall and mostly brown from a lack of seasonal rains that fell here during that time of year. There were no settled peoples or communities around, not on this side of the passes anyway. No one seemed to know what, or who, lived on the other. Besides themselves and their baggage train, there wasn't any sort of life about which they could see, except for the occasional flock of birds. Instead, there was only the inexorable slide deeper towards that great unknown, which always seemed to lie in wait just beyond the next horizon.

"Not talking much today, are we?" Grieves tried chatting across to Yusri while trudging along.

"I've nothing much to say," Yusri deflected the attempt.

"No, well, you really never do then, do you?" remonstrated back Grieves like an apt ignored spouse.

"No, not usually," persisted Yusri, much to Grieves's dissatisfaction.

"Aren't you at least a little curious to know what's on the other side of those mountains?" Grieves tried baiting him out, pointing off into the distance.

"I'll find out when we get there," came the respondent's passionless reply.

"You've got no excitement in you," Grieves scorned towards his neighbor. "It's very lackluster, you know."

"Hah," escaped Yusri. "I'm just not as easily excited as you are," he tussled back mildly. "And this is hardly the first mountain I've ever had to march over either."

"Yes, but did you ever go over not knowing what you'd find on the other side?" Grieves's entreaties continued, easily betraying his hopeful excitement.

"We never knew what we would find on the other side, you damned fool," upbraided Yusri unflinchingly. "That's why we went!"

"No charm either," Grieves carped at him further. "It's a wonder your Mrs. can stand to live with you at all," he marveled. "And three children as well? Pah! Hyra of Ur could do no better, I'd wager."

This brought Yusri into some humor. "Well, I haven't been home very much," he chuckled, though not without some regret. "And besides," he issued with his tense smile, "she's a whole lot prettier than you are."

The two men shared an easy laugh between them.

"Well, I for one am curious," Grieves continued, speaking in his turn. "I want to know what we'll find there."

"Well, we'll find out soon enough then, won't we?" Yusri answered him by way of question as they continued their marching from out of the mountain's valley and up towards the slopes above.

Chapter 7

Back inside the tabernacle, violence ensued. One of the men present, a rotund and dark-clothed individual, came charging out from across the crowd. His heavy feet stomped furiously with every step as he nearly flew across the ground and unto Pan's person without either stopping or slowing down. The force of his impact slammed Pan's small body backwards where it was flung against one of the wooden support posts, making a dull thud. Almost instantly, he was then lifted up from off the ground and put into a vice grip that wrapped around his entire neck.

Hearing the sudden commotion from outside, Beocca turned around and fled headlong back in retreat the way she'd come.

Underneath the tent's canopy, however, as Pan's face reddened into shades of blue and his dangling legs kicked harder for survival, General Ballista did finally intervene. "That's enough," he stated plainly, loud enough for all to hear.

The strangler, either from being too caught up to listen or else too incensed to care, continued with his affair, unabated.

"If you do not remove your hands from my property, Juba, then I will have to take them off of it myself," informed Ballista from behind to his man in resolute firmness, yanking his own blade's handle from Its scabbard, producing the metallic melody of his sword's song.

Juba gave Pan another hate-filled look, squeezing even harder than he had at any time previous before releasing him suddenly and suffering Pan to crash into a heap on the floor. Once there, Pan began immediately clutching at his throat in terror and gasping for air as fast as was humanly possible. Both body and mind tried desperately to recover themselves from the acute effects of prolonged asphyxiation.

"Well now," General Ballista started, looking down dourly upon the frightened and half-choked youth who was lying crumpled next to his tent post. "Whatever am I to do with so complete and utter a fool as you?" he wondered aloud to his audience. "The way you burst into my chambers like this, unannounced and un-invited, in order to display such, such, Gods be praised, such a profound lack of wit; why, it almost seems wrong to have you beaten," he surmised with a slight semblance of pity, as one does prior to striking an incontinent dog which has wet upon the rug.

"Still," he gave Pan a small, merciful sigh. "It would be unseemly not to."

"Guard!" Ballista retempered himself. "Do as I have ordered previous," he in-structed him. "Only do ensure that my property is not permanently damaged or put long into disuse—two or three days and no more," the general finished flatly prior to returning himself back to where they had left off before the interruption started.

"Yes, General," the sentinel snapped to, throwing a salute to his already turned and walking backside.

Pan Shepherd bowed his head into pitiful submission and went silent, filled with angst about the upcoming punishment.

The sentry, accosted the boy with rough vengeance, immediately manhandling him out of the tabernacle and back into the light of day.

"Masonista," General Ballista called in the direction of his most senior at-tendant, a slave who was nearby, upon reseating himself. He motioned for him to approach.

"After the watch has been changed," the general spoke low upon his confidant's arrival. "I want those two sentries outside to be punished," he tasked him formally.

"Sir?" Masonista questioned through inflection while still standing, stooped beside his chief.

"They were derelict their duties," impatiently edified the commander. "They could not even guard me from a simple child, a fool no less," he reasoned with a growing condemnation. "I won't have it," the general laid on, loud and severe, ending Masonista's need for crouching and sending him back into a retreating silence. "The men must know that there are consequences for failure," he declared his mantra to all those who were present to hear it while peering at their faces in turn. "They must learn to fear those consequences," the instructor explained his philosophy. "They must learn to fear those consequences more than they fear death," the general ordained. "Then they will not fail," ended Ballista savagely, leaving little room for doubt.

"Yes, General," conformed Masonista with the rest, nodding their heads in various degrees of acquiescence. "And what of the other two, Korballa and Tarwin?" Masonista inquired further after regaining his master's ear in isolation.

"I will think on that for a little while," he answered him with an adjoining nod of dismissal in advance of calling back into session the assembled officers who were present.

Those inside made to gather themselves once more around the heavy wooden table in order to view and hear their plan of action for the upcoming maneuvers through the pass.

"Not you two," the chief spoke with a frosty bite towards the other two breaches in discipline who were there. "You both wait outside," he ostracized them, pointing towards the exit with an unflinching stare.

Korballa and Tarwin each felt their necks catch fire as their public rebuking was carried out in so blatant and shameful a fashion. Both men's minds seemed to go blank under the intense scrutiny of what felt to be at least a thousand eyes upon them, all disparaging or uncomfortable, like two bad apples in a bunch. The two lepers, thus shunned, then stuttered and stammered their complicit obedience before tucking tails to run. Korballa, during the embarrassing retreat, tripped slightly over himself, causing a misstep and stumble which led to even more ignominy.

Back outside into the light of day, the guard, who had dragged Pan from out of his trespass, began to half pull and half carry him over towards a hitching rail on which he intended to lash the boy rancorously with a horse's whip.

"What happened?" the other posted sentry entreated worriedly to his comrade. He had stayed put during the recent disturbance, but now started to follow the other guard.

"Stay there!" compelled the latter to the former who threatened to leave the entranceway unattended by his trailing.

"Do you know what you just did, you little shit?" the angry, afraid sentinel fumed once they had reached the post. "Do you have any fucking idea?" he demanded emphatically, making way to grab hold of some rope to tie him with.

Pan looked around, helpless and alone, at the few curious onlookers who'd stopped or slowed to spectate in his upcoming beating.

"Stop!" came the ferocious halt from Tarwin, who Pan had seen just leaving the tent with Korballa in tow. They were both now storming straight across to meet him.

The guard made moves to resist them, saying, "But sir, I have orders from the general to—"

"We'll do it," Korballa cut in, looking like death.

"Give him to me," Tarwin issued again, not asking.

"General Ballista said the boy was not to be damaged permanent!" the guardsman pleaded, concerned that their response would be too unrestrained. "Two or three days out of work and no more!"

"We heard him," Korballa spat. "Now hand him over."

With mixed sentiments, the sentry obliged to do as he was told by his superior officers and passed the slave boy to them. It was a strange bedfellow to be so concerned about that which he had just before harbored such animosity.

Tarwin snatched Pan by the outstretched wrist and immediately turned, posthaste, to haul him away while Korballa followed.

Once more the trio made their way through the vast encampment towards a destination unknown. It was less busy and crowded than last time, he noticed, most likely because of the youngness of day. Cooking pots sat or hung above small fires which burned and mixed with the aroma of what was simmering inside them, causing Pan's stomach to pang in hunger despite his present deep concern. He had been genuinely distressed about his coming beating by the guard, but now he was positively fearful. His mind raced to catch up.

"Where are you taking me?" he mustered up enough courage to ask them after walking another few hundred feet in silence.

"To where no one can hear you scream," Tarwin answered him, smiling down sinisterly as they reached the camp's outskirts and continued going, following along the riverbank.

"I didn't mean to get you in trouble," Pan tried reasoning with them. "I was only trying to help."

"Don't bother," Korballa complained. "It's too late for that now."

The two cutthroats walked their mark further out of hearing until reaching a natural depression in the embankment where they couldn't be seen.

"Here we are then," Tarwin recorded with nonchalance as he stopped walking forward and turned around to meet the shepherd face to face.

"Looks like a good spot to me," Korballa agreed, following them up from the rear.

"General Ballista will be more angry with you," Pan tried arguing. "He said he only wanted me hurt a little bit," the boy continued on, growing flustered as the two ravenous dogs began circling their prey. "I didn't do anything wrong!"

"The general doesn't care about you, welp," Korballa enlightened him while pulling the net closed. "You're as good as forgotten by now."

"I won't be forgotten by tonight!" Pan's dam finally broke as he watched the noose tighten further.

The predators hesitated, sharing a quick glance between them.

"What about tonight?" intimidated Tarwin first. "You're nothing but a half-wit slave," he relegated. "Fit for only sweeping up floors and dumping out piss pots."

"By tonight, the general will call me back into his quarters," he divulged his nectar for them both to feed on. "And if I am not there, then he will find out that you two are the reason for it," the little shepherd boy envisaged to his captors with clarity. "And then he will kill you for it."

Incredulous at his response, Korballa himself laughed heartily. "God's alive," he said over to Tarwin, who was himself brooding quietly. "I've never heard such a mouth on a slave before."

"If I'm not telling the truth, then all you have to do is wait until tonight to come and find me, and then you can do with me as you please," Pan spilled his beans. "But if I am telling the truth, which I am," he restated positively, "then if you two kill me now, by this time tomorrow you'll both be dead."

"What in the three winds would general Ballista want with a pompous little Podunk peasant like you in his private quarters, filth?" castigated Korballa spitefully. "You think he fancied you for a trollop do you?" he lampooned further. "You think he wants to bugger a sweet little lad like you?"

"He will call for me because of the men who are going to die today in the passes," Pan guessed with confidence. "He will remember that I tried to warn him when he hears of it, and then he will send for me."

Korballa and Tarwin both paused to take counsel within their own minds about the plausibility of what they were hearing. There was just enough possibility of it being true to restrain their original murderous intent.

"You must think you're pretty smart, don't you?" Korballa inflamed angrily. He was growing even more incensed at his vengeance becoming thwarted.

"You don't seem very foolish to me," hypothesized Tarwin thoughtfully towards the pair. "Sure doesn't seem so now anyway, does he Korballa?"

"Nope," Korballa played along nicely. "Seems like he knows plenty to me."

"Indeed he does," corroborated Tarwin.

"Say, I've got an idea," Korballa offered while looking over towards his companion with a twinkling eye. "I bet I know something we could teach him that he doesn't know about yet."

"Oh yeah?" fired back the accomplice who knew all too well his partner's meaning. "What is it?" he wondered aloud as Pan followed intently the discourse that was flowing back and forth between them.

"If we can't kill him," orchestrated Korballa, "then we can at least bugger him instead."

"Sounds like a great idea to me," Tarwin agreed, nodding his smirk.

Pan had heard that word before, but he didn't take its meaning, and so only repeated again, for their own sakes too, that he should not be harmed. "At least wait until tonight and see for yourselves," the shepherd boy bartered, believing himself close to an unscathed extraction.

Korballa reached over and gripped Pan firmly by the shoulder. "Don't worry, dove," he told him. "We're not going to beat you," came his almost comforting reply.

Tarwin stepped nearer, grabbing Pan by the front before laughing. "You can take him," he smiled across to his friend. "I'll help hold him down."

Pan tried to resist, but it was hopeless against the two grown, war-trained men. Before he knew what was happening, he was down on his belly with Tarwin sitting upon his back and Korballa fumbling with his tunic, lifting it up above his midriff.

"Stop!" Pan cried foul, scared and uncomprehending. He still didn't know what was happening to him. A very short time later however it was forcefully explained as he began to suffer himself being ravaged by Korballa until passing out.

Chapter 8

"Hey," her rhythmic voice carried gently into the blackness like small waves lapping against a moonless seashore before dawn. "Hey, Pan," chirped the little songbird once more. "Pan can you hear me?"

As if startled awake from out of a nightmare, Pan Shepherd came to suddenly and found himself lying prostrate on his stomach. After lifting up his head for a brisk search around, he discovered that it was the same tent which they had previously been inside of. Maybe it was all a dream, he thought to himself until the pain of his body's first movements quickly made apparent that it wasn't so. He laid his head back down, accompanied by a long sigh, and looked shamefacedly towards the golden-haired Beocca who had awoken him, their eyes intermingling in thoughtful unison.

"I told you that you would get in trouble," Beocca told him, fighting back tears. "I didn't want to take you there," she scolded him softly. "You made me to do it!" the kind soul grieved whilst beginning to cry.

"Don't cry, Beocca," Pan comforted her from across the short distance which separated them. "It's not your fault that this happened."

"I know," she whispered endearingly through her sniffles, her little heart beset by strong emotion as if some favorite toy had been badly damaged. "It still makes me sad though."

Beocca's natural kindness touched Pan, who looked at her like a sliver of light that finds itself a well-watered seed down deep between the folds.

"How did you get here?" he inquired of her through quiet conversation whilst staring over sideways from his prone position.

"I snuck away from my work," she grinned back mischievously, betraying a rebellious streak hidden somewhere within her.

Pan simpered at her fondly. "Not here again, silly," he countenanced for a moment of good humor, causing her face to light with joy. "I mean how did you get into this camp."

"Oh," Beocca again sobered, the shadows reforming just as fast as they had disappeared. "The army brought me here," she disclosed with clear unhappiness.

"What about your family?" Pan's interest piqued further. "Are they here too?"

Beocca cast down and began tracing doodles with her fingertips onto the ground. "They got killed," she informed him delicately without looking up.

Despite the divulgence coming as no surprise, it was still displeasing. "By who?" Pan revisited, having been desirous about learning that specific detail.

"By the army," she revealed what he'd already expected.

"I see," answered the shepherd boy from his same stilled position upon the cot. "I'm sorry," he offered her sincerely.

"Me too," she injured, still tracing with her fingers into the dirt before eyeing up. "What about you?" she shifted the focus, seeking out now to find her own discoveries. "How did you get here?" she asked him.

"By the army," Pan copied her with a grim smile.

"Oh," she repeated in downcast murmur before venturing out with the last straw. "What about your family?" Beocca tepidly questioned him while feeling ill at ease, as one does when expecting to hear bad news.

"Same as yours," Pan confided with the same sorrowful regret, confirming her gut's belief.

Beocca shook her head in pity. "I'm sorry," she commiserated with him, from one orphan to another.

"Me too," he echoed back her sentiments once more.

The two forlorn creatures each stared upon the other for a hair's breadth of time as an amalgamation of mutual friendship through shared misery became forged into being.

Beocca changed the subject first. "Did you get to see the general?" she wondered at him.

"Yes, I saw him," Pan confirmed. "I told you that I would," he added on with a bit of boyish bravado.

"What happened then?" She impatiently awaited details.

"I told him what I told you," the shepherd boy dispatched neatly.

Beocca paused for a moment's recollection, sending her eyes upward towards the tent's ceiling before guffawing out with a tickled laugh when she remembered what Pan had told her prior about the men and his sheep.

"But you don't even have any sheep!" she accused him in jovial astonishment, putting her small voice high and casting both palms out and open towards him.

"I used to have lots of them!" Pan defended himself like a child being tickled.

That made Beocca curious, but she was already too distracted by his present story to sidetrack herself now. "And did he believe you?" she inquired with incredulity after becoming captivated by his fantastical tale.

"No, not really," Pan admitted with a friendly ganter. "At least not yet."

"What do you mean?" Beocca sought remedy to his enigmatic response.

The shepherd smiled over to her. "I'll tell you in a few days," he promised.

Beocca grew serious. "Is that why they hurt you?" she checked with a heartfelt compassion.

"No," Pan told her. "Well, not directly anyhow," he said before breaking off his steady gaze and looking away depressingly.

"What did they do to you?" dictated her childhood curiosity.

"I don't want to talk about it," Pan returned abashedly, tears of shame and anger both mixing in equal parts.

Beocca sighted down once more, nudging her toes through the dirt, sand, and grass as she did so.

"Well if there's anything I can do to help," she attempted to rekindle his fire's warmth. "Just let me know," Pan's new friend extended kindly, peering back up with her orbs of emerald.

"Thank you," the shepherd boy offered meekly as a return, bringing his eyes back to hers as well. "I will."

"Ok," the young girl proffered up with a blushing grin, as good-natured as could be. "Do you need anything right now?" she sought to aid him.

"Maybe just some water," Pan requested kindly. "I'm very thirsty."

"I'll get some for you!" Beocca brightened, genuinely pleased that she could be of service before alighting off. She came back almost as quickly as she had gone with a half-filled copper ladle that was carried over to him as he lie there. "I'll help you," Beocca insisted, holding it out for him to drink from.

"Thank you, Beocca," Pan relieved while lowering his head back down to the cot in fatigue. "I'm feeling very tired," he conveyed to her through half-closing eyes. "I think I'll try to sleep now."

"Of course," Beocca rose with a nurturing beam, making herself ready to leave. "You get some rest," she prescribed sweetly, giving his head a light pat. "I'll come back later to check on you."

"I'd like that," Pan appreciated. "Thank you again."

Little Beocca's face shone with delight as she turned to make her haste back out into the throngs of moving masses teeming by just outside his quarters. Pan's cheerful caprice lasted all the way up until she was gone. With her left the sun, and in its place not even the stars remained to light his way. A profound state of ruinous despair flooded over him as that morning's events came cascading back into the forefront of his mind, beating incessantly, like a migraine throbbing inside the skull. Salty tears made his face damp as he lay there, empty and alone, desperately seeking the false reprieve of slumber.

Chapter 9

"Hey now, that's some nice view, that," panted a sweaty Grieves towards Yusri. "Wouldn't you say so?"

"Aye," agreed his stocky counterpart who was half-breathless himself from exertion after a short gander towards the sprawling expanse of mountain valley stretching outward beneath them. "It's a fine vantage to be sure."

"Eye'll say," Grieves carried on with being wholly absorbed. "Look, Yusri," fired off the next directive. "Yew can even see our camp from 'ere!" He pointed across the elephantine valley with his exclamations. "Sure is much bigger in person though, iddnn't?" tacitly checked his compatriot for agreement. "It seems so much smaller from where we are now."

Yusri grinned slightly from his new friend's child-like ease of excitement. "Aye," he copied back over once more after taking in another glance at the scene.

"Eye'v never been so high off the ground before," continued Grieves, reporting where his mind had wandered.

"You're on the ground right now, you silly bastard," Yusri shook his head in mock contempt.

"You know what I mean," returned Grieves with a snap of ginger. "It feels much cooler up here as well," he weathered the observation. "It's not near so hot as it was down in the valley, thanks be to gods."

"That's on account of the altitude," informed Yusri knowingly.

"What's that?" requested his unlearned friend with interest.

"It means how high up we are," the latter instructed. "The higher up we go, the colder it gets," he explained. "And that's not all either," Yusri looked towards Grieves with an edifying expression worn about his face.

"What is it?" Grieves intrigued further.

"It gets harder to breathe too," mentored Yusri. "So much so that eventually a man can hardly catch his breath while sitting down."

"God's alive!" flew out Grieves, first impressed, and then more fearful. "How high up do you think we'll be going then, Yusri?" he worried to know next.

"Not much," Yusri reckoned with a light smile. "The front's already going through the top pass now, and then it will be all downhill from there."

"Well, that's good news," Grieves expressed happily in advance of issuing a complaint. "It's no easy task lugging this here gear around on an upward slope all afternoon," he lamented matter-of-factly.

"That's called incline," Yusri tried improving upon him further.

"What is?" Grieves sought for notice after one again losing his bearings from the unknown vernacular.

"Never mind," discounted Yusri with a short laugh. "It doesn't matter."

The mountain they now traversed was heavily wooded with alpine timbers that formed a dense patchwork on all sides, except the cliff face. Their battalion had meandered its way up to the passes top by that time after a long and arduous day's journey from the valley floor. It was already late in the afternoon then, and both the men, with their officers alike, were wearied by fatigue. Much thought was given to making camp and satiating their hunger, but little was taken for anything else.

Scouting reports had already given the all clear, leaving defensive measures light and discipline lax. Their chosen path had funneled and narrowed the higher up it wound along the mountain's side so that in some places it was difficult to march in any kind of formation at all. In short order, the entire column had become spread out and thin as it stretched its head up and over the peak like a snake out of coil before beginning its slithering descent down onto the other side.

"What do you think they'll have at supper time?" imagined Grieves over to his comrade in arms, full of big dreams and appetite.

"Beats me," shrugged Yusri without any extra foresight.

"Hm," opinionated Grieves longingly. "Well I hope whatever it is that it's as least as tasty as whatever it was that was in that stew last night," he recalled fondly. "That was savory."

Just as Yusri made to respond, an unexpected call was shot up and down the line like cracking ice.

"Shields! Shields!" Grieves and Yusri heard their officers shouting frantically, betraying that this was not a drill.

"To arms, to arms!" they heard from their own commanding officer, who came running down the path past them, flapping his arms wildly like some beleaguered duck.

"What's happening, friend Yusri?" Grieves turned to him for solace beset with a fast-growing tide of alarm.

"We must be getting attacked," he answered him with his hairs standing on end, looking both backward and front for any sign of trouble. The rest of their company's soldiers were quickly clambering together for a semblance of order and reason as they tried to make themselves ready against the unknown threat.

The unready soldiers could hear them coming before their eyes could see any shapes take form. Through the woods they came, hurtling down the mountainside like some terrific avalanche, screaming like banshees who howled and hooted uproariously in a fast-oncoming wave of death.

Grieves had a sudden urge to defecate that was almost unbearable, and Yusri's entire body tingled all over as the butterfly effect that preludes the start of combat took hold.

The trumpet sounders, off somewhere in the front, blew their horns obstinately, signaling first that there had been contact and almost right after that they were being overrun.

"This isn't good," appraised Yusri to Grieves while the fever pitch reached a deafening crescendo just as the rushing hordes came screaming from out of the tree line dressed in their animal skins and helmets of antler.

"What do we do?!" shouted down Grieves to Yusri as the first wave prepared to strike head on.

"Fight or die, fool!" Yusri managed to reply just as the hammer struck.

Their thin line was slammed by one at least three times as thick and in other areas much thicker still. Hot and dirty breath, stank rotten by decay and old alcohol, blasphemed towards them under a hail of swinging arms and metal blades which dinged and clung against the polished bronze that repelled them.

At first, Grieves didn't know what to do, and it was all he could manage to avoid being simply bowled over.

Yusri himself suffered from no such indecisiveness. Hesitation will get you killed, and his was a hand well practiced. Even before sense arrived to the melee, his muscle memory had already taken one life.

Grieves's fumbling defenses, however, were quickly foundering beside him; he was taking all and giving none.

"Fight, Grieves!" Yusri screamed at him from the next shield over as he ducked and parried the man nearest to him while pushing his sword's blade into another's abdomen who was just behind. "For gods' sakes, Grieves, fight!"

The panic of their men around them, his own terrifying fear, Yusri's pleas for help, and watching death approach from slaughter as it was already reaching so many of the others nearby, these things and more conspired to cause something within Grieves to snap, to give way from reason. His mind went completely blank and thought of nothing as though transcended by some tranquil master's thoughtful meditations. He detached from his natural state of being and quite literally lost control with both ears ringing. A berserker's cry erupted from his massive frame, rallying up towards the heavens, before he dropped shield and gripped his long sword with both hands held firmly around the handle.

The lion roared, fierce and loud, defiant against the pack of overwhelming hyena who were fast closing in. Then he started to hack at anything that moved that was not bronze-clad. Great, beastly strokes with both arms and the weight of a rhinoceros behind them were let loosed upon the group of lightly armored warriors who opposed them. His first chop nearly cut a man in two, and his backstroke almost sliced another completely asunder.

Yusri could just see a glimpse of what was developing to his right as he himself busied with facing down his own insurmountable odds. He took an ax to his shield before dropping it hard on the shaft of a spear which was aiming for his ankles, breaking off its head. His next move was a lunge up from the quick crouch which banged his metal shield out against the face of the spearman just as Yusri hooked his arm up and over with his short sword into the shoulder of the one who had swung his ax in the first place. Then he gritted his teeth and fought on for survival.

Grieves himself was fighting like the furies scorned. His war drums constantly blared the blind ferocity of savage combat as he screamed and struck indiscriminately with his sword, killing or maiming with every bite. He was an animal, devoid of sense or reason, surviving on instincts alone.

A bubble started to form around the two natural born killers as Grieves became increasingly avoided by the attacking masses.

"Move, move!" Yusri ordered him amidst the screams and shouts of complete chaos happening around them just as soon as they were not directly engaged.

They witnessed their company commander get struck down, and another of his officers who had tried to escape being caught up from behind and butchered into pieces. Behind them could be heard the shouts for a formation to form while the rest of the division appeared to be completely overrun.

"Go, you big son of a bitch, go!" Yusri screamed without fear of reprisal towards the blood-soaked maniac who was still fighting madly beside him.

Grieves gave Yusri as crazed and demented of a look as Nemesis himself, his chest heaving wildly with neck and eyes both bulging at the seams.

"Go!" Yusri shouted again, this time physically pushing him in the direction from which they'd come before becoming entangled once again into the brutal and wild realm of feral hand-to-hand combat.

Tuck, parry, that slice nearly took off his head, lurch to the right and reach for the Achilles tendon, made two with a wrist turn before twisting back up into a thrust that punctured the other man's lung beneath the clavicle. Grieves was in it deep too, he bellowed like a raging bull as he violently hacked through both the shield and helmet of a man who'd initiated an attack before turning his massive broadside and charging towards two others who had until then been rushing unto him. He collided with them at full kilter, slamming together in a crushing blow that stilled him and flung each of the two onto their backsides whereupon Grieves flew atop them like an eagle and sent them both into oblivion beneath the monstrous blows of his long sword delivered from on high.

With those five gone, Yusri pushed him down further. "Move, you bloody imbecile!" he blasted. "Titan's wrath, we have to go!"

There was mayhem all around them.. Men screeched from the pain and agony of being gouged and sliced open by sharp metal or else beaten to broken by way of blunted objects. The sounds of weapons, shields, and helmets striking together filled the arena with a deafening clatter that was broken only by the raucous yells and battle cries of those still engaged in the struggle. Whistles could be heard from behind, and next to them were soldiers whom Yusri recognized to be from the adjoining company while to the rear remained what was left of their own but which by now had been completely enveloped and almost destroyed.

"Listen to me!" Yusri yelled to those who would listen through the fast-moving hurricane's eye. "We have to move back!" He pointed towards the battalion's supply train.

Grieves himself heard none of it. He only looked right and left while constantly shouting out obscenities at the top of his lungs, near to foaming at the mouth. Three others there who had heard Yusri's exhortations, as well as seen the so far indomitable bastion of protection who was with him, agreed to his plan with wide eyes and nods of affirmation just as the clearing halted.

"Shields, shields!" Yusri commanded as the four readied themselves to put up a concerted effort against the new incursion. Eight, nine, ten, there was not time to count them all before the wave hit, smashing against their little fortress like a storm tide on jutted rock.

"Brace!" blared Yusri as the four planted their back feet and were collectively slid rear from the charging warriors' initial inertia. At the first instance of relief in the pressure, he called out to them from within their outfaced shell. "Enaut! Enaut!" he cried. All at once, he and the outside man hooked their swords up and over the tops of their shields into the neck and shoulder of their enemy while the two inside men uppercut their own blades through the middle of the cracks to disembowel those who were opposing them.

"Back step!" Yusri bawled as the four defenders retreated in unison by a few feet to leave an obstacle of freshly minted corpses for their attackers to stumble and fight over.

Grieves had taken no such cover or defense, however. Indeed it seemed as if he did not know the word's meaning. He only and always just attacked, and those who tried to assault him were themselves blitzed so that each and all became bloodily dispatched under Grieves's unabating slaughter.

He screamed in blood-thirsty ire towards the heavens while swinging with enough might to fell small trees in a single stroke, smashing through wood, fur, meat, and bone alike. A crushing blow was landed onto a man who had just managed to get his wooden shield up in time and which collapsed him to his knees from the force of impact. Then Grieves turned and immediately met an incoming man low, catapulting him up and over himself through the air before coming up at a lunge which led with his shoulder that took another attacker in the chest who then himself flew back and onto the ground just as the first man who had been crippled under the initial strike regained his feet. He shrieked as death came.

"Stay together now!" Yusri ordered his gaggle that had begun to form wings as two more men came upon their small outcrop of relative safety and began clinging to its sides like a pair of shipwrecked sailors. "Enaut! Enaut!" Yusri repeated again as the maneuver replayed itself once more, felling multiple of their opponents and giving a moment's doubt to those still piling on.

The intensity lessened as their perimeter grew, in large part due to Grieves continuing to make his presence felt to both friend and foe alike.

"Who is that?" asked one of the soldiers to all the rest present from within the confines of their bronzed cage during a small respite in the action, causing Yusri to flush with a sudden pride that almost burst him into tears.

"That's Grieves," he enlightened them before quickly regaining his composure and rejoining the fray. "We have to keep moving!" Yusri banged the point home. "That way!" he yelled, directing down the line to where some semblance of order could still be seen. The front was in complete shambles. They had no more lines there. It had been completely swarmed, and every man therein fought for his own life now. It was a situation which was burning down towards them like a fast-moving wick so that soon the hopeless chasm of death would reach their location as well.

"Move together!" Yusri ordered his gathered soldiers who now amounted to upwards of ten, and that began growing more rapidly as the retreating troops from towards the front found refuge in their allies' numbers.

Grieves continued to fume and fury, but the enemy had seen enough of his prowess for the time being, so none dared get close enough to add anymore to his already exceptional tally. That, plus the added defense of Yusri's command post, put off any additional attempts there as the raiders made off in search of easier prey.

They were thus able to move in a group three or four hundred meters down towards the rear to where the supply train was kept. A few of the battalion commanders who were still alive stood around there fervently discussing orders. One of the company's commanding officers nearest to Yusri's squadron called over for them to join in with his formation.

"This way!" he hollered to them through the ongoing pandemonium. "Fill the line! Fill the line!" the exhortation was repeated at an up-tempo shout towards all the incomers who were falling in.

Yusri grabbed his friend and yelled for him to follow. "Stay with me!" he directed at full volume.

The two made it into the fast-filling formation and took to their assembled places side by side within the new front line. They recognized the faces of men to their left and right, but they did not know them. Grieves saw Quiminax hobbling past with some gaping wound, but it was much too loud and he much too far away to do anything other than watch him go. Orders were barked and blasted while the soldiers who were already assembled stood by, watching solemnly the demise of so many of their brethren.

In front of them was a growing massacre as sheer numbers overwhelmed the small pockets of resistance that were left. They had formed as Yusri's had but remained sessile from where their opening stands were made. The anterior of their force was, in all likelihood, completely destroyed; it could not even be seen from this side of the pass. For as far as could be seen, however, there was only fighting. Men locked inside of mortal struggles that stretched off into a dusty void of ceaseless noise and mayhem.

Yusri and Grieves stood in a mostly observant silence on account of Grieves's uncontrollable heaving. His giant body was all a tingle from the horrifying exhilaration of the previous twenty minutes of ferocious combat.

The company officer present relayed their rear-guard commander's instructions. It was hopeless to continue struggling here, he told them, and with night fast closing in, they had decided to make an organized retreat back the way they'd come.

"Riders have already been dispatched with word of the ambush at its onset," they were told. "And by now are racing back towards the encampment at full gallop."

The surviving commanders knew well enough already that it was too late in the day, and there would be no possibility of their remnants making it back onto safe ground before nightfall. They therefore knew that it would be a running retreat until the cavalry arrived with reinforcements and they needed to move swiftly. Staying where they were meant certain annihilation.

Slowly, the rear guard started inching forward in order to descend its way back towards the mountain's base. The slingers and archers, of which there were still a good many since the majority generally marched towards the back, grouped at the newly-formed front where Yusri and Grieves were mustered to help keep the distance between themselves and any incoming marauders. The rest of their division was left where they were, fighting it out in the passes to the last man, hacked and butchered into pieces, or worse. Over an hour passed before the sounds of their screaming could no longer be heard off in the distance.

Soon after they were called to a halt.

"Why have we stopped moving, Yusri?" asked Grieves anxiously to his battle-hardened companion while still himself being covered in the blood and gore of more than a dozen men.

"I don't know," came Yusri's concerned reply. "We should be moving, though," he reasoned. "Can you see anything up ahead?" the vertically challenged warrior asked from his building of a friend.

"Eye can't say for sure," Grieves spouted with difficulty. "But it seems to me like the way is blocked."

"What?" Yusri asked, shocked. "Are you sure?" he doubled down with his alarm bells ringing.

"Certainly looks it," Grieves told him. "There's big trees lain flat all in the road like."

Yusri glanced around to his feet as if struggling with some inner demon before forcefully casting it aside. "Lift me up," he said to Grieves, who looked down upon him warily, the way a lion does a honey badger.

"What?" he sought for clarification of the request.

"I want you to lift me up," Yusri shooshed vehemently before adding, "I cannot know if I cannot see, and I cannot see because I am too short, and I do not trust your eyes to tell me, so I need you to lift me up," admitted the stoic with a stiff embarrassment.

"Ok, Yusri," acquiesced Grieves willfully, careful to not cause offense on account of his friend's small stature.

Yusri sighed with resignation from his observation tower a few moments after. "Ok," he said, disappointed. "Put me down." Once replaced on firm footing, he allowed himself to admit the truth. "You were right," came his deflated judgment. "The road is blocked."

"What does that mean?" probed Grieves, full of apprehension.

"It means that we're trapped," came Yusri's resigned reply before sighing mournfully. "I told you that marching was the easy part."

"Yea," remarked Grieves back glumly. "Now I know what you mean."

Chapter 10

The small expeditionary force who'd been dispatched back into camp carrying news of their attack rode hard beneath a waning moon. Each one assigned pushed their straining stallions to the breaking point in pursuit of winning the race against time. Second watch was almost halfway past when the first rider amongst them to arrive did so at an enfeebled trot, his mount having been made lame during its final stretch.

"Horse!" the black-guard courier yelled loudly to the stupefied watchmen after dismounting at a run and headed straight towards them from out of the pitched blackness.

"Whose that?" one of the sentinels started to challenge before being promptly broadsided.

"Horse! I said, get me a horse!" the purveyor of bad news ballyhoo'd from ten steps closer. "Our men are dying in the passes," he choked out upon reaching them, clearly one of their own. "I must get to the general," he demanded. "Now!"

Dispelled from their stupor and brought back into being by this sudden damnable illumination, the guardsmen closest to him turned around and whistled over shrilly towards the guard house behind. The others who were there then began immediately chattering amongst themselves or else seeking for more detail from the out of breath rider.

"Bring out the lieutenant's charger, on the double!" alarmed the whistler towards the sentry who'd just stuck his head outside to see what was the matter. Judging by his director's foreboding expression and the desperate appearance of the man standing nearest him, he did not add any of the usual snark or bluster which would have normally accompanied such a request, opting instead to immediately turn to heel and head off running towards the stables.

The agitated messenger did not remain idly by, however, and went chasing after the errand bound soldier directly after. The others who were there and that'd been congregating about the area chased after him haphazardly, the way a crowd follows some unfolding tragedy. Soon after, a guardsman who was still looking outward called back to them. "There's another one!" he claimed, causing those who'd been trailing the initial arrival to stop in consternation and turn themselves back around.

"What's that?" checked an initial member from inside of the first group just as the latest night-cloaked horseman began to dismount from his own hobbled steed. His message was a near repeat of his predecessor. "A horse!" he shouted towards the gathering spectators standing clumped around the camp's front entranceway, eyeing his approach. "Get me a horse!"

This second such occurrence in as many minutes sent a buzzing throughout the encampment, which provided notice to the general's headquarters that something was amiss even before the initial dispatcher burst upon the scene. He himself appeared there soon after, riding at a tear atop the gate commander's freshly borrowed stallion.

"General Ballista, sir!" The courier came running in before stopping dead at a respectful distance and snapping to attentively with his salute.

"Proceed," the general commanded while standing up from the table at which he'd just been sitting in order to confront head on whatever bad tidings had sought to injure him. The attendants who dressed him daily could attest that his bulging body, nearly covered in scars from head to toe, was without marks on only his back alone.

"General Ballista, sir, we are under attack!" the horseman spat out. "Ambushed," he reported with a quick glance over at Masonista, who was standing behind his chief with several others. "While crossing over the pass."

Ballista breathed. One breath, deep and full, held in for a miniscule pause before its exhalation out of the nostrils. A second after, likened to the first, except that he released it more slowly this time. Followed in succession by a third, and final, which granted him all the seconds that were needed in which to formulate his plan of action.

"Vega," he spoke over to the cavalry officer who'd until then been sitting on a skin laid bench staring down thoughtfully while spinning his sword's tip into the ground from around its handle. The bespoken man's head shot up and over intelligently towards its summoner.

"Take both wings of the cavalry and provide reinforcements to fourth division as quickly as you can," challenged Ballista. "Leave only enough men behind as is needed to defend the camp adequately," ended this first decree as Vega bowed flamboyantly and without reply prior to making resolutely for the exit. General Ballista then turned to another of his commanders who was present with him at the table.

General Juba was assigned next. "I want you to take third division and route them up towards the passes," Ballista instructed him. "Try to reach them by morning."

"We will have reached them before the sun has warmed the sky, General," Juba boasted cockily in advance of throwing his salute and marching out martially with his attending staff present.

"Masonista," General Ballista delegated following the formers' departures. "Have a few of your men see to it that carts are made ready for the wounded and sent out as soon as possible with food, water, and medical supplies behind third division," he appended. "Have two cohorts from second division to go as escort and send the surgeons along with their accompanying physicians as well."

"Yes, General," Masonista heeded the call. "I'll see to it personally."

General Ballista watched him go prior to rejoining the bearer of bad news. "Now then," he let hang while returning himself towards the messenger, "tell me everything."

A short time later, when the second and then third envoys began to materialize at his tabernacle's entrance, General Ballista understood well the current situation on the ground. He allowed the others their chance to speak out of respect for their zealous exertions, but neither had any additional information to offer. What all could be gleaned had already been done so from that quarter, at least for now.

"Masonista," General Ballista signaled to him upon his return arrival from the medics' station. "Have Captain Faroh fetched and brought here from whatever he may be doing," the edict was passed. "And while you're at it," he attached, following a second thought. "Bring in Tarwin and Korballa as well."

"Yes, General," Masonista complied without dissent, glancing towards the wall of the tabernacle where an upraised eyebrow sent two men along on their way to retrieve them.

"The rest of you may go," proclaimed General Ballista to the remainder of his commanders and their officers.

While the two old comrades were thus left waiting, Masonista spoke to his general in confidence. "Do you think that the reinforcements will arrive in time, General?" he queried him.

"Maybe," Ballista replied informally. "It all depends on if they can make it out of the pass or not," he explained. "The attackers, whoever they are, wouldn't be so foolish as to follow our men out from their redoubts on the high ground," the well-seasoned commander lessoned from experience. "No," he figured most likely, "whoever planned this operation knew well what they were about."

"How can you be so sure?" Masonista was curious to know. "Even dogs can get lucky sometimes."

"This wasn't luck, Masonista," explained the general via his introspections. "They hit us at the end of a long day's march when we were most vulnerable and while it was still light enough to see," he detailed. "And besides," Ballista reminded him, "those routes were just cleared yesterday."

"How do you think it happened then?" perplexed Masonista to his unquestioned leader. "Captain Faroh has never failed you before."

"We'll find out soon enough," foreshadowed the general brusquely.

"And what of the boy?" Masonista passed over on further reflection.

"Let us deal with this first," Ballista sounded just as Captain Faroh was being brought in.

"Captain Faroh," the general greeted him as does a lictor the condemned. "Please, wait a few moments, if you will, while the rest of our group is assembled to join us."

"Yes, General," the captain nervously replied with a swift salute while standing there racking his mind for why he could possibly be there at that time.

When the other two were eventually brought in, it did nothing to help quell his intrigue. He looked at them both carefully but could not see any connectedness between them and so slowly began to relax his guard. The captain already knew through the grapevine that there had been an occurrence, but he still didn't know what it was. Must just be some new orders, he told himself as Tarwin and Korballa each took their spots beside him so that they were all standing next to each other in a row facing General Ballista with Masonista behind him.

"Captain Faroh," the informal tribunal started. "What orders did you receive from me yesterday?" General Ballista asked him bluntly.

Captain Faroh, who could still not see where any fault may lie, answered the question openly. "Sir," he commenced himself to speak. "The general directed that I should take my squadron into the valley and up along the ridgeline to patrol the mountain passes," he dutifully reported.

"Indeed," concurred the general disappointedly. "And what was the result of those directives, captain?" posed Ballista with a first push upon the needle.

Captain Faroh felt unease, but not guilt, and so continued on with his erstwhile narrative. "Sir, it was reported to the general that the mountain passes were all clear, sir, fit and ready for maneuvers."

"Fit and ready for maneuvers," General Ballista repeated back slowly, putting an emphatic mockery on each word.

"Yes, General," Captain Faroh confirmed once more with a small bit of pleading confusion in his voice as he sought reason for this hard press.

General Ballista stared at him with clear disfavor while the awkward silence was brewed more potently.

"Tell me then, Captain Faroh," he bit deep after the pause was done, exposing the truth for the first time. "Why then is one of my divisions under attack right now as I speak in those same passes that you just told me are, how did you put it, 'ready for maneuvers'?"

Faroh was thunderstruck. His olive skin immediately flushed pink at the harbinger. He glanced to Korballa and Tarwin, who were both standing there next to him but each looked away fast from the newly-ordained pariah that was even more leprous than they were.

"Go on," Ballista prodded him. "Tell me."

Poor Captain Faroh could not connect the sudden dots which had shown themselves so unexpectedly. He could only stand there in a murmuring stammer as though a cat had hold of his tongue.

"An entire division, Captain," the general charged with his vexation mounting. "Two thousand trained and well-equipped soldiers, along with their supplies and officers," he winced at the catastrophe. "That's a very expensive bill for one man to make."

"I, I," the bewildered captain struggled to speak. "General Ballista, I don't know, sir," he managed the thought. "I just can't see how it can be true."

General Ballista smarted at the insinuation. "You're not seeing it is the entire problem, Captain," he deposited with judgment nearing. "Do you have anything at all to say for yourself?" The burning torch was held nearer.

"General Ballista, sir, please," Captain Faroh pleaded his case. "In all my years of service to you, I've never once—"

"Stop there," the general intervened, cutting him off completely. "Captain Faroh, it's your many years of experience and high rank which afforded you the position of being a lookout for my army in the first place," Ballista declared. "Your negligence, incompetence, or worse," the general eyed him harshly for a traitor, "has now cost my army dearly." His monologue continued. "The punishment for such a failing, Captain, cannot be anything less than death," pronounced the judge his sentence. "The soldiers themselves would not accept anything less for the infraction," he summed it up succinctly. "And neither will I."

"Guards!" General Ballista called out to the soldiers whom Masonista's well-oiled associates had placed waiting inside the wings for just that occasion. "Take Captain Faroh into custody immediately and see the sentence carried out," he ordered them, without breaking his gaze from off of the damned.

Captain Faroh was still in shock when the two sentinels first took his hold, snapping him out of the trance. "General Ballista, sir, wait!," he cried while being dragged away by force. "General Ballista, sir, please, have mercy!"

Ballista despised the word, instead giving a flippant shooing away towards Faroh as if the captain had been no more than some annoying insect to be squashed. Upon the departure of his caterwauling, General Ballista's inner sanctum fell once more into a solemn stillness as the commander directed his iron gaze upon those two victims who were left remaining.

"And so," shifted the commandant, "what do you two have to say for yourselves?"

Engulfed by terror, the pair who had just watched another man of high repute being hauled off for death, each trembled when they gave thought that they too, in all likelihood, would be about to share in the same fate. Korballa dropped to his knees first with Tarwin immediately following suit as they began prostrating themselves onto the carpeted floor, begging for their lord's forgiveness.

"We didn't know the boy could hear us!" Korballa lamented with a beggar's passion. "We believed him only to be a fool."

"We thought he was sleeping!" Tarwin threw in as additional support.

General Ballista cracked an unobtrusive simper into the creases of his mouth which none could see.

"The only fools here, clearly, are you two," the general scolded them in a conversational manner. "And that one especially," he jerked a thumb over towards the place where Captain Faroh had been standing.

"Yes, General," Tarwin fell on his blade further. "A thousand apologies, your grace, and we most humbly beg your pardon."

"Stop your groveling," disdained the general towards the pair after he'd had enough of their pathetic capers. "Now rise," he directed them both.

The two pitifully bedraggled characters stood up slowly and in sad resignation as they prepared themselves to be dragged away like they had seen happen to the man preceding.

General Ballista announced their fates. "I should have both of your tongues," he told them sternly. "And I would too," threatened the consequence to its intended victims. "Except that the shepherd boy turned out to be right," circumvented the dictator ponderously. "Now I cannot very well punish you," declared Ballista whilst softening his tone and looking at them both the way an awed spectator does after some stunt performer's miraculous escape from danger. "And if I cannot punish you," enlightened the despot, "then I must reward you instead," he finished, looking at them each in turn. "Else I may seem weak," the explanation was over.

The troubled pair did not know what to make of what they were now hearing, so they remained steadfast and motionless, waiting for the bow to crack.

"In light of your 'services,'" remarked the general glibly. "Each of you will be allowed selection of an equine from out of the corrals," he gifted them wryly, like a cook handing out extra sweets to a fat child.

Korballa and Tarwin were astonished. Each just stood there, stupidly mute, with their mouths falling open.

"Did you hear what I said?" General Ballista asked them, plainly taking pleasure in his ready ability to still deliver shock and awe, regardless of the tactics.

Korballa broke first. "Y-yes, General Ballista, sir," he sputtered out awkwardly, still grossly unsure of whether or not he was understanding things correctly.

"Off with you then," Ballista governed with a depreciating nod. "You can go and take your picks first thing in the morning," the general added, "then report back to me here after."

Still overwhelmed by surprise, but also now more confident that they would somehow be leaving alive as free men, the two soldiers regained military composure and struck hard to heel at the same time before throwing a salute and making their departure.

After the miscreants had been dismissed from the tabernacle and it was once again cleared of all people except for Masonista and himself, the latter moved to inquire further about what they'd just heard.

"Do you really think Captain Faroh is a traitor?" he inquired.

"No," Ballista believed sincerely, "I think him unlucky is all."

"Then how do you think it happened?" Masonista extended his petition.

"Goat paths I imagine," general Ballista sighed unhappily. "Speaking of," addressed Ballista over to his confidant, "have Faroh's scout called for, the one whom I purchased the shepherd boy from yesterday."

"Yes, General," acceded Masonista, always ready to obey. "Shall I fetch him myself?"

"That would be best," acknowledged his leader. "I should like some time to think, alone, before the rabble rouses.

Chapter 11

Glowing candles burned low, causing melted wax to drip down hotly from their half-departed wicks by the time Matrius arrived.

"You're just the man I wanted to see," the great grizzly informed him upon his entrance inside of the tabernacle. "You will have to excuse this late hour, Matrius; it is Matrius, isn't it?" Ballista paused to wait for confirmation whilst inviting his guest to come nearer.

"Yes, General," the surprised scout attested from his appointed spot, who, like Captain Faroh before him, was anxiously going over all of the reasons why he could possibly have been summoned into the supreme commander's headquarters during the middle of night. Considering that he has already seen Captain Faroh's head on a spike, his assessment was not a good one.

"Excellent," Ballista engaged amicably before striking closer to the point. "Tell me, soldier," he made to ask. "Have you heard any news regarding that of our comrades in the passes?" the general probed him under an inquisitive eye.

Matrius wisely begged off. "I give neither time nor ear to the gossipers, General," the scout reassured him.

"As you say," the general stabbed passively. "Very well," he conducted like a man of business in meeting. "Allow me to be the first to inform you, then, that fourth division has been ambushed inside of the passes. "There was a short intermission. "Your former captain was held responsible for the failure." Ballista stared up at him.

Matrius felt a sudden shiver go down his spine as he imagined himself about to be implicated in his captain's affair.

"I'm promoting you to take his place," the general ordered him instead, out of the blue. "Starting now," he added, "to avoid any interregnum."

Matrius was nearly toppled over by this unexpected gift horse, and it took him more than a few seconds of thought to recover enough of his wits to look inside its grill.

"Thank you, General, sir," Matrius jawed with credulity. "I am deeply honored by your confidence in me, General, deeply honored," Matrius humbled himself. "You will certainly find no reason to be disappointed in me, sir, of that I assure you."

"Oh, I have no doubt in your abilities, Matrius," parted general Ballista with confidence towards the replacement part. "I am quite sure you will be up to the task." He feigned a smile. "As a matter of fact," Ballista saddled him, dropping the other foot down. "There is one such task which I would entrust to you now," relegated the delegator. "Your first assignment, if you will."

"Anything, General," his new fanatic submitted loyally. "Only give it name and watch thy will be done."

"Rest easy, Matrius," soothed the general his ardor. "I can see plainly that you are eager, but it is no great service that I require from you yet," he explained. "I wish nothing more than to have you go and retrieve for me the shepherd boy with whom you returned with yesterday," the directive continued. "The one I had purchased from you,' Ballista post scripted. "He will be inside of a tent within my slaves' quarters, I presume."

"Yes, General," acquiesced Matrius without hesitation, snapping to briskly and making ready for his departure.

"Hold," Ballista heeded him, much like a dog pining to get off its leash. "There's more," he renewed. "I want you to be unusually kind and gentle with the boy, Captain," the general complimented by addressing him for the first time in his new rank. "I had him beaten yesterday, a mistake it turns out, and so I wish for no more harm to be done to him at present," he concluded with both brows beating. "Do we understand each other?"

"Of course, General," smiled the newly minted captain with as pronounced a grin as the situation could allow. "I understand completely," Matrius accorded him.

"That will be all for now then, Captain," Ballista adjourned with a slight nod of felicitation as acknowledgement of the step up. "You're dismissed."

Matrius bowed low in homage before striking a hard salute and turning himself to depart mission bound for the boy.

With new-found gait in his step and a beaming pride to boot, Captain Matrius strolled his way through the starlit encampment enroute to his particulars. He found the general's slave quarters, which were a great deal nicer than the general slave quarters, near the outskirts of camp. Upon Matrius's arrival, the newly or-dained leader of men sought to search for his desired quarry. A short time later he discovered his culprit after checking unsuccessfully inside a few of the other tents there first.

"Here you are, little fool," Matrius greeted happily the back-turned boy whom he recognized to be the shepherd by torch light. "Now I've found you." Pan was lying alone on a cot that was lined up against an edge of the cloth enclosure before he rolled over to meet the voice and see from whom it came. When he recognized Matrius standing there in the flame-lit darkness, a troubling concern kept him muted.

"Come now," Matrius quipped from outside of the tent with one hand on the torch and another on an open flap. "That's no way to greet an old friend like me, is it?" he joshed.

"Why are you here?" accosted Pan through the flickers, his mind immediately beginning to imagine the worst.

"Ease your nerves, sprout," Matrius settled him, looking about in the shadows prior to taking hold of a nearby oil lamp that was hanging unlit and within reach. "I was sent here to take you back to the general," he informed him. "So grab what you need to and let's go," directed his appointed chaperone whilst providing some light to see by way of the newly lit lantern.

Pan breathed a small sigh of relief in advance of his mind's promptly rejecting it back again. "I can't go now," he abashed in demure.

Matrius laughed. "It's not a request, little lad," he pressed upon him, still in a good humor. "The only reason I did not just walk in here and take you without asking was because the general specifically requested that I avoid your further injury," elaborated the newly appointed captain while beginning to look the boy over. "General Ballista said that he had ordered you beaten," second guessed Matrius aloud after his cursory inspection had ended. "So, far as I can tell, though, you look fine to me," his observation continued. "Looks like you got off easy, in fact," the horseman spited "Now let's go," Pan was ordered for the second time.

Pan's timidity was palpable as he began looking around in search of an escape. It was the same look that Matrius had seen the boy make yesterday after having hopped down from his horse upon waking. "Come now," he scolded impatiently. "What is the matter?" intrigued the increasingly flustered captain, dropping off the torch outside and entering the tent's interior. He walked over to the boy's cot and yanked him roughly into standing, whereupon Pan fell straightaway back down onto the floor, crumpled by a searing flash of pain. The young shepherd threw back up a countenance full of hurtful tears towards his interloper "I told you that I can't!" he shouted out defiantly. "Ok?"

Taken aback by the child's sudden schism, Matrius at first responded with consternation. "What's wrong with you, boy?" he berated him with a scornful glare. "Your legs aren't broken," the captain accused. "There's barely a mark on you!"

At this, Pan burst into tears. Matrius was even more confounded by this strange exchange and so for the next few seconds glanced around the tent in search of any open containers that may be lying around. However, as the little boy's body became racked by uncontrollable sobs whose intensity and volition only seemed to increase, the hard man started to soften and grow concerned. 'He's certainly not drunk,' Matrius determined through second thought.

"Okay, lad, okay," the fellow human comforted him. "There's a good boy now, aye?" he eased in while crouching down next to him and rubbing his backside. "Where are you hurt?" the scout sought to remedy while unsuccessfully continuing to search the boy's body for any obvious signs of trauma.

Pan's only response was to reach over and grab hold of the horseman, burying his small face inside of Matrius's expansive chest and wailing louder.

"Pan," Matrius used his real name "Listen to me, lad," he said while pulling the still sobbing child away from his chest and looking down upon his wet and snotty face with some compassion. "What has happened to you?" the captain sought answer to his riddle. "Why do you cry thus?"

The boy sucked and heaved a little longer as he tried to make his body untensed enough to speak. In a short time however, and under the continued support and protection of the unexpected comfort that was Matrius, he quieted down enough to whisper in a hate-filled shame.

"Korballa," he gritted his teeth in barely suppressed outrage and indignation before beginning to cry again. "And Tarwin helped to hold me down," he hiccupped out after.

It took Matrius a few moments of ponderance until the pieces fit. "Mmph," he grunted in acknowledgement of the names after the fact, as if to say that he was not surprised.

"Well," the horseman imparted with a sincere pity. "I am sorry for your troubles," he delayed the response, "but still, you must come."

"But I can't," Pan pleaded and made gesture from his broken position upon the floor.

"I will carry you," the captain, who now understood the boy's incapacity to walk, said kindly.

"But everyone will know," the sheepherder reacted quietly, both embarrassed and guilt-ridden.

"Yes, yes that's most likely true," Matrius agreed after thoughtful rumination. "Nevertheless, there's nothing to be done about it now," he determined, though not without some regret at the boy's predicament. "You still have to come," finalized the captain. "I'll carry you forcefully if I have to."

Pan looked around dejectedly, tinkering about his mind in search of a solution to the quandary. Suddenly a plan was formulated. An idea arrived so as to give Pan reason for his crippled state and abject demeanor.

"I will go," agreed the shepherd in advance of looking up at Matrius full upon his face, boy to man. "But I want for you to beat me first." He was deadly serious.

Matrius observed the youth strangely, contemplating his little person in a new light. "I thought that you were just an idiot," he charged suspiciously with senses heightening. "What are you on about boy?"

Pan defended himself through a waterlogged face. "Would you want others to know if it had happened to you?" he checked.

This arrow struck close to home with the honor-crazed captain who could readily understand such a sentiment as that. After placing himself for another moment in Pan Shepherd's shoes, he made up his mind to agree.

"Are you sure about this, shepherd?" Matrius made doubly sure. "It will be very painful," he said, solemn and stern.

"I'm sure," agreed Pan readily and without hesitation.

Matrius decided to accept the odd job, but not before suddenly bursting out into laughter as he remembered clearly his general's instructions to him about not injuring the slave boy.

"Why are you laughing?" fumed the shepherd, growing upset again.

"Gods smite me," Matrius answered back after wiping away his tears. "No worries, little lad," he chuckled towards him. "I wasn't smarting at your expense."

Pan did not reply.

"Alright, then," the captain pulled himself up, making ready to do violence. Before Matrius moved to begin, however, he prompted the boy by asking, "You know my doing this won't stop it from happening again, don't you?" The horseman callously informed him, "This is only a temporary solution."

"It will never happen again," fired back Pan like a spear thrown by Hercules.

"Okay then, lad," Matrius finalized while shaking his head at his supposed naivety. "This is your last chance," he warned. "Are you sure?"

Pan gritted his teeth and nodded in the affirmative that he was.

"As you wish," Matrius granted him. "Courage now."

Without any further pause or delay, Matrius flew into beating the boy on his face and body. He was careful to strike with only half strength or less, and he aimed to leave only superficial marks and not serious injuries but still the pain was very real nonetheless.

Pan could not help but shed tears as he was being struck, bloodied, and bruised by the powerfully-built full-grown man who was laying into him. He did not, however, cry out as he had that morning. Only the outflow of pursed air escaping his lips from the impacts gave sound to his inner turmoil.

Upon thinking him banged up enough to pass as beaten, Matrius stopped his waylay and gently aided Pan Shepherd back onto his cot. He then helped to brush off the extra dirt and grass from around his contused and puffy person.

Pan sniffled and heaved, doing all that he could to suppress the tremendous sobs that wanted nothing more than to explode out of him.

"That's a good lad," Matrius patted him respectfully, clearly taking a bit of shine to the tough nut who refused to crack. "Come now," he said while smiling fondly. "I'll not beat you without a reason." His face smirked as he reached down to scoop the boy up gently into his arms before starting to carry him.

Pan continued to snivel and whimper, but he did not cry. He allowed his body to rest on the way to the tabernacle, but his mind was racing.

"You made me a tidy sum you know," Matrius informed him by cutting into his busy thoughts while they walked.

"What?" Pan wondered at him from his interrupted cognation.

"The general's man paid me a nice sum for you," the captain provided some clarity. "So I suppose a bit of thanks are in order," he extended the manner before speaking on. "I don't know why the general wants to see your scrawny person in the middle of the night," Matrius questioned until opportuning an inopportune thought and having the decency to nearly blush. "Whatever it is, though," his dance around the subject was divine. "You'll probably not want an empty stomach for it no doubt."

Pan's midsection immediately tightened with hunger at this bona fide true supposition. It had been ages since he'd last eaten. "Yes please," the shepherd boy meekly responded.

"That's a good lad," smiled down Matrius. "Let's get you some food then, before we go," he suggested. "It won't take us long."

"Thank you," Pan Shepherd quietly relieved back towards the unforeseen benefactor who continued to carry his injured person towards a fate unknown.

Chapter 12

"Gods eye'm starved," complained Grieves over bitterly towards his forlorn friend, Yusri, who was still standing next to him in the front of their rear-guard formation. "It's been morning since we've 'ad a crumb."

"Aye," Yusri agreed, shaking his head like a king in check. "That's the way they wanted it."

"The way ew wanted it?" Grieves sought to have figured.

"Whoever's attacking us," his tutor unambiguously decided.

"What do yew mean?" the inexperienced giant strained his wits to keep up while the latter instructed him.

"Think about it," he connected the dots. "They hit us as the perfect spot." The first line was drawn. "Right when we were crossing over the top of the pass with half our strength on either side," the second intersected the previous endpoint and kept going. "And at the end of a long day's march to boot," his shape was nearly finished. "Pah," he spat. "Those trees down there blocking the roadway are all you need to see to know that this is true," Yusri's macabre design was completed.

"So, what will 'appen now?" the unsettled Grieves sought further prognostication from out of his soothsayer.

"They will wait until later," he rendered his pupil. "Until we are even more wearied by hunger and fatigue," the alluding continued, "Then they will hit us again to finish what they've started," he depressed in sad resignation at the apparent facts yet proved.

"But won't elp come?" persisted Grieves, who was still yet unwilling to resign himself so soon to destruction. "Surely someone from camp would ave known by now that something was amiss and sent for reinforcements?" his inflection made a question of the statement.

"Aye, it's likely so," granted Yusri while some of the others around started to listen in intently to their conversation. "But they will not reach us before morning at the earliest, and by then it will be too late."

Grieves looked down and around at the ground unhappily, clearly disappointed by the news.

"But ow do you know?" he raged like the final glowing of a red-hot ember before it cools into ash. "Ow can you be so sure?"

"Because it's the only thing that makes any sense, Grieves," Yusri scolded him mildly. "Look at us." He waved a hand. "Look at where we are at now and what has already happened." Stock was taken of the situation. "Most of our men are already dead," the hard truth was spoken harshly. "Their work," Yusri offenses while pointing towards the woods which harbored them, "is already well more than halfway finished," he tallied. "So why would they do anything different?" challenged the lecturer who was frustrated by his own calculations.

Grieves gravely nodded his acceptance of the diagnosis in advance of seeking out a cure. "So what can we do?" He searched for a remedy.

"There's nothing that we can do here," Yusri sighed, deflated. "We're hemmed in on three sides with a horde of bloodthirsty barbarians whose hackles are raised, clamping down on the fourth," he reported sober mindedly. "We have no dispersed provisions, and it's already too dark to attempt doing so now under the constant threat of an imminent attack," the realist turned pessimist.

"So yur saying that we should do nothing, then?" Grieves surprised over, still unbaptized by his friend's new doctrine.

"I'm saying that you should make your peace with the gods," Yusri softened a small smile upwards as a consolation. "I don't think that either of us will live to see the sun's rise tomorrow," he winced in pain from the mournful thoughts that his wife and daughters brought. Of the son whom he had never met, but which he was sure was already born and waiting on him who would never come home. The warrior sighed heavily through his melancholy but found only small relief.

"What if we tried to sneak away?" clawed Grieves desperately, seeking for any branch, however big or small, that he could use to help pull him from out of the swiftly moving river which was fast carrying him closer towards a precipitous demise.

"That would be desertion, Grieves," Yusri hissed over towards him, dismissing the notion out of hand.

"Ow is that desertion if we're all certain to die ere anyway?" Grieves challenged back with the vigor of a person who wants to live. "We're much better off to the army alive than dead any ow," he reasoned, not without a point. "It does none of us any good, except our enemies, for us to sit around ere, waiting to be killed, and besides," he added on for good measure, "we wouldn't be deserting, we'd be retreating." The difference was emphasized emphatically.

Yusri allowed his rigid mind to entertain Grieves's line of interpretation.

"Think about it," he pushed on doggedly. "What if no one knows what's appened ere, and we're the only ones left to tell 'em? And your family too," Grieves poked for a reminder, "what about your wife with the new infant and two girls?"

Yusri shot Grieves a look of pure fire and brimstone. "Do not try to have me desecrate my sacred honor by dangling my family in front of me," he nearly snarled.

"Desecration he says," grappled back Grieves contemptuously. "Sacred honor," he snorted. "Well that's easy for yew to say while we're way out ere," argued the proponent. "Meanwhile poor Heidi's off alone with those three little uns, all by erself in the world," denigrated Grieves whilst continuing on with vim. "Forced to struggle in the ways that yew and eye both know most widowed women often must." His face contorted into an upturned and knowing expression. "And for what?" the inquisitor accused. "For the awner of being slaughtered ere? Upon some nameless rock?" There was a small pause. "Tell me, friend Yusri, where is the great awner in that?" the litigator drove his point home.

Before the two sides could dig in any deeper, however, the scales were weighted down in Grieves's favor.

"I'll go," a soldier who was right behind them said who'd been listening in.

"Me too," seconded another who'd fought beside Yusri in his shield wall earlier.

"I don't want to die here," a third man beside Grieves chimed in. "Not cut off and surrounded like this, waiting to be massacred."

Despite being hounded on all sides, Yusri continued to stubbornly resist. "We cannot just walk away," he admonished them. "Besides," the reasoning went further, "if we were seen, our own officers would have us caught and executed."

"The officers would," one of the unknown soldiers agreed, "but not the men."

"So, you want to just leave them here then?" Yusri shamed. "To simply abscond and run off?"

"It's these officers' fault that we've been left behind," another of the strangers asserted, much to Grieves relief. "Instead of trying to afford our escape like this fellow advises," he respected a motioning towards Grieves direction. "They have us sit around here in the dark, without either food or water, awaiting our certain demise," the critic impugned their grievances. "It's ludicrous!"

The others, except Yusri, all concurred with the speaker's assessment.

"We should quietly pass word that there's a soldier-led expedition out of this place," one of the unnamed faces suggested to the group in discussion.

"There's an idea," satisfied another. "We can go around and pass the word," he volunteered. "Those who want to join us can."

"Come now, Yusri," Grieves exhorted before the others left. "Let us live today so we can fight tomorrow!"

"There is no guarantee that we will live!" argued back Yusri, who was clearly losing ground. "Or that we will even make it out of formation!"

"Well ere there's no chance at all!" Grieves grew increasingly upset. "At least out there we av a chance!" he impassioned. "And if we do die, then we'll still die fighting, so what difference does it make if we die right ere or if we die trying to retreat back into camp?" His reasoning turned personal. "Don't you even want to try to make it back to see your wife and children?" Grieves stung before Yusri immediately punched him in the face, threatening to cause a scene.

The strike hurt Grieves, but so too did it dispel whatever final doubts had been keeping Yusri on the sidelines. He stood himself down without further comment or incident as the blow's recipient gingerly rubbed its point of impact without a word.

"We would have to move quickly," Yusri finally relented. "There won't be much time."

A wave of deliverance washed over Grieves, who had until that moment increasingly believed that he would be relegated to die there terribly as he had seen and done himself to so many others in the previous hours.

"Pass the word quietly to those you know and can rely on," Yusri told the rest of them as they started to depart. "Make sure to keep a tight lid on it!" he further warned from behind them. "If any of the officers find out, then our goose is cooked."

As the minutes passed by and the darkness thickened, the sounds of night emanated all around them in whispers and echoes from the masses of unseen nocturnal creatures that called that place home.

A little while after, while the crickets still chirped and the owls hooted, the unknown accomplices from earlier began to come back in and report on their initial successes prior to seeking out further instructions.

"Tell them to meet us near the tree line on the flank," Yusri decided for them.

"Which flank?" Grieves tried to be helpful.

"The one that isn't next to the cliff face," Yusri pointedly retorted, causing Grieves to lower his head from the mistake.

"When?" another man asked, much more pertinently.

Yusri looked up towards the crescent moon's arching position in the sky, judging approximate. "Tell anyone who wants to join us to be there within an hour," he issued them.

"An hour?" the third soldier challenged. "Why so long?"

"I need time to get some supplies first," Yusri settled the matter.

Each man thus tempered, they one and all nodded their heads in joint resolution before leaving to pass along the word.

"You stay here while I go to see what I can find," Yusri relegated his companion.

"But why do eye need to stay?" perplexed Grieves. "Why can't eye go with yew?"

"Because you're as big as a damned house, you fool," Yusri sniped, "and I need to be stealthy."

"Oh," the big oaf figured. "Ok then, Yusri," he submitted. "Eye'll wait for yew ere then."

Yusri waved back his understanding and set off towards where the supply wagons were located.

Grieves himself was starting to become very concerned by his extended absence, even considering that he had been abandoned before half an hour later, with two brown leather sacs in tow and a limping man behind him, he saw Yusri returning.

"Look who I found," grinned Yusri while dropping his load as Grieves discovered with good cheer the person of Quiminax being brought to join them.

"Yusri told me you two boys were planning to make a run for it," Quiminax teased. "Since I don't like the way things are looking around here, I told him that I'll join you!" He laughed over jovially towards Grieves, causing him to do the same.

"What's this then?" Grieves checked his friend's serious injury after their laughter subsided. "The bastards managed to get one through, did they?"

"It was the man on my left's fault," Quiminax blamed. "Never did much like the bastard," he added strength to the excuse. "They managed to get an ax down on my thigh while I was fully engaged to my front, the cunts," storied the teller. "Damn near knocked me right over then and there!" his highlight ended colorfully.

Grieves smiled back, sincerely happy to see his friend alive and mostly well. "And what of the others?" he inquired of him next. "Av yew seen them too?"

Quiminax quickly lost his look of luster and only shook his head sadly in the negative that he had not. "I saw Sillius get swarmed," he told him dolefully. "I haven't seen any of the rest."

The group of reunited mercenaries paused in grievant silence before Grieves changed the discussion's tune.

"What's all this then?" he checked with Yusri while feeling through the leather bags as a child would unopened presents.

"Not enough," Yusri chagrined. "But better than nothing at all," he truthfully added. "Come on then," their self-appointed leader next ordered while picking back up his baggage and tossing one piece over to Grieves. "We need to start making our way towards the tree line."

Fear, that great irrationer of men's souls which conquers reason and swallows courage, had taken tight hold over the remaining members of the once proud and indomitable fourth division. Now, down to a quarter strength or less and trapped on all sides, it seemed as though initiative and daring had all but disappeared into the vaporous void. Whispers and looks, sometimes even hisses of menace, accompanied the exit bound trio en route to the tree line.

Upon their arrival, they found only a small group of nine congregated and awaiting them. Without comment, Yusri laid down the sac which he had been carrying and removed from it a rope that he instructed the men to hold onto as they walked so as to keep as small a path through the enemy lines as possible. "We must move quickly but quietly," he continued briefing them. "No talking, no calls," the rules were listed. "If the man in front of you stops, you stop, understand?" His unflinching gaze checked each of them for compliance.

"Okay then, let's go." Yusri waved them forward from the front of their column once he was satisfied. "Remember," he reminded them, "stay close and keep tight."

The men in attendance agreed to his plan and took their positions along the rope with Yusri at its head and Grieves following second behind. They managed to break off from the formation's side and sneak off without incident. A few of the array waved back to their comrades for the last time as they disappeared into the wood's swallowing blackness.

Yusri led the way through the trees following his sense of direction as well as gravity. He moved up first and then began quietly curving downward to skirt the no man's land between the hastily fortified remnants of their division and the amassing army of annihilation that was preparing to rain down death upon them from above.

They traveled like that for a little while and were making good progress until quite suddenly, behind them, a terrible and terrific set of noises erupted like a screeching volcano. The high pitched yeets and shrill squeals of the amassed warriors preparing to attack were meant to incite fear and trepidation in whomever was on the receiving end of those calls. They caused Yusri and his fellow fugitives to freeze solid and drop low into a crouch. They each listened through the darkness but did not have to strain their ears very hard to make out the sounds. There was the familiar cry of the whistles being blown preceding contact and a short while later they heard the shouts and cries of the careening charge sweeping down off the mountainside to collide with the leftovers of their division at full force. The sounds of intense fighting could then be heard as another last stand was made.

Yusri had heard enough. He tugged along the rope's length and began to continue leading them on their path back down the slopes. As they silently crept, each man listened for as long as the sound would carry their comrades being exterminated. Even without the order for silence issued earlier, none of them would have dared to speak. There was nothing at all to be said.

Yusri continued leading them for many hours, and without further issue, until a spot was reached where he felt safe enough to stop and take a rest. He broke out from the sacs some stolen provisions which were dutifully passed around and distributed amongst the muted men without any word or comments spoken. After fifteen minutes or so, Yusri signaled to them that it was time to continue moving and they each gathered themselves back amongst the rope and prepared themselves to go.

It was still completely dark when the first sounds of hoofbeats could be heard reverberating through the ground towards them. Not wishing to be either trampled or skewered, Yusri quickly led his string of beads further up off the pathway that they'd been following. The rumbling sound grew louder until the unspecified and fast-moving shapes of charging cavalry began flooding past them the way water does in a storm creek upon receiving its first rains after dry season. The men stood back in the trees and watched them ride by, thousands of them thundering along, until finally the long train ended with the last stragglers struggling to keep up.

Yusri gave another tug upon the rope to set his own caravan's wheels back into motion. They slanted downward from out of the woods and began walking into the roadway since it was obvious that the rest of their way was now clear. A shooting star canvassed across the sky overheard which many took to be an omen; some thought good, others bad. Still, they walked on, traveling as before with the rope in hand as a sort of comfort, despite no longer having a need to do so since leaving the forest.

Suddenly their column came to a stop as Yusri halted them. Something else was coming their way now; he could hear it. He crouched low and began to lead his men back off the roadway once more and into the tree line. As the sound grew nearer, Yusri realized what it was. It was the sound of infantry marching on the double.

"Come on," Yusri broke the silence, "they will be our guys."

Grieves felt so relieved that he could cry, but he instead kept mum and said nothing, only following behind silently like the others. They fell into the roadway and stood there in a disorganized gaggle just behind Yusri until the approaching point man noticed their obstruction and called out.

"Halt!" he cried behind to his own men before demanding his way through, thrusting out his torch light. "Identify yourselves!"

Immediately the entire formation behind him could be heard yanking up the uppermost part of their swords from their scabbards in preparation for an attack.

"Survivors from fourth division!" Yusri answered, calling back towards the light. He could see the torch man gesticulating with his free hand at the reply whilst speaking words that were indistinguishable because of the distance between them. The reinforcements relaxed their aggressive stance and a very large man, second only to Grieves in girth, though nearer to average in stature, could be seen angrily headed towards them, followed closely by several torchlit attendants and a few guards.

"What is this?" he roughly accosted upon first reaching the group of supposed deserters until his torch light better showed the picture in front of him. He first saw Grieves, as everybody does, because he's generally the largest person there by far, but this time it was also because he was caked in so much blood and gore that the readied accuser could not figure out by what miracle he was still standing. Then he saw Yusri, who was also well painted, followed by Quiminax that had nearly been cloven in two and so he was forced to momentarily change his tune.

"What happened?" he wanted to know.

Yusri spoke for them. "We were ambushed, sir, right as we were crossing over the pass's top."

The fierce man nodded ahead of continuing on. "Where is the rest of your division?" he pinned Yusri down.

"Still inside the passes sir," Yusri reported regrettably.

"Then why are you here?" the torch-lit tiger accented his last word before eyeing them once more with a deep suspicion.

Yusri could feel the others' stares behind him as each man wondered intently what he would say.

"We retreated sir," he bristled under the contact, "to live and fight another day."

"Who ordered the retreat?" the judge began to quickly sour. "There are two thousand men in fourth division soldier, yet here," he commented insultingly while looking around. "I count less than ten."

The insinuation was clear, but Yusri didn't budge. "Three quarters of our battalion were wiped out during the initial onslaught sir," Yusri venomed towards the unknown assailant. "We had less than five hundred left when they came at us the second time."

"Gods alive," the aggressor stated prior to turning and messaging with one of his aides. "Get those men back on the march," he ordered, directing over towards the assembled troops behind. "Post out sentries on the perimeter to sweep for more survivors and keep alert for any possible intrusions to the flank."

"Yes, General," the subordinate complied with a half bow before turning and running back the sixty or so feet which separated the survivors from their reinforcements. A horn was blown next, followed by the mass of armored soldiers recommencing with their quick time, clanging and clattering loudly as they went by.

"How many attacked you?" strong armed the unnamed commander tersely.

"I can't say, General," Yusri respected the rank. "They hit us from all over and at the same time, but if I had to venture a guess then I would say many thousands at least."

The general took what was offered without giving thanks before circling back to his earlier inquisition. "And who ordered the retreat?" he solicited.

Yusri was once again pigeonholed, forced to choose between either his principles or his head. The choice was easy.

"I did, General," confessed the stoic. You could almost hear the collective gasp escaping from the group behind him.

"I figured as much," the general scoffed scornfully whilst turning to another aide de camp.

"Take these deserters back under guard to the encampment for General Ballista to interrogate before execution."

"Yes, General," the second attendant complied, moving with all haste to call upon some lower ranking associates in order to help procure the required equipment and men needed for transporting the prisoners back into camp.

The general waited until the culprits were being put into chains before spitting on the ground contemptuously and walking off after third division.

"Now you've gone and done it, Yusri," Grieves chastised him miserably as they were being shuffled away under armed supervision.

"I had no choice," the defendant shot back, distempered. "A man's either got principles or he hasn't, okay?"

"Cack!" Grieves cried out incredulously. "It will be hard having principles with no head," he responded.

"It was your idea to leave in the first place!" Yusri reminded him blamefully as they reached one of the ox drawn carts that had been assembled to transport the wounded in. "I was a fool to listen to you," he embittered. "Now instead of dying as heroes and having my family paid upon my death I shall be shamed and then executed as a deserter with the likes of you!" he insulted while being pushed inside the cart by one of the guards.

"Let's go, big man, it's your turn," another of the escorts said warily. "We don't want any trouble now, okay?" he respected on account of Grieves's size and blood-soaked appearance. "We're just following orders."

"Out of the frying pan and into the fire," Grieves sighed heavily while climbing in.

Chapter 13

The first gray light of dawn was just starting to creep up over the horizon when Matrius arrived back at General Ballista's headquarters with the young Pan Shepherd in tow. He was still carrying him as they were admitted into the commander's presence with an ever-present Masonista posted right by his side.

"Ah," Ballista concerned upon his first sighting of the youth, regretful at his mistake but not of its consequence. "They have not beaten you too badly I hope?" the general inquired, as would the owner of a sick horse that was being sold off for the slaughter. He motioned for a chair to be brought over.

Upon its ready placement, Matrius sat Pan down in the provided seat whereupon the shepherd boy looked every bit the injured victim that he'd intended. "No sir." He winced for added effect. "Not too badly."

"Good," the general earmarked for a return while studying the youth without comment for some time. "Yesterday you tried to warn me," Ballista's opening remarks recalled with a piercing gaze. "Today I will listen to what you have to say." He settled in like a bribed magistrate preparing to hear a case.

The contused, puffed-up, and bloodied young Pan responded meekly that he was willing. "Yessir," he sided without appending further.

General Ballista nodded like a bureaucrat who finds that all of his parchments are in good order before proceeding.

"I understand how you knew where my army would go," the general gathered his intelligence. "But what I want for you to explain is how you knew what would happen to them once they got there."

Pan Shepherd had been listening attentively to the general speak and was doing his utmost to appear respectable despite his shoddy and downbeat appearance. "I told you." The rustic's inexperience with speaking to gentry showed through as a natural impertinence. It was not done intentionally, however; it was merely a habitual over familiarity with those who felt themselves to be his superior. "My sheep showed me."

General Ballista kept his calm. "Yes," he grated. "I remember that." His tone grew more exasperated and severe. "What I want is for you to tell me how."

Pan walked along the razor's edge as does a tightrope artist when he spoke.

"Oh." He loosed the arrow towards its center mark. "Sometimes when my sheep are lost, I have to find them," the shepherd boy plainly stated in his prepubescent tone. "I saw the men waiting there while I was looking for one."

"When?" Ballista abruptly cut in.

"On the day before yesterday," he delivered openly.

"Why did they not stop you when you came upon them?" Ballista continued perusing the carousel. "Why did they just let you go away again?" He peppered the boy with questions.

"They didn't see me," Pan weaved. "I used the trails to go around them."

General Ballista's ears shot up at the news. "What trails?" he fixated sharply.

Pan looked confused by the question but did his best to interpret its desired response. "The trails over the mountain?" He answered as though it were a question.

Ballista directed a sideways glance up towards Masonista, who himself smiled back down from the shared sentiments.

"Careful boy," the general warned gravely. "Are you telling me that you know another way to get over this pass?"

"Yessir," Pan admitted eagerly. "I do it twice a year at least."

A victorious smirk spread itself over the cruel lips of General Ballista after he'd heard the report. "Tell me," he then asked with a well-disposed disposition, "do you also know what's on the other side?"

"Yessir," the shepherd continued to be helpful, "that's where I'm from."

General Ballista gave a thankful look up towards the heavens as he appreciated this good fortune.

"What is your name, boy?" the general made to inquire whilst eyeing him with a new-found value, the way that one would a pile of black coal possessing diamonds.

"My name is Pan, Pan Shepherd," he introduced himself with a half bow followed by another wince.

"Pan?" Ballista reiterated, still unrepentant at the damage that'd been done on his account. "How peculiar," he commented. "Tell me, Pan," the inquisition continued. "Why do you care what happens to my army?" the general confronted him directly whilst looking hard over the well-beaten youth. "Why did you try to help me?" Ballista sought to find out.

The sheepherder looked abashed before responding with the candor of a child. "I thought that if I helped you, that maybe you would give my sheep back to me," he lied innocently enough.

"Ba hah!" General Ballista let escape a sudden quip of laughter. "My gods," he said while shaking his head with a deprecating smile. "Masonista," said the general. "Whatever am I to do with so foolish a slave?" the commander commented rhetorically and in good humor.

"We shall try to find something useful for him, General," Masonista spirited back, clearly entertained as well by the youth's unrefined simplicity.

"Have one of your attendants check with the cooks, Masonista," Ballista directed. "See how many of the boy's sheep we have left remaining," he humored the shepherd.

This order was immediately carried out by a single look delivered from Masonista to one of his well-trained associates. The man responded without hesitation and exited out of the tabernacle enroute to complete his task.

"Now then," Ballista rejoined in an almost conversational manner after finishing his side chat with Masonista. "I'm sure there may be something that can be done," he reported hopefully, causing Pan to flash a busted smile.

"However," the general lost his easy demeanor and replaced it with a more businesslike approach. "There is something that I need you to do for me first."

Pan had the presence of mind to look concerned without replying, clearly disfavoring the proposition.

General Ballista gave another short laugh at this response. "Do not look so worried, boy," reassured the lion to the mouse. "I will give you back your remaining sheep once it is done."

The shepherd could not very well refuse. "What do I have to do?" he surrendered.

"I want for you to show my men how to move behind the pass without being seen," the general demanded by request. "Do you understand?"

Pan looked both unhappy and unwell. "Yessir." He nodded timidly. "But it is very far from here and I cannot walk it," the shepherd boy issued forth with an undue apology at his having been rendered disabled.

General Ballista regretted his decision's consequences for the first time until quickly coming up with a solution. "That's no matter," he dismissed. "I will have Captain Matrius carry you," the commandant solved whilst looking over towards the captain for an acquiescence that was quickly given.

"Okay then," Pan accorded. "I can show you."

Ballista pounded a heavy fist upon the table in a preemptive triumph that startled Pan backwards into his chair.

"Captain Matrius," the general addressed neatly.

"Sir!" Matrius snapped to in an instant, more rigid than a pole of lead.

"I want for you to take my horse and ride this boy back up to the passes where Generals Juba and Vega are both located now." His mind was working too fast for him to slow down his train of thought. "Once you arrive there you are to give General Juba this," Ballista directed him towards a hastily written scrap of parchment which he was scribbling away on. "I want him to take you and this boy with all quickness and to move as many of the third division as can make it around behind our enemies to attack."

General Ballista finished his first message and tore the piece away before starting on another right after. "These orders are for General Vega," Ballista further
explained. "I want for Vega to push a frontal assault with the cavalry as a decoy,"
the strategist planned. "Once the enemy is engaged and committed," Ballista told
him, "then General Juba will drop down behind them like an anvil and smash into
their rear to break our way through." His stratagem was complete. "Are all of my
orders understood, Captain?"

"Yes, General, right away, sir," the horseman dutifully complied as Ballista finished with his second message and then passed them both along to Matrius for
safekeeping.

"Good," was again restated. "Then take this boy at once and be off immediately," he commanded. "Ride like the wind, Captain," the general enjoined with
vigor. "You will find the Red Hare is well up to the task." He smiled knowingly
before their dismissal. "Like the wind!" Ballista's voice trailed after him as he and
Pan left outside the tabernacle to make all haste towards the general's stables.

"You!" Matrius shouted at a lackey who was standing outside preparing that
morning's feed.

The servant looked up only to become rudely accosted by the charged and impatient Matrius, who had suddenly appeared there before him like some angry
apparition. "Bring out General Ballista's mount, as quick as you can!" he barked.

Without a second thought, the footman hopped to, nearly tripping over the
food bucket, and ran over to complete his task of preparing the great stallion.

A few minutes later the majestic red equine was led out of the stables and
walked over at a trot towards Matrius and Pan by the still running stable hand.
Matrius could not help but have his mission's ardor momentarily checked as the
great thoroughbred came nearer. It was a work of art, he adored, the most perfect
horse he'd ever seen.

Matrius regained his composure by the time the fiery beast arrived. The lackey
was surprised enough to protest when Matrius climbed aboard it himself and then
pulled up young Pan behind him to sit between his legs.

"What are you doing?" the slave started to challenge him before being silenced at the end of a whip.

"General's orders!" Matrius menaced back as he threw out his legs and kicked them hard into the steed's sides, causing it to immediately dig in its powerful haunches and launch out at run.

By Jove! Matrius thought to himself as he struggled to hold on. He'd never rode a horse like this in all his life. It seemed as though an immortal strode beneath his person. The Red Hare was a flawless specimen of beauty, strength, and speed.

Pan Shepherd was enjoying the ride as well. Despite his many injuries, both physical and otherwise, he was carried in relative comfort aboard the living arrow that'd been shot by an unseen bow. The champion ran so hard, so fast, that it seemed to be on clouds of air as its hooves barely touched the ground at all. It was a level of speed that was wholly unknown to either man or boy alike and which stayed miraculously constant, like the burning of a star, as it charged itself across the grasslands enroute to the mountain's passes.

"We sure are going fast!" Pan yelled out to Matrius through the whipping wind and rising sun as the famous Red Hare bellowed out great huffs with every stride.

The captain laughed aloud in joy. "That we are, lad!" he shouted back. "You'd better hold tight!"

On and on the indefatigable beast raced, unchecked and untampered, as it made its way ever closer to their goal. They arrived an entire hour earlier than they would have had he used his own mount instead. Matrius finally idled back the great creature upon reaching near to where the outermost posted sentries were standing on guard.

The pickets there, however, quickly noticed General Ballista's Red Hare, and they took him at his word that it was urgent. Matrius and Pan were promptly let through and given directions as to where to find the two commanders.

Following those instructions, the captain and his shepherd came upon the first grizzly remains of fourth division as they moved past the now cleared trees which had been blocking the roadway. Now it was the site of their last, last stand. Pan

Shepherd was horrified by the gruesomeness of it all. He gripped Matrius's thighs hard with each hand but still could not tear himself to look away.

As the two plodded their horse further up the pass, the scenes grew only worse and more horrid. The higher up they went, the more time their attackers had had to do their work. Bodies had been cut apart and mutilated, some flayed, others half burned. Expressions of agony could still be seen on many of the victims' twisted and contorted faces of death. All around them were deceased soldiers, bloating in the hot sun. A quiet but savage anger reigned supreme in all of the men there in response to the barbaric and ignominious treatment towards so many of their friends and comrades.

Generals Vega and Juba were spotted amongst the carnage directing some burial and recovery operations there.

Matrius set the Red Hare back into a gallop and made his way hastily towards them.

"Generals!" he shouted whilst riding nearer, catching their attention as he did so.

"You ride the General's horse," General Vega noticed with a curious concern upon his reaching them.

"I do, General." Matrius lifted up Pan and hopped down with him off the red stallion to deliver his news.

"What is it?" General Juba sneered, a hair's trigger away from violence. All of the men there were boiling with rage.

"General Juba, General Vega," Matrius addressed them each in turn as he handed over their respective correspondence. "My name is Captain Matrius, and General Ballista sent me with orders for third division to move behind the enemy lines as quickly as possible to cut off our enemy's retreat while General Vega's cavalry holds them in place here with a frontal assault."

"Masterly if feasible," Vega spoke with a refined delicacy after finishing his reading. "And did he happen to provide us with further instructions as to how?"

"This boy here is to guide us," Matrius informed them, inviting an immediate look of surprise and indignation.

"The general wants me to follow behind this welp?" Juba insulted him with an incredulous defiance bordering on insubordination. Neither man took any notice of his injuries.

"Yes, General," Matrius replied gingerly. "This shepherd boy is from the mountain's other side and knows of a way which can be taken to put us behind our enemy's position undetected."

"Horse shit," Juba spat, hardly mollified but willing given the circumstances.

"How long will it take the boy to get into position?" Vega expressed a more helpful thought.

Matrius looked to him for an answer.

"It usually takes me around two hours when I go," the shepherd responded meekly.

"You'd better hope that you're right about this, boy, or I'll have you skinned alive and roasted when we return," threatened General Juba with death and agony.

"Alright," Vega led. "I'll hold my men here for two hours before we try to take the pass," he formulated. "That should give you plenty of time to get around and move into position," his calculations figured.

"Agreed," Juba hardened before calling out loudly to his second in command. "Demetrius, have the men immediately mustered to set out," the general dictated with a vindictive relish.

"Yes, General," the second in command acknowledged before bowing out and moving on to reform the men.

"Alright then, lad," Matrius informed him while reaching down to pick up his light load. "It's time to go."

"Gods favor you, brother," Vega clasped Juba by the forearm. "I'll meet you in the middle," he smiled confidently before releasing his grip.

"And you," Juba replied with a moment's grace before stamping off. "Let's go, Captain!" he shouted at his behind for Matrius and the shepherd boy to come follow.

Chapter 14

Korballa harried Tarwin into reaching the corrals that lay outside of the encampment before breakfast was even taken. An exceedingly rare occurrence for the incessantly voracious Korballa, who was now leading their way like some conquering hero in the midst of a triumph.

"Our pick," he kept repeating over and over to himself. "Can you believe it, Tarwin, our pick!" The sprightly fellow near frolicked on account of his exuberance. "Look!" directed the happy Korballa with an enlivened excitement, "there they are!"

Stretching out before them were multiple pens of horses. Each of the wood bound enclosures held many hundreds at least. Despite the early hour, there was already a beehive of activity taking place around the grounds when the two subordinate officers arrived to collect their prize.

Tarwin had, despite the occasion, been walking along with a strange silence and reservedness that morning. It was as though he were brooding over some inner machinations which Korballa could not fail to miss but which his present circumstances allowed him to ignore.

"Good morning, Master!" greeted Korballa with an unfamiliar cheer and friendliness to a master of horse who was just then berating some young idlers who'd been caught lounging.

"Get back to work, yuh bunch of mangy loafers," he derided them. "You 'ont find no time tuh be goppin uhround ere!"

The set-upon shirkers scattered like roaches exposed to sunlight as Korballa and Tarwin both reached him.

"Good morning, Master," Korballa entreated for the second time upon reaching the spry elderly man with a jubilee that was not contagious.

"An juss ew are yew to decide wut kind of got damned morning it is?" the cantankerous old horse trainer gutted out. "Whadda yuh want?"

Taken aback but hardly put off, Korballa related to him the purpose of their visit.

"Ell," the master quipped as if it were no concern of his. "Go inside an choose un then," he imparted impatiently. "This isn't a boarding house," the terse notice continued. "U've got tuh make ur own way around ere," he ventured out to them both before tipping his hat and walking away to oversee more goings-ons. "Let un of my boys know from which'd pen yew'd picked um frum," he called back with a final instruction. "I've got tallies tuh keep updated for thuh feed count."

With permission granted, Korballa shrugged off the rude reception and exhorted his friend to come join in with the hunt. "We're about to become equites!" he celebrated ahead of turning on his heels and speeding off. He began moving around the holding pens methodically, in constant survey and attention to detail. Tarwin quietly went his own way, separating himself from his erstwhile companion like some self-imposed prisoner in exile. At times, when Korballa would shout out or signal over regarding some especially fine thought or specimen, Tarwin would only nod or return some other halfhearted gesture as one would be apt to do when being either disinclined or disinterested.

After about an hour or so had gone by and both men had viewed and studied dozens of horses between them, a choice for each was finally made. Tarwin, for his pick, had chosen a lovely, staunchly built chestnut carrier with a high-born prow while Korballa for his selected a vigorous yearling with speckled gray and black markings. It looked as though it had been rolled in soot.

As the two new equestrians gave notice to the stableboy on watch there from which pen each of their mounts had come, Korballa finally allowed Tarwin's melancholy to incite his attention.

"What's eating at you?" He investigated the storm clouds gathered around his friend's downcast horizon as they approached the exit to leave and return back to camp. "You've been quiet as a field mouse all morning," Korballa harried him. "I thought you'd be more pleased."

Tarwin's rain fell heavily from out of its swollen clouds. It was like the arrival of a monsoon that blotted out the sun. "I've been thinking about what the general's going to do when he finds out that you raped the slave boy," he got off his chest, staring over disapprovingly towards his friend.

"What do you mean?" Korballa immediately went on the defensive.

"I mean that the boy turned out to be right," Tarwin explained. "You heard the reports this morning," he pertinently reminded. "That means the general will want to see him again," the brighter one among them poked the point's tip in deeper still. "But with the way you buggered him," recalled the witness, "I don't think he'll walk right for a week." There was no seeking for humor in his statement. "And what do you think General Ballista's going to do when he finds out why?"

Ice shot through Korballa's veins like a polar blast while at the same time an immense heat broke out like a rash on his skin that then began emanating off in waves. "But the general wanted him punished!" defended the rapist.

"Yes, you dumb animal," Tarwin let loose with a wither. "He wanted him to get beaten, not fucked."

"Why would that matter?" Korballa tried to reason.

"You think that it won't?" Tarwin argued back assuredly.

"But you helped me to do it!" Korballa fired off, shocked by the sudden sortie. "You sat on his back and laughed while it happened!"

"I know!" Tarwin yelled in exasperation, igniting some attentive stares and glances from the passersby.

"I always told you that your prick was going to get you into trouble," Tarwin denigrated, "but now you've gone and fucked us both!" The speaker sighed with a pronounced resignation before stopping with his new horse next to the encampment's front entrance.

Korballa'd had the wind taken out of his sails also and so now sought to stop and loiter by the roadway as well.

"What should we do?" he asked remorsefully.

"What can we do?" Tarwin answered back plaintively. "By now I'm sure the general already knows." He sighed again, looking down heavily upon the Earth where he figured he may soon be resting. "As soon as we go into headquarters this morning we'll have these horses stripped and probably our lives taken as well."

"For a slave?" Korballa gasped incredulously, his appetite once again whetted by overriding concern and fear.

"It appears as though he may be much more than that," Tarwin was the first to figure.

"Then we could lie," Korballa pecked at a glimmer of hope. "We could just say that it isn't true and that the boy's a liar."

The newly minted horseman lost his patience. "By all the gods I swear you really are a degenerate fool," Tarwin lambasted him. "All they would have to do is check!" he snarled, frustrated. "Plus we took the boy directly from the guard, remember?" the accomplice prodded. "And still others saw us when we delivered him back into his tent afterwards, unconscious." The litany of evidence was rattled off one after the other.

Korballa was again made to see clearly the error of his own judgment. He thus allowed the latest strike to go unchecked after having run out of useful ammunition in which to return fire.

The two men stood there in their brewing silence, thinking no more about gift horses, breakfast, or well-endowed whores. Now their thoughts were centered only on the bleak horizon of severe punishment or execution looming large over their doomed heads, like the executioner's blade before the fall.

Tarwin ended the stalemate first. "Well," he figured with a depressing smile whilst rubbing down on his new mount. "We should at least take them for one good ride then," he gave his depressed opinion on the matter.

Korballa reciprocated with the sort of smile that precedes a last hoorah before nodding his agreement. "I suppose you're right," he admitted while giving his new-found prize some fond attention as well.

"Let's go then," the counterpart spoke as he climbed awkwardly aboard his own mount like an unpracticed person would, patting down gently upon its neck.

"I'll follow your lead this time," imparted Korballa with a little bit of black humor as he pulled himself atop as well.

Tarwin looked forward and then dug in his heels hard to start the races. They then careened at full gallop towards the grasslands which were running alongside the river enroute to nowhere. Korballa came riding next to him in all haste and looked over sideways as the two old friends shared a laugh while cutting capers before retribution's time had come.

They sprinted about, to and fro, forgetting their troubles enough for a short time to give both new vigor and spirit. After their steeds had run hot, however, and they themselves were made sweaty, Korballa motioned towards Tarwin during a short respite to look at something odd which could be seen setting off in the distance.

As the two stared over, they could make out the general's stallion moving at a blazing speed as it cut its way across the landscape in front of them, about a quarter mile off, near the roadway.

"That's The Red Hare!" Korballa exclaimed whilst peering harder.

"So it is," Tarwin readily agreed. "But who's that riding it?" he perplexed. Even from that distance they could tell plainly that it was not Ballista. "And who's that riding with him as well?" The horseman's interest piqued further.

The two mounted riders sat perched upon their own horses' backs, scrutinizing intently The Red Hare's passengers.

"It can't be," Tarwin broke first.

"You think so too?" Korballa exclaimed hopefully.

"It looks like the slave boy!" he nearly shouted.

"What in Numa's wrath could the slave boy be doing riding upon the general's horse?" Tarwin wondered in incomprehension.

"Do you think it means he doesn't know?" Korballa checked hurriedly.

"Maybe," Tarwin ruminated deeply. "But probably not," he decided and cast down again. "It's time to go and find out, though," He sighed before making himself ready.

Korballa looked across with pursed lips and resigned himself as well before the two horsemen turned their slickened steeds and made to move them at a trot back inside camp.

"Let's eat something before we go, at least," Korballa ruefully suggested, his body finally overpowering his mind on the matter.

"We can," Tarwin agreed with indifference as he led their way back into the enormous encampment, riding high but with spirits low.

Chapter 15

The prisoners came filing in, one after the other, into General Ballista's headquarters during mid-morning. There was a steady stream inward until the last man there had entered and taken his position inside of the line that was then facing their army's commander.

The general viewed them all with a stern disdain that bordered on open contempt as they were being led in. His attitude gradually shifted, however, in accordance with the results of his looking each man over individually.

"I was told that you all were deserters," General Ballista issued to the group at large, like a judge reading off an arraignment to the mob. "Your appearances here would appear to suggest otherwise," he noted with an upraised brow. "In any case," the talk continued, "I need to know what happened to my division." Ballista paused while looking over the bloodied and roughshod survivors. "Who speaks for you?" cast about the fisher of men with his net spread open wide.

After the earlier episode had occurred between General Juba and Yusri, one of the men there who was present took it in his mind to try and speak for himself. His oration hadn't gotten off the ground more than two words before Grieves stepped forward with a heavy clank from his armor and anointed from his blood-caked person that, "Yusri speaks for us, sir."

The other man fell back into line without further comment.

General Ballista looked from Grieves towards that of whom he spoke, taking him under consideration for the first time.

"Alright then, soldier," Ballista started toward him, "tell me what happened to my men."

Yusri straightened himself up to as tall as possible, which was not nearly so tall as he would have liked. He then stepped out in front of the others to relate unto the general through simple soldiers' speech what had happened and how. From the enemies first charge until their own imprisonment, his story was related the

way that a combatant would tell it—not a runaway. Yusri gave details and observations which showed his experience and leadership under duress. General Ballista
was particularly impressed with how he used the rope to exploit the darkness and
more than once his eyes glanced over to Grieves upon hearing of his martial prowess as well.

General Ballista listened to the accounting given by Yusri with full attention,
seeming to live vicariously through the ordeal. He grew softened to the story's
teller as the accounting wound on, understanding full well the type of picture that
was being painted in front of him due to his own wealth of knowledge on the
subject. At times he sat there with his eyes shut tight while listening to a certain
point or detail being given, the same way that an audience member might if lost
by captivation during some composer's heightening crescendo. By the time Yusri
had finished speaking, the general had taken quite a shine to him.

"You and him," Ballista gave another notice over towards the elephant in the
room, "managed to do all that?" He hung the question there like a picture on the
wall to be stared at.

"I have reported it as it happened, General," Yusri defended them. "No more
and no less," the laconic stoic recorded dryly. "Though we did not do it alone, sir,"
Yusri gave credit like a good leader should. "Every one of these men here did their
part."

"So it would seem," Ballista nodded before leaning back in his chair to con-
template again the group at large.

"Well," the general then stated directly, "so far as I understand it, you did in
fact leave the division without receiving any orders to do so." The truth was spoken. "Is that correct?" Ballista checked, causing Yusri to slightly wince at its effect
before affirming that it was so.

"I see," their commandant furnished with severity. "Generally, the punishment
for desertion is death, gentlemen." Ballista eyed them each in turn, meeting their
gazes fully. A sudden sweat broke out on more than one man's back from the
notice given.

"However," the general broke his long silence after the proposed sentences had sat low inside their stomachs like massive stones for a full stop. "It wouldn't go very well with the men were I to execute the last survivors of a massacre." He afforded some thought to his soldiers sentiments. "It would do more harm than good," the reasoning extended further. "That and I agree with you as well." Ballista surprised his entire audience before bringing Yusri back once more into the limelight.

"Were not my pig-headed and muddle-brained commanders as clever and prone to initiative as you, a mere foot soldier," he commended out loud to the tabernacle at large, breaking his gaze from Yusri and looking around towards all those who were present with an outstretched hand pointed towards him. "I would have still many more warriors alive than I do now," the general regretted remorsefully.

The prisoners, Grieves especially, were beginning to feel less of a chill in the air from its apparent dissipation as their outlooks improved.

"Given how many officers I've just lost," General Ballista aimed his sights upon Yusri once more, "I'll be in need of some good replacements." The commander stared with both eyes prying.

"What's your name again, soldier?" sought out the leader of men from his inquiry.

"They call me Yusri, General."

"Not anymore they don't," ordained Ballista with a genuine smile. "Now they'll call you Major."

"Sir?" came the flabbergasted and flummoxed reply of incredulity from the newly advanced infantryman who'd just been risen high above his natural rank and status.

"You heard me, Major," Ballista addressed him by his new title. "I need officers who know how to think and lead when it counts," he told him. "Have I not chosen my man correctly?" the general searched out expectantly for an answer.

The newly promoted Yusri was nearly overcome by that tempestuous ocean of emotions that lives within all men and which constantly fights to not be governed. Now it threatened to roam freely, raging about his soul like a bucking bronco so that it was all he could do in order to simply say, "Yes, General," as a response. He was half afraid his eyes would start to well with tears.

Grieves, by his own account, was made full of cheer by the happy news and even Quiminax, who was beginning to suffer mightily as the hours passed and his wound was left largely untreated, gave satisfaction at the dealings.

It was during this scene that Tarwin and Korballa both slunk back into the general's headquarters, fully expecting the worst. Instead, they were met with an unconcerned glance in their direction which was neither troubled nor venom-filled. It went back to its original purpose about an instant after.

"And you," General Ballista spoke to Grieves next. "The gods have rarely made so fine an example of a soldier," he complimented most graciously. "Nor as blood covered but without injury it would seem," the general added on as polite humor. "You there," the commander spoke over to a slave in waiting, "bring this man a chair to sit down upon." He was referring to Quiminax.

The big man, Grieves, nearly blushed before opening his mouth to speak, self-deprecating himself to his own detriment like that of a cat which shows itself to be without claws to the mice.

"It wasn't much really," Grieves mis-truthed. "Certain as rain, I can't even re-ally remember it!" He was much too fresh. "Twas my friend Yusri ere that pushed me from out of danger in the first place." His commentary next included, "With-out m pushin me down the line with the others," Grieves jerked a thumb over towards the rest, "eye'd be still back on that mountain lyin still with death." He grinned with a width that was much too unseemly before finally bringing his vo-luminous circumlocution to an end. "E'll make a very fine major, though, your grace, av no doubt."

"Indeed," was all that General Ballista stiffly replied after the untoward display was over. "Is there anything else?" The general had by then turned himself back towards their group's leader.

"No, General," Yusri shot out before pulling back in. "Actually, my apologies, sir, but if I may," he humbly begged pardon, "I'd like to request that Grieves here be assigned to my detachment." He put his loyalty on full display. "And Quiminax too, sir."

"Very well," the general acquiesced willingly. "In fact, you may have them all, seeing as how you've already led them so well thus far," he doled out another admiration. "See that your man here is taken to the aid station at once and then head to requisitions to get the rest of these soldiers squared away; we break camp today."

His volume raised loud towards the tent at large. "We move out today," he told them. "We'll half days march towards the valley floor and then begin crossing over the passes tomorrow at dawn," the edict was announced. "Begin gathering your men and materials together," the general's pronouncements carried on. "We will depart by this afternoon," the late notice was given, causing a flurrying of activity to start.

"Major Yusri," the general addressed him.

"Sir!" Yusri saluted hard and sharp.

"You and your men are dismissed, Major," General Ballista announced to him before turning to start a conversation with Masonista, who was by his side.

Yusri gave a half bow in homage before turning and ordering his men to move outside. "You heard the general," he directed them, "let's go."

As soon as they'd officially reached outside of the great, tent Grieves accosted Yusri jollily from behind. "Major now, is it!" He clapped his friend's back and smiled as broad as his large face would allow. "Gods alive," he cried out. "Eye thought we was gonners for sure, and now ere yew are, a bloody major!" His mind still couldn't reckon it. "Eye must be dreaming!"

"Juno's cunt," Quiminax spit as well. "Grieves is right, Yusri," he seconded. "I never in a million moons saw that one coming."

"Nor I," Yusri admitted truthfully. "Part of me feels like the gods must be toying with me." He smiled wide and then thought about his family and how proud it would make them.

"What are your orders, Major?" one of his unknown troopers broke into his revelry.

This sudden imposition startled Yusri back into the present. It made him realize for the first time that he was now on a different playing field than a short time ago when he was led inside the tabernacle as a prisoner. Now he was no longer simply an enlisted man, a soldier with three tours of experience. He was now an officer, a leader of men.

Yusri's rigid sternness took command as he made to give his first official orders.

"Grieves and I will take Quiminax by the medics to get his wound sewn up and cleaned," he led on. "I want you men to go and get cleaned up yourselves, take some chow, and then get some rest," their new major endeared himself immediately. "In three, no make that four hours, I want you all assembled with your gear here at this same spot ready to move out, understand?"

Nobody shouted, as that would have been uncalled for given the situation. Instead, the men all agreed with a few, "Yes, Majors," sprinkled throughout. Yusri did not need to lord his rank over them; he was from the trenches and had proven himself capable many times over. Each man felt glad in their hearts, some even lucky, to have him as their leader.

"Off with you then," he dismissed, sending them all on their way. "Come now, Grieves," Yusri then said over to his friend; there would be no rank between them. "Let's go and get Quim here stitched up."

"Thank you, Yusri," Quiminax offered sincerely. "My apologies," he laughed, "I meant Major."

Back inside the general's headquarters, other business was being attended to. Tarwin and Korballa, both with much inquietude, approached their general to report in as was ordered of them the night before.

"General Ballista, sir," Tarwin spoke for them two. "Korballa and I are here reporting for orders," he spoke uncertainly, trying his utmost to resemble that of an invisible and inanimate object.

"Ah yes, it's you two," came the ambiguous acknowledgement which sank the two men deeper into their stressful concern. "And have you each now a new mount?" he asked them, looking up from his parchments.

"We do indeed, sir," came the short reply. "Thank you, General," Tarwin offered with Korballa joining in right after.

"Yes, thank you, General," he added.

"It was nothing," General Ballista brushed aside their thanks. "Go and prepare your gear," he issued them his orders, "then report back here ready to depart with the attending staff no later than noon."

The two men stood there like condemned men who'd just had their sentences commuted at the final hour. They were unable to compute any alternative to what they'd worked up for themselves into believing was a certainty.

"Well?" the general inquired impatiently at their non-response. "Have you something to say?"

"N-no general," Korballa nearly stuttered. "Twelve o'clock, sir," he reiterated back before saluting, causing Tarwin to do the same.

"Good," Ballista noted before facing back down to his maps. "You're both dismissed," he remarked whilst waving them off without looking.

Once outside the tabernacle, Korballa nearly burst with excitement. "He didn't know!" he exclaimed. "He didn't know! Otherwise he would have said something, right Tarwin?" his ardor momentarily dampened in case he were again mistaken.

Not believing it himself, Tarwin could only nod his head in the seeming acceptance that it was so.

"I can't believe it!" Korballa sighed another huge relief. "You see!" he accused. "It was nothing to worry about!"

"It must have something to do with the general's horse we saw earlier," Tarwin thought out loud, trying to piece the disordered puzzle together. "Or maybe the boy was not so hurt after all?" He shrugged, skirting the first smile that he'd had since the previous night when the consequences of their day's actions had first appeared themselves in his mind, preventing him from further slumber.

Korballa followed the good humor with his own snarkiness. "Maybe it wasn't his first time!" he joshed wryly.

"Or maybe you've just got a small prick," Tarwin jabbed over, causing both men to laugh.

"By gods, I really thought we were done for," Korballa admitted, shaking free the last worry before Tarwin stuck it back on.

"We still may be," he opined, "if the general ever does find out what we did then we'll most certainly face punishment for it."

Korballa considered the matter over in his mind carefully, causing a cloudy countenance to reappear.

"So what should we do?" he solicited his ready accomplice, searching for a cure to their malady.

"Kill the boy," Tarwin resolved.

Chapter 16

The savage caravan of armed killers with a murderous intent swarmed swiftly through the side passage shown to them by the shepherd boy whom Matrius still carried with him whilst pointing their way. General Juba was the third in line, carrying his large battle ax with both hands held full around the heavy handle. The low clatter of jostling and jangling men, weapons, and armor rattled to shake free the small stones and pebbles from out of their many hidden nooks and crannies along the craggy goat's trail.

They kept moving, in some places having to pass in single file so that the column of soldiers again became spread out and dispersed. Like ants in a line, they each moved ahead, one behind the other, following blindly but full of malevolence. It was a race against time to arrive and spring the trap closed.

For a long stretch, their meandering continued on unabated. Pan Shepherd quietly directed the way, and Matrius carried him forward like a rucksack, huffing and puffing all the more the farther they went. General Juba himself was the first to break silence, interjecting a foul tempered check from the boy's behind.

"How much farther?" he growled with an angry impatience.

"Not much now," the shepherd boy meekly assuaged.

Within ten minutes, Pan Shepherd began to have Matrius slow down. They were approaching a clearing in which their current path emptied out into the way that a stream feeds a river.

"That's it," Pan whispered. "It's through that way." He pointed to the right. "That's the direction of the pass," their guide told them before then turning towards the opposite pole and adding further, "and down that way is the jungle."

"Jungle?" Matrius was surprised.

"That doesn't matter now," Juba cut in irritably. "Keep moving into the clearing."

Matrius instantly obeyed, carrying himself, along with the boy, guardedly out from their sidewinder path and on to the open ground beside it.

Once there, Juba immediately began ordering his officers about in muted signals to assemble their respective troops into an attack formation. It took more than the usual little while for all of the well-armored and ready soldiers to come filing out from the goat path. The delay was made even longer as they worked to fill inside of the line which ran exceedingly deep on account of their location's narrowness. Eventually, however, and after much quiet cajoling, they were all there, high-strung and expectant. None of the enemy had so far spotted them, which led Juba to suspect that something was amiss.

"How far up the pass are they?" The general moved over to wrought answer from out of the boy whom Matrius still held like an injured calf. He was clearly referring to the enemy, but the way that he spoke to Pan made it clear that they were both considered one in the same.

"Half a league I think." He wilted under Juba's withering stare.

"We'll move closer," the general decided himself upon the intel's reception. "I want my men to be charging distance." He smiled brutishly. "General Vega should be starting his attack at any time," Juba calculated over to Matrius whilst looking up towards the sun.

"Be sure you keep this welp out of my soldiers' way, Captain," the threatening tiger snarled towards the horseman's charge. "We may still well have a use for him yet when this is done," he concluded by way of a final disdaining sneer in young Pan's direction before brusquely turning away and stepping off.

General Juba marched out, cutting as silent and intimidating a figure as death itself to the front and center of third division. He swept his merciless gaze from one side to the other with a vicious pride and indomitable spirit. His earlier orders regarding silence under pain of death were still in effect. There would be no raucous shouts or cheers of approval as would have generally been the case. Instead, they would continue to move on, muzzled, before swooping down like birds of prey from on high upon their unsuspecting victims.

The general turned with purpose and, leading by example, began to slowly jog up the passageway carrying his double-headed battle ax with both hands wrapped tight around the pole. Juba himself never carried a shield. The rest of third division shuffled slowly after him while Pan and Matrius stood aside, allowing for them to mostly pass until heading up with the rear.

Juba halted his division with a single upraised arm once they had moved into a better position. From the back of the formation, nothing could be heard except the sounds of men trying to be quiet or of nature when the wind blows. Closer to the front, however, the signal was clear. There was fighting up ahead. The sweet release that Juba felt could not be tamed. With a flourish of flamboyance, he turned around to face his men, bringing on level his imposing grin to greet them.

"Soldiers!" the firebrand shouted. "Soldiers, the enemy are over there!" he pointed towards the sounds of combat that were now reaching them. "Our brothers already fight alone without us!" the general shamed them. "And now they wait for our blades to join them!" Juba rallied his men. "Remember the fourth!" their indomitable leader cried. "Remember the fourth!" the impassioned exhortations continued.

"Ah-oot!" General Juba then released a bellicose and ferocious roar towards his bloodhounds like raw meat thrown to the wolves. "Ah-oot!" The battle cry was repeated, this time with an ax thump to the chest. It was immediately followed by the two thousand other members of third division who'd intentionally had their hackles raised. "Ah-oot!" they copied their leader in a voluminous eruption of noise and demonstration which was certainly heard by those at whom it was directed.

"Ah-oot!" Juba heaved out once more, deep and heavy, working up his horde into a murderous frenzy before letting them off the leash. "Follow me!" he led them. "Come now," the call went out, "let us go show those horsemen how real fighting is done!"

His last order was as clear as crystal. "Attack!" he screamed demonically. "Attack and kill them all!"

General Juba turned his powerful body and began to lumber it at a trot leading up to a run at the front of his small army. The men of third division, on seeing their leader's vigorous display and martial spirit, watched him charging headlong into the enemy alone for only another moment before their own dams broke as well. There was nothing that any of the officers could do to maintain any semblance of order to the formation. The entire mass simply pushed forward in one giant swell that was soon running off at full speed in chase of their ax-wielding commander.

All at once they saw them, right as they came flowing over the small bumpy outcrop skirting the edge of the ridgeline. Down in their front could be seen General Vega's cavalry locked in a head-on struggle inside of the pass's choke point, fighting to get through. Large groups of armed men could now be seen being pulled away from that altercation and hastily assembled into a new line which faced the direction of Juba's war cries.

The aforementioned stood atop the vantage point for less than a moment before continuing his rumbling charge towards the hastily-assembling new line. Ever closer behind him, and eventually passing him by, came the less portly and quicker steps of Juba's foot soldiers, each vying desperately for the honor of drawing first blood.

The hunters had now become the hunted as the outraged and vengeful bronze mercenaries came from out of nowhere to crash into their enemies' half-assembled rear. Juba saw one of his armorers, a soldier from Kinzalla, take first blood after he launched himself through the air and into a breach that was found within the still-forming fighters, taking the man's life who landed beneath him before he himself was slain.

General Juba and his men came on like the arrival of a thunderstorm in summer. First there were only a few fat and interspersed droplets striking hard against the ground, kicking up dust as they fell. Before long, however, the downpour started, and with it came the wind and the hail. Juba was like a hailstone that drops before the rain arrives. General Juba was an unnatural man who preferred the chaos and freedom of battle to the dreary, hardly palpable peace of everything else, women and drink excluded. War was what he was best at, and his reputation preceded him.

The heavy sounds of his footsteps approaching were lost through the din of growing battle. Juba charged their line as if he intended to bowl right over them, but with surprising nimbleness and speed he checked himself at the last moment and brought down his ax instead. The aim was not to chop, but to hook, as he reached out and caught the top of a man's wooden shield who was at his front.

With a single, well-practiced move he jerked down hard causing the caught shield to lower before shoving the ax head forward and crushing the man's face behind it. Juba then pulled back with his left hand, sliding the ax's heavy pole through the loose grip of his right to make an arching swing directly through the space that he'd just created in order to catch another man's now unprotected ribs. They splintered like split eggs crushed underfoot before Juba pulled with his right arm, now swinging his ax using only one hand up and over his head before grabbing its handle with his left hand just as he was bringing it down like a man chopping wood for the fire, splitting the intended victim right through to his trunk.

In seconds, Juba had already taken three men out of the fight and made a gaping hole inside the enemy's line that faced him. Reinforcements next came pouring into the gap like a torrent, screaming and charging in from behind as they went so that in only a few moments' time the fight had transformed into a rout.

As soon as the fighters engaged with General Vega's cavalry felt the pressure let up from their rear and realized that it was because they were being attacked there, they panicked. Within seconds, a general flight ensued as the enemy force lost all cohesion and began to splinter away into many multiples, the men scattering to and fro in every direction as they attempted to save their own skin.

General Juba and his men continued to kill indiscriminately and without mercy. A few of the lightest-footed combatants who smartly took to the mountain's side instead of attempting the pass were able to survive and thus escape, but the rest were all slaughtered.

"Good to see you made it, brother," General Vega's voice greeted warmly through the eerie calm of death as he hopped down off of his horse and sought out his fellow general's embrace after the fighting was done.

"And you, brother," Juba reciprocated with a soldierly affection through still-winded breathing.

"I thought there would be more," General Vega made his feelings known while looking around the pass.

"I'd hoped the same," Juba agreed, though with differing sentiments in mind.

"Fabian," Vega called for one of his horsebound, lower-ranking attendants. "Go and send word to General Ballista of our victory."

The bespoken rider clapped to with a crisp salute before turning around on his steed and racing off at full gallop back down the mountain.

"Get me a body count of the enemy," Vega directed towards one scribe in particular, "and bring me a count of all our wounded and of any dead as well."

"Yes, sir," came the quick and ready response that was followed by swift actions.

Juba's second in command, Demetrius, also then arrived on hand.

"General Juba, sir." His man saluted with a chest that heaved from all his recent exertions.

"Have all the men been accounted for?" General Juba started.

"The count is being conducted now, General," responded Demetrius from his position of attention, still trying to catch his own breath.

"And has their leader been found?" Juba followed it up further.

"Not yet, sir," the second in command reported what he knew.

The general was slightly disappointed. "Very well," he told him. "Have some detachments start moving these carcasses out of the way," Juba began issuing orders. "Have first and second battalions sent forward to that escarpment," the general pointed over, "and start fortifying our position there." To avoid any later surprises he also added, "And send half of third brigade to go and block the goat's path that we used to skirt around the enemy as well."

"Yes, General," Demetrius accepted the responsibilities unquestioningly.

Captain Matrius appeared soon after through the masses of moving men and horses who scurried about, moving the dead and stripping their poor and battered bodies of any meager wealth which they could find. The shepherd was still being carried along with him.

"Well done, Generals," Matrius congratulated them both jovially upon his arrival.

"Why do you still carry him around like a newborn, Captain?" Juba unappreciated the compliment, addressing his attention instead to the spurned child.

"Juba," Vega laughed at his friend's ill humor. "Did this boy not just help guide us to an easy victory?" he reasoned fairly.

"Pah!" Juba spat, unwilling to admit the truth.

"General Ballista had him beaten yesterday, General," Matrius respectfully explained his answer to the initial question. "He still cannot walk on his own."

"They went too easy," judged Juba harshly towards Pan, who was frightened and could only look up in search of assistance from the two others.

The subject was changed on its own by the arrival of the attendant who'd been sent to get a count. "Nine hundred and seventy-one confirmed dead, General," reported the subordinate dutifully.

"That's far too low," Juba turned his attention away from Pan and focused on the provided number instead.

"Yes, that does strike me as odd as well," Vega intervened with his own thoughts on the matter. "They must have pulled most of their forces out before we got here," he opined. "It couldn't have been just these."

The counter was dismissed.

"Not even a thousand," Vega thoughtfully stated.

"You must be right," General Juba agreed. "They must've believed that they could hold the pass with just a token force," he assumed.

"Without that boy's shortcut they may very well have." General Vega gave a nod towards the shepherd. "You can't fit more than ten men through there at a time," he said whilst pointing back at the narrowest point in the pass. "And even fewer horses," he added as an afterthought.

Chapter 17

Pan Shepherd became something of a celebrity around the soldiers' camp. Once word had gotten out that it was he who had tried to warn the army about its earlier ambush and that it was also him who had led Juba's division around behind the enemy, the shepherd boy became an instant success. The youth was quickly transformed into a sort of well-appreciated mascot and lucky charm all combined into one. Juba himself maintained his resolute dislike towards the youth, but the rank and file particularly relished in Pan's presence and often cheered him whenever Matrius would carry him past.

General Ballista, they had received word, was on his way with the remainder of the army. He had passed instructions that General Juba's men should continue fortifying their newly won position while General Vega and his men were directed to begin probing the downward path for any signs of the enemy.

Matrius himself was afforded an easy position of sinecure by his two superior officers and had only to maintain his watchful eye over young Pan Shepherd until the general arrived. The boy was not pampered, but he was certainly indulged as Matrius allowed himself and his charge to be given every manner of food, drink, and attention made available by the surrounding soldiers. The captain was very careful to limit the boy's wine intake, however, less he suffered a repeat of what had happened before.

The atmosphere was still very much muted but the defeatism and feelings of vengeance which they had carried along with them like chips on their shoulders were now satiated for the time being. The dead of fourth division, and a few from third, had to be carefully collected, cleaned, and laid out for the funeral pyre which was set to take place that night. The enemy dead, by comparison, were simply tossed over the cliff face or otherwise heedlessly discarded as food for the wolves and carrion.

"Why do they do that?" Pan asked whilst looking upwards towards Matrius, who was carrying him past a group of soldiers that were still cleaning and wiping down the bodies of their dead comrades.

"Why do they do what?" Matrius dealt freely with young Pan after having by this time developed a fondness for the boy.

"Why do they clean the bodies before they burn them?" the shepherd clarified his curiosity.

"It's a mark of respect," Matrius informed him. "And to ensure that their spirits are not sullied while leaving the body through the flames," he detailed as extra.

Pan absorbed the thought before thinking next, "But why do they burn them?"

"We have to," the horseman answered knowingly. "If we didn't, then in a few days their dead bodies would bring on a pestilence to the living."

"But why does that happen?" Pan's train of thought continued down the same road.

"Because the dead become filled with many ill humors," his edifier patiently explained. "Ill humors which can then get passed on to the living, causing them to fall ill or even die as well."

Pan Shepherd nodded his head in understanding as they continued their stroll around the top of the mountain's pass, taking in the sights and sounds of all that went on about them. Men dug redoubts and chopped wood, carried bodies or equipment, talked, and ate together in small groups or else otherwise moved about in order to carry on with the usual activities associated with mass funeral arrangements and fortification.

One group of laboring soldiers stopped what they were doing and approached Pan Shepherd to see firsthand the little cripple who had sought to warn them and then who had later also pointed their way.

"That's a good'un!" The first man approached with his breath smelling strongly of alcohol to give Pan a vigorous rubbing on his head for good fortune. The others who were there with him also each crowded around and wished to touch upon him as if he were a lucky trinket.

Pan himself very much enjoyed the attention and kind treatment though sometimes, as with the head rub, the endearments could become too rough. His many
injuries had caused him to become very tender and sore.

"What is your name, boy?" another one of the jovial spectators greeted him.

"My name's Pan, Pan Shepherd." He smiled back at them.

"Strange name that," the speaker replied without any ill intent.

"We three ere, which it is that I'm Durn," he said with a well thickened dialect.
"Weez urd et was yew ew was leedin our train this afternoon," the soldier garbled
out. "In frunt of ol' Juba himself," his tone became incredulous. "S'dat true?" He
hung on the question like a hooked fish with no teeth.

Pan wasn't entirely sure what the inebriate had asked him but the gist seemed
clear enough. "I think so," the boy responded.

They were each and all amazed. "You see!" an unnamed man fired off towards
the one who'd asked. "I told you it was true!"

"Gods alive," Durn impressed. "Eye can ardly magine it!" He broke off, starting
to give a good guffawing along with the others. Pan Shepherd simply maintained
his pleasant demeanor, being unsure of what all the fuss was about but still undis-
turbed, nevertheless.

"Where you going to lead us to next, Pan?" another of the soldiers inquired
unexpectedly.

"Right into battle he will!" slack jawed Durn before bursting out into fresh
mirth, causing all the rest to do the same.

"You men get back to work now," Captain Matrius intervened, using his rank
for the first time in an official capacity. The group was becoming far too familiar
for his liking.

"Aye, Captain." The mercenaries obeyed his order with knuckles touching to
scalp. They were still chuckling amongst themselves as they walked off waving
towards young Pan Shepherd, well entertained by the idea of General Juba being
led by a handicap.

"Why were they laughing like that?" Pan asked Matrius once the men had disbanded back to their task.

"Because General Juba never follows behind anyone," the captain made known to the child. "Besides General Ballista," he made an exception. "So the men found it funny that he had followed behind you."

"But he followed behind you too," Pan expressed truthfully.

"I know," recalled Matrius. "But it isn't thought of the same," he let out with a grin.

"Aren't they scared of him?" the young youth wondered.

"Everyone's scared of him," Matrius blanketed. "I don't even think General Ballista would wish to fight Juba alone in a one-on-one fight."

"I'm scared of him," Pan confessed with his voice quieting.

"So am I," the captain admitted freely while passing another smile.

"Now what will happen?" Pan continued the conversation as Matrius walked them both between and around the many busy scenes of activity.

"What do you mean?" Matrius did not take fully his meaning.

"I mean what will happen with the army and with you?" the shepherd boy made plain his meaning.

"Ah," Matrius responded downward after having now comprehended. "We will finish crossing over the mountain very soon I imagine," the horseman answered. "And then we'll move down into the lands on the other side."

"But why?" Pan really wanted to know.

"Why what?" Matrius began to grow slightly irritated at the inquisition.

"Why do you want to go there?" perplexed the youth. "To the other side."

"To see what's there of course," illuminated the captain brightly, "and to take what we find."

"But what if what you find isn't yours?" The shepherd simplified his train of thought.

"Something is only really yours, lad, if you are strong enough to keep it," the seasoned veteran lessoned wisely. "There are no other real arbiters of peace in this world, Pan," he professed profoundly. "It's power and resolve alone that dictate."

Pan remained quiet for a time as he considered his transport's reasoning while all the time continuing to be assailed by high marks and praises by those they passed throughout the burgeoning encampment.

"Why did this happen?" The shepherd boy led out next in another direction. He was seeking a reason for the massacre.

"Because men who are used to ruling themselves do not so easily prescribe to being ruled over by others," Matrius provided the explanation.

"And now you want to rule over the rest?" Pan's inquisitive nature remained untamed.

"You either rule or get ruled boy," Matrius instructed his pupil.

"But what if they do not want to be ruled?" Pan mused aloud.

"Then we will kill them," Matrius answered easily. "We would first make a desert, and then call it peace."

Chapter 18

General Ballista turned his gaze upward, looking past the large funeral pyres that were in front of him and into the celestial sphere above. There were many lit torches that remained held in a sort of silent vigil which was spread out solemnly around the occasion. The imposing general cupped his face with both hands spread wide, hiding himself completely from view. Slowly he slid them down again, uncovering his eyes and nose in turn until only his mouth remained shielded in a very public display of distraught commiseration.

After a short pause, their commander made a sign to the gods before indicating by nod that it was time. Spread out over a handful of seconds, the torch bearers, one after the other, began tossing their flames onto the stacks. The accelerant made from pitch and flax did its work quickly as the superstructures alighted and began to burn. At first, they combusted sparingly and interspersed, but within a few minutes the different flames had joined together into one giant inferno which lit up the night sky close by like a midday sun. The intense heat radiated outwards in all directions like ripples on a pond.

After a few minutes spent watching the leaping flames, General Ballista turned away and addressed Masonista, who was standing near to him. "Pass word for Captain Matrius to bring me the shepherd boy down to my quarters," he gave instructions, "and then seek out Generals Juba and Vega and have them brought to join me in about an hour as well."

"Yes, General," attentively listened his most trusted counterpart. "Here, let me," Masonista offered as he reached out to hold still The Red Hare whom his commandant had long since gotten returned to him.

"Easy, Red," Ballista patted, rubbing his great thoroughbred lovingly before swinging himself up and over upon its high back, taking full control.

"I'll see you down there," the general imparted towards Masonista as he made to turn off and began descending in the direction of their base camp with his companion cavalry in tow.

At the foot of the mountain where General Ballista's main army now sat encamped, the soldiers were waiting for the first light of day in order to begin traversing up and over the alpine pass. It was still early into the second watch when Pan Shepherd, along with his recently appointed chaperone Matrius, arrived as ordered inside of the tabernacle.

"Fine work by you two," congratulated the general with regards to each upon their arrival. "We've managed to strike two birds with one stone in part because of you," he heaped more praise towards the pair before turning a bantering expression towards Captain Matrius.

"They tell me that you made good time, Captain." General Ballista openly brandished a knowing smile towards his onlooker. "So, tell me," he was fishing for a compliment, "how was he?"

Matrius knew right away that General Ballista was referring to his mount, and so with all the respect and decorum appropriate for the situation, he began to gush in glowing terms about the great red stallion.

"Never in all my years did I ever feel such speed, General," the captain of the scouts reported grandly. "It was all I could manage to simply hold on!" He almost showed his teeth through the grin.

Ballista allowed himself to let out a sincere laugh, genuinely made happy to hear his prized possession spoken about so highly. Everybody knew that The Red Hare was a once in a lifetime horse. He was equine perfection of the highest order.

"It pleases me to hear that you enjoyed your ride so thoroughly, Captain," his general chimed in gloatingly. "There have only been a few so fortunate as to experience it firsthand."

"Indeed, General." Matrius well understood his good fortune. "I thank you very much for the privilege, sir," he appreciated. "I'll remember it for the rest of my days."

General Ballista accepted this last piece of flattery with good graces and a tipped head before forcing himself to then return to more immediate and pressing concerns.

"I've need to speak with your charge, Captain," his commander informed him. "You may either take your leave here or else wait outside while I do so," he finished, just as Masonista entered and gave acknowledgement to them both in advance of moving over to take his usual spot of council behind the general.

"Well then, shepherd," Ballista started out on an easy tack. "You've done well today it seems," the purveyor of destruction and doom loomed across optimistically.

The general's mood was encouraging enough that Pan felt emboldened to ask, "Does this mean that you will give my sheep back to me?" The boy clasped hopefully at the notion from his seat opposite the great lion.

The general continued to allow himself to be amused. "Yes, boy," he relieved and excited simultaneously. "You will come to find that I am a man of my word." Ballista's look changed from that of relaxed to one of intense meaning. "I always do what I say."

Pan readily felt the threat conveyed.

Ballista then resettled the scene. "You will join my army and I as a guide tomorrow while we cross over the pass." He let this news sink in. "I will have Captain Matrius carry you alongside of me while we go."

"My humble apologies, General," interjected Matrius upon hearing. "I have still yet to meet with or muster my men since the appointment." He was referring to his recent promotion.

"I am aware of that, Captain," General Ballista proffered like an immovable bulwark from behind his table. "However, you must be aware that you are the only one in this entire army who has had any dealings with the boy at all, and that he is also still currently unable to ride or else carry himself." He paused before confirming, "Are you not?"

Matrius glanced over to the still handicapped shepherd who was seated, looking back at him. "Yes, General," the horseman capitulated.

"And you can hardly expect that he should ride with me?" his dubious tone coupled with a questioning brow.

"No, General," Matrius retreated further. "No, of course not."

"Good." Ballista held the field firmly in his grasp. "So it's settled then."

He looked back towards the boy. "The last time that you were here you told me that you grew up on the other side of the mountain," the interview began. "Is that correct?"

"Yes, sir," Pan confirmed. "That's right."

The general nodded. "Good," he repeated. "What I want for you to do now is to tell me what it's like there."

"What do you mean?" Pan requested for more clarity.

"I mean, how many people live there?" Ballista gave as an example. "What is the weather like?" he also wanted to know. "Is there abundant food and water?" the questioning continued. "These are the types of things that I am interested in learning," the general specified more clearly. "Do you understand now?"

"Yessir," the youth acknowledged. "I understand."

After a brief moment's thought, he made to answer. "Well, sir, about the people, I'm really not too entirely sure," Pan struggled to comment. "But I do know that there's a whole lot of 'em," the rustic answered vaguely. "The weather, though, is always hot and no matter what time of year it is, it usually always rains at least once on most days."

These details were more helpful. "What about the availability of food, such as livestock and wild game?" the general mined further, seeking out a vein of gold from amongst the quarry.

"The jungles are full of many animals and all kinds of sweet and sticky fruits as well," Pan described from pleasant memories.

"Jungles?" Ballista stalled upon the word. "What do you mean?"

Pan was slightly bemused by the question, but he did his best to answer it anyway. "I mean the kind of forest that grows there," the boy explained. "It's very much different from this side, you know," he continued his telling in a conversational manner. "Over here there's hardly any trees at all once you get off the mountain, and for most of the year it hardly ever rains," he recorded. "On the other side, though, it's nearly always wet and everywhere you look you're surrounded by trees!"

The general brooded over this valuable piece of intelligence for a time before proceeding with his enquiry.

"What of the people?" the general sought for more details. "How do they live?"

Pan began to take on another look of uncertainty so that General Ballista elaborated further. "Do they live in villages, in towns, or in cities?" he continued asking. "Do they have roads and thoroughfares or are footpaths and trails mainly used?"

"Footpaths and trails mostly," Pan answered readily enough, much to the general's chagrin. "What's a city?"

With that indirect response given, the inquisitor pressed on, "How many villages are there all together, and who controls them?"

At this request, Pan was forced to stop and think again for a time before shaking his head in the negative and replying that he didn't have an answer. "I don't know," the boy responded. "A very great many, though," he added on before going further. "Every village has its own leader," the shepherd told them. "Sometimes they work together and other times they work apart." He shrugged and turned up his palms from a lack of any understanding to the goings on of tribal politics.

While imagining this loose confederation of uncivilized barbarians, General Ballista continued to work out his intended course of action. "What about your village?" the inquirer investigated. "Where is it located?"

"It's along the shore of the black lake," Pan informed him, "about a ten day walk once you reach the other side."

"Why do you go to the other side at all?" the general focused in on that point specifically. "Why do you go back and forth across the mountain with so many sheep?"

"Because they don't like all the heat and the rain," the shepherd boy expounded. "That's why I keep them on this side of the mountain and then twice a year I take them over to be shorn by the weavers so that clothes can be made," Pan added on. "They're not mine, though," he explained. "They're everybody's." His depiction went further. "All of the villages in the region use the wool because we have nothing else good to make clothes out of." Pan's story was sensible. "That is why we never eat them," the shepherd boy condemned slightly by the remark. "They're much too valuable to us alive."

General Ballista nodded his understanding before pressing on. "Tell me about the men, the fighters," he wished to have inspected next. "How are they led, and who trains them?"

Pan continued sitting there in the seat, which was much too large for a child's body, and thus left his legs dangling up from off of the floor. "Every man is a fighter when he has to be," the boy shed light upon the subject. "The village patriarch tells them when to do so."

"Do they fight together or alone?" Ballista's inquest deepened.

"I don't understand," Pan admitted honestly.

"When they are told to go fight," the general detailed more plainly, "do they fight all together as one or does each man fight for himself?"

"Each man fights for himself," relayed back Pan once he understood, "as soon as they are told."

Ballista was able to read between the lines in order to glean off the information that he was seeking despite the boy's nonintentional ambiguity. There was only one more thing of note to ask then.

"And what of gold or other valuable objects?" the general prospected. "What do people use to trade with?"

"Oh yes," Pan's face shot up at the news. "There is lots of gold," he told his receptive audience. "Sometimes people even find it lying bare in the riverbed."

Now it was the general's turn to straighten. "Speak sense, boy." Ballista grew serious. "Are you telling me that your people possess this?" he asked while holding up as an example an unevenly engraved gold coin.

Pan peered at it just long enough to get a good look before he nodded his head in the affirmative. "Yes, sir, just like that." He then drew the noose tighter. "Most all people have it."

General Ballista turned to Masonista, who peered back at him with just as surprised and feverish an expression.

"You've been very helpful, Pan," General Ballista afforded him the compliment after returning his focus. "I have many things to discuss here amongst my officers," he revealed as he made to end their meeting. "I will send to you one of my physicians when they return from the summit, and in the morning," he wrapped up, "Captain Matrius will fetch you to ride alongside with me at the front."

"But what about my sheep?" the boy whined with all the frankness of a child who understands neither rank nor decorum.

Ballista smiled at his insolence. "What's left are yours, shepherd," he told him. "After we have crossed the pass tomorrow, you may take them as you please."

Pan happily agreed.

"Good," Ballista concluded the affair. "That will be all for now then." The general looked back over to Matrius, who was examining some of his displayed weaponry. "You may take the boy back to his tent, Captain," arranged the general. "Masonista here will have one of my physicians sent along after a little while to check on his injuries."

"Yes, General." Matrius left off from his observations and moved to obey orders. "What time shall we report back in, sir?" he requested notice.

"Before the dawn has changed from gray to colored," relayed his commander.

"Aye, sir," Matrius snapped to and threw up his salute.

"Dismissed," General Ballista relieved, sending them both back out into the starlit camp of a new moon.

"It seems like you made a good impression," the captain announced to the shepherd whom he still carried with him everywhere they went.

"I hope so," Pan said truthfully.

Upon reaching his place of slumber, they found that the tent was deserted. "So much the luckier for you then," Matrius accorded him. "The other slaves are probably all tasked with getting everything ready for the morning's move," he figured. "So tonight it looks like you may have the whole place to yourself," congratulated the horseman.

"I don't so much mind the others," refigured Pan, "except for the snoring." He smiled through his complaint.

Matrius grinned. "We've got an early day tomorrow lad," he told him. "You'd best to get some rest while you can," the horseman recommended while placing Pan on his cot. "There'll be a doctor in to check on you soon."

"Okay," Pan heard himself say, as the long day finally came to an end. He was already fast asleep before Matrius had left his tent.

Chapter 19

"What do you think?" Masonista inquired of his chief in regards to the shepherd boy's most recent deposition.

"I think that the god's favor us," returned General Ballista with a favorable impression.

"But what if the boy is lying?" articulated his right hand.

"Do you believe him to be?" answered Ballista by way of a question.

"No, no, really I do not, but that is hardly reason enough for us to trust him completely," Masonista well argued. "He could be mistaken by accident," the adviser cautioned. "He is after all still only a child."

"Indeed," Ballista agreed. "Yet is it not also true that this child has been proven right about everything else said thus far?"

"That is exactly why we should be more hesitant, General," worried Masonista. "Where did this boy come from?" he challenged. "And what of his family?" The next inquiry followed suit. "Where are they now, and why has a mere child been left tasked with so important a role?" His many petitions remained unanswered. "We should check into this," the adviser warned.

"And tomorrow we will," Ballista soothed his man's ruffled feathers. "For now, however, let us assume that what he has said is once more accurate."

"In that case, it still sounds very much like a dangerous expedition to me, General," Ballista's confidant conferred with him. "Our supply lines are already dangerously overstretched," Masonista reminded before adding yet further another bone of contention. "The tropical climate alone will cause our soldiers' equipment to rust, and the increased heat will bring disease and with it, sickness and death."

"I have considered it," dismissed the commandant. "We will not be staying long enough for either to be given a chance to take root, however," he expressed his intentions clearly. "This year we will perform a brief reconnaissance to make contact with the tribal groups and get a lay of the land," he elaborated the details.

"We will afterwards move back here to spend the winter resupplying, fortifying the pass, and making the necessary alliances for next spring's campaigning season. And besides," Ballista figured, "if what the boy says about the gold is true, then it should not prove very difficult to procure enough wealth to keep the men well paid up and content over the winter months."

"As you say," Masonista allowed. "But what of the lack of roads and transport?"

"We shall just have wait and see when we're on the ground ourselves," Ballista retorted. "With such a loose network of tribes it should not prove very difficult to find out their petty grievances and play one group off the other, and without a unified and well-organized field army, any real danger will be limited to guerilla tactics alone."

"But we have no idea about their villages sizes or populations," remonstrated Masonista. "Or even of their numbers and locations, for that matter," he rebutted further before offering his commander a forewarning. "I believe that we should proceed very carefully, General," he looked him on fully, "especially after what has just transpired."

"It is your job to prattle so, Masonista." Ballista smiled through his self-assuredness. "Even if you do sometimes nag me like an old woman."

"Some may call your confidence a hubris, General," Masonista threw back the barb without being stung.

"It is only hubris if I fail," Ballista defended himself defiantly, just as general's Juba and Vega arrived and began to enter the room. "I will ensure that control is maintained over both sides of the pass, Masonista," his general told him. "And with an open supply line and overwhelming force, we will crush ruthlessly any and all opposition against us," he finished speaking before turning to stand up and warmly greet his men.

"Generals!" he congratulated. "You have done the entire army proud today with your splendid service."

"I only wish that there had been more to serve," macabrely humored Juba in his usual blackguard manner.

"Indeed." General Ballista smiled. "As do I," he seconded whilst ushering in his guests. "Please, take your ease gentlemen," invited their commander to sit down. "Masonista, will you call the rest of the general staff to our assembled council?"

"Yes, General," his helmsman acquiesced readily as he made a move to depart out of the tabernacle.

"They tell me it was a slaughter," Ballista spoke over towards the two generals who remained.

"Indeed, sir, it was," came the genteel voice of General Vega. "On both sides."

"How many dead and wounded?" inquired their chief.

"We lost four and seven respectively," Vega recorded the figures, looking over to Juba for his confirmation, which was affirmed by nod. "Two scores of our own men were injured, and we counted 973 amongst the enemy dead."

"Nine hundred and seventy-three?" General Ballista harped on the number. "Is that all?"

"We thought the same, General," Juba included himself into the conversation. "We believe most of the enemy force was moved out of the area before we arrived," he said disappointingly.

"I see." Ballista paused in an equal regret. "Tell me, Vega," he took up another line, "what do your scouts report of the other side?"

"No contact with the enemy was made, General, but the terrain is not at all conducive for large or even mid-level cavalry operations," Vega reported. "The tree cover is too thick and the visibility too low."

General Ballista was taking all of this into consideration as the first arrivals began to trickle in for their rendezvous.

"Welcome, Generals," Ballista greeted them amicably. "Please, find yourself a seat," he told them. "We will be beginning shortly."

A small yet lively chatter filled the air while the various officers spoke amongst themselves as still more arrived to join them. Before long, Masonista himself returned with the last of who was expected to be present.

"Commanders," General Ballista esteemed with the zealous vim of a frightening populist. "You will, I hope, excuse the lateness of this meeting which I have called at this hour," he began. "But in the morning there will be no time for such matters, so I wished for every man here to know his duty now," their leader addressed the room, finding the eyes of each and every member of his audience at least once, except for Masonista, who stood behind him as usual.

"We have suffered a most cruel blow, gentlemen." The general touched somberly upon the nerve of their recent defeat, causing many of the other officers present to divert their eyes downward. "However," he came back on strong. "Thanks to the efforts of Generals Juba and Vega here," Ballista gave notice to where the two men were seated by way of an outstretched arm in their direction, "we have almost managed to return the favor." He bared teeth towards the crowd, allowing them a moment of congratulations and thanks to be directed at their victors before curtailing it by speaking further.

"Our brothers are irreplaceable," Ballista's words quieted the scene. "But, nevertheless, we must try our best to account for their worth," he moved on to elaborate. "Our initial intelligence reports that conditions on the other side of the pass will likely be very different from what we have grown accustomed to," Ballista informed them. "It is expected to be hot, humid, and with dense terrain possessing little roads or infrastructure."

He paused to look around the faces of his cabal.

"With that being said," their general continued, "and especially after what has already happened, we must remain ever vigilant against the threat of further ambush or guerilla attacks." The officers in attendance all shook their heads in varying degrees of accordance and agreement.

"Further," Ballista drilled, "you are to ensure that your own junior officers keep their men well-watered." The commandant provided reasoning. "The heat, coupled with the dampness and heavy armor, will cause profuse sweating to occur so that each man should be directed to drink double his normal ration." He paused once more to add weight before proceeding.

"Masonista has already been directed to ensure that fresh reserves are continuously resupplied, which reminds me further," General Ballista's countenance turned sour, "there is to be a strict observance to the wine allotment and dilution as well." He searched about his generals keenly. "Make no mistake about it, gentlemen," the counselor pressed on. "Tomorrow we will be venturing into unknown enemy territory." General Ballista's quick glances darted around the tabernacle like a fish escaping danger. "Vigilance will be critical not only for our success," he cautioned, "but for our survival as well."

The other generals voiced their support and understanding as General Ballista peered about the room. "Now then," he told them. "If there are no questions, then these are tomorrow's dispensations."

With no objections raised, their orders were handed out.

"General Vega," Ballista started with first. "You and your division of calvary will act as a buffer between our force's front and any enemy or civilians that are encountered there," their commander added. "Your forces are to move back and forth in an arcing motion from one side of the line to the other with regular dispatchers sent out to keep me well apprised of the situation there," he concluded. "Is all that understood?"

"Perfectly, General," replied his trusty lieutenant. "You need not worry about us."

"I never do." Ballista nodded before turning his attention towards the others. "Generals Lysander, Ziggurat, and Alaric will lead the fifth, seventh, and ninth divisions respectively as the forward group. You will be our center push, gentlemen," he shared with them his formation's design to their ready agreement. "Generals Uddica and Thymistacles," he addressed next. "Each of you will lead your own division on the flanks," their commander assigned. "Thymistacles," the speaker looked at whom he spoke, "you will take the left flank and Uddica." His head turned towards the other. "You and sixth division will cover the right."

"Aye, General," they each responded with their understanding in turn.

"Generals Augastene and Phocus will form the center group of our army and shall be afforded the additional benefit of my company," General Ballista's last comment elicited an easy laugh from amongst his assembled officers.

"Juba," the commandant then affectionately referred to his most fearsome warrior by name alone. "It will be your job to keep our rear secured," Ballista afforded him this most critical task. "You will be responsible for keeping our supply lines open," he spied his general in earnest.

"They will not be closed, General," Juba guaranteed. "You have my word."

"I wish that every man's word afforded me as much assurance as yours does, Juba," the general complimented him openly.

"Lastly, General Vega," Ballista revisited once more. "I want for you to detach a small force to assist General Juba in keeping our back flanks well scouted."

"Sir," Vega responded by affirmation.

"Good," General Ballista recorded. "Then are there any questions?"

"None, sir," came the ready answer from the seasoned core of veteran officers.

"Very good," their commander readied to end the assembly. "I won't keep you any longer then," Ballista made to release them. "Have your men ready and assembled to move out at first light," he dismissed. "We leave at dawn."

Chapter 20

At first, Pan felt that he must still be dreaming. Very quickly, however, he realized that it was not a dream at all. He was being suffocated. The shepherd boy began to flail and scream, but the covering that pressed down over his mouth and face muffled the sounds so that he could not be heard. Everything was blackness and despair as a desperate alarm began to make his heart beat furiously from the combination of fear, adrenaline, and a fast-emptying supply of air. Pan began to feel his thoughts fading as consciousness tapered away. Then, quite dimly, he made out a sound. It wasn't clear, but he thought he heard a person yell, "What are you doing?" before the pressure suddenly lifted off his face just as quickly as it had arrived. This gave Pan the opportunity to gasp for air through his pronounced dizziness and haze.

The shepherd flew up in an instant, throwing off the woolen blanket which had been used to try and suffocate him, whilst at the same time hearing a tremendous commotion going on in the shadows right beside. There were multiple people fighting in what was shaping up to be a desperate and brutal struggle for supremacy inside the tent's darkness.

Pan did not wait around to determine the victor and instead darted off the cot with a speed and agility that made his many injuries seem frivolously light. Springing out of his shelter to a star-filled night sky, the shepherd boy began shouting loud and desperately. "Help!" the boy erupted into a passionate cry. "Help!" he screamed again at the top of his lungs. The frantic struggle inside of the tent continued, but there was much less banging and ruckus than there had been before. Pan could hear the sound of feet squirming in sand.

"Help!" Pan continued to holler as a few angry voices cut through the blackness to find out what was the matter.

"We're being attacked!" the boy wailed, causing all within earshot to immediately rise and begin jumping into armor.

Men started falling out of their tents all around him in a desperate struggle to gain their gear and weapons before the fighting started. A tumultuous upheaval began as the incitement spread around the entire camp like a lightning strike that shocked all over, including the central tabernacle where General Ballista was awoken and put on high alert that another attack was imminent.

Back where Pan was located, the fighting inside of the tent had finally subsided and two shadowy figures burst out of its front to try and seize him. Seeing that the entire encampment had been aroused, however, and that many torch lit figures were now running in their direction as well, the two attackers turned instead and tried to flee.

"There!" Pan's voice chased after them, pointing towards the two fast retreating culprits who were able to disperse into the crowd of frantically moving soldiers that were all trying simultaneously to take up a defensible position.

"What's this?" a stranger angrily grabbed Pan by the shoulder and jerked him around to face him. "Where is the attack?" he listened impatiently.

"In there." The shepherd pointed over towards the tent which he'd been sleeping in, causing the unknown soldier to become even more intensely irate.

"You woke up the whole gods damned camp for a bad dream, you little shit?" he raged in disbelief.

"It was not a dream!" Pan vehemently refuted. "Go look inside and see!"

A crowd was fast arriving at the boy and his tent with many angry murmurs and grievances being aired at the entire affair. After the tent flap was opened, however, and the still warm body was discovered lying there inside, there were more than a few gasps at the surprise.

More people came as the encampment was now in full alert, searching everywhere for any sign of danger.

"Who is it?" asked one from the crowd.

"I can't see yet," another voice announced as the unknown person was being dragged out by his legs before being turned over.

"That's the general's doctor!" one of the torch bearers exclaimed once the flickering light had found the corpse's face clearly.

"It is!" affirmed another. "That's Dr. Pubble!"

All eyes turned to the boy, who was immediately carried under guard to the general's tabernacle under a litany of questions. The rest of the camp, meanwhile, was in the process of being slowly disarmed and quieted after the false alarm had taken place.

Very soon after, Pan Shepherd found himself delivered back in front of the army's commander within his great rotunda. It had begun to almost feel familiar to him now from his many recent trips inside.

"What happened?" General Ballista wanted to know as soon as the briefing had been related to him by Masonista.

"I don't know, sir," the shepherd boy truthfully reported before relating all that had transpired in as much detail as he could recall.

"Do you know who did this?" came the second advance.

"I do, sir," Pan surprised, causing the general to lift up a brow in expectation of the answer. Gods help him if he mentions his sheep again, Ballista glimmered the thought.

"Well?" he asked impatiently after a few seconds of silence.

Pan swallowed hard. He had been looking into Ballista's eyes directly up until now, but at this point, he turned them away in shame and began to look abashed instead.

"Out with it, boy!" the general began to come unglued. "Who killed my physician?" he demanded an answer.

"Tarwin and Korballa," Pan whispered, still looking down towards the ground.

General Ballista did not understand the answer and so inquired further. "Tarwin and Korballa?" he repeated the names aloud with a confused expression.

"Yes, sir," Pan confirmed once more with a timid demure.

"Explain yourself, boy, and be quick about it," Ballista growled. "I've got no time for a child's foolery." The lion grew fierce. "Tell me why in the seven furies would Tarwin and Korballa try to kill you?" His question was posed as serious as death.

Pan again sat there, muted and disturbed.

"Out with it, damn you!" General Ballista roared his displeasure whilst slamming an incensed fist down hard upon the wooden table, causing both Pan and Masonista to startle in an alarmed fright.

The boy began to sob. "Because," he choked out, "Korballa put his manliness in me."

The general's face took on a look of angry bewilderment as his mind did not immediately make clear the shepherd's meaning.

"He put his manliness in you?" General Ballista repeated back the statement before suddenly understanding.

"Are you telling me that my attendants raped you?" the general stripped away all finery.

Pan continued to stream tears down his puffy cheeks as he silently nodded his head in the affirmative that it was so.

"Gods alive," General Ballista sat back in his chair, flabbergasted, looking over to his confidant, Masonista, who only shook his head in disapproving silence. It became even more outrageous as his agile mind worked out what had happened after and why.

"Those lascivious fools," spat hard the general. "Furies slay me." He shook his head in disbelief. The offense given to the boy was of small concern to him, but the disrespect shown to his own person by their actions was unconscionable.

"I'm sorry," Pan apologized unnecessarily before wiping his eyes and nose with one arm, still refusing to look up.

Korballa and Tarwin ,meanwhile, knowing full well that their jig was up and that they were soon to be discovered, decided to make a run for it. They used the cover of their camp's confusion that'd been generated by the shepherd boy's call to alarm in order to grab their most important belongings and mount up. Before all had been resettled, the two fugitives were already setting off their horses into a sprint towards the fast-enveloping darkness.

Back inside the tabernacle, General Ballista fumed. "I want them both found and brought here immediately, Masonista," he ordered his most trusted counterpart, who moved instantly to obey while Ballista was left bristling at the outrage.

"Why did you not speak of this earlier?" the general maddened a look of red-hot rage towards the sullen youth.

"Would you?" was all that the shepherd boy meekly responded.

The general bit his tongue from this well-placed rebuking, so that they both sat there in silence for many minutes until Masonista's return.

"Tarwin and Korballa have fled, General," Masonista reported to his commander and chief upon his return arrival. "Their tent is empty and appears ransacked, and both of the horses which you so recently gifted them are missing as well."

General Ballista just managed to choke back his anger, which threatened to explode at any moment, like the top off a heavily smoking volcano.

"I want for you to find them," his intense fury rapidly boiled to just beneath the surface. "And I want you to bring them to me, alive," the general put heavy emphasis on the last word.

"Yes, General," Masonista dutifully complied, as he again ducked away to quickly begin assembling men for the pursuit.

"Well, boy," the general returned his focus to him after a few moments spent softening his nerves. "It would appear as though I need to keep a closer eye on you." He grimaced a smile. "You will sleep in here tonight," Ballista informed him. "Tomorrow I will work out something better."

Chapter 21

By dawn, Tarwin and Korballa had already spotted the general's horsemen approaching from their rear. Teams of riders had been sent out in all directions, including the newly promoted Captain Matrius and his detachment. They had all been given clear instructions to capture and return the two disgraced officers back into camp. Each squad had thus set out in a different direction from the encampment so that it was only by lucky chance that one of the intrepid scouts of Matrius's troupe picked up on the two fugitives' trail and so put them all on the chase.

"Damn you've got good eyes, Finnigan!" complimented Matrius, his new chief, after he caught sight of the outriders' hoofprints in the starlit darkness. They'd been following them ever since so that by the sun's early light, the two specks riding off in the distance could clearly be seen.

The sight of their quarry only quickened the pace of the pursuers whilst for the pursued, it sank their hopes like a vessel holed.

"What are we going to do, Tarwin?" Korballa yelled worryingly over towards his horse-bound neighbor as they both continued to push their near exhausted mounts to the breaking point. They had been running them since leaving camp, but with no clear direction or destination decided until sometime after exiting, they had wasted near to an hour of both time and energy, which their pursuers had made up to great advantage.

The situation was not yet hopeless, but it was fast becoming so. If they were unable to break off from their pursuers fast, then in the near future they would find them too close to shake, and eventually their own mounts would run themselves lame and stop as well.

"We've got to get off the plain," answered Tarwin through the wind. "We'll try and lose them up in the ridgeline," he directed forward to where their two horses were now headed.

Tufts of grass and dirt continued to fly up in chunky wads from their animals' hooves as the sun rose gently, bringing color again into the vivid world.

Matrius could see where the two outlaws were headed, and figuring out their strategy for himself, he ordered half of his force to break off and start pointing themselves farther up, at a slant, in order to cut them off. He and his men would then continue on for themselves, following up on their current path to close the door behind them.

Eventually Korballa and Tarwin's worn out mounts made it to where the wood line started. It led up into a heavily forested series of ridgelines stretching back into the mountains. They pushed them on, kicking and whipping ever more strongly to keep the two depleted beasts moving forward despite the strain.

Matrius and his party reached the same entrance point that the two escapees had taken no more than twenty minutes later. He then immediately led his force up and into the trees to find them.

"Keep a sharp eye out," the captain forewarned towards his men, who nodded as they began traversing the slope.

They came across the abandoned horse of Korballa first. It was lying on its side, rattling deeply with every breath, while a blood-tinged foam bubbled out through its open mouth.

The riders dismounted. Their own horses were also extremely tired, and the steep terrain would risk laming them as well if they were not careful. As the group walked farther up the wooded ridge, Tarwin's horse was also discovered panting by a nearby tree, its leg clearly injured.

"Fan out," Matrius ordered them. "Make sure to keep in sight of the man next to you," he added as they moved to form a line that was spread wide to cover more ground.

A few hundred yards further up the ridge, Tarwin and Korballa spied the approaching picket line from behind some boulders. They had gone up as far as they could go and were now blocked from going any further by a cliff face that dropped down sheer on the other side. Their chosen path had ended.

Tarwin sighed heavily as he removed himself from his peering. "It's over," he carried over to Korballa in a voice of melancholy that was filled with regret. "We're done."

Korballa was unwilling to resign himself just yet, so he continued moving back and forth to look at both the approaching bounty hunters on the one side and the impossible wall dropping down on the other.

"But maybe he will let us live!" Korballa hoped on a prayer towards his more rational counterpart, referring to Ballista.

Tarwin shook his head in the negative. "No, Korballa," he told him morosely. "It's too late for that now."

Korballa refused to listen, and despite Tarwin's truth, his own deaf ears were immune to its value. He continued to pace around like an animal caged while the troupe grew closer. "It was an accident," the condemned man tried self-reasoning. "If we explain ourselves well, he will understand."

Now it was Tarwin's turn not to pay any mind. He tuned out the noise and instead turned to walk up to the edge of the cliff face where the view was most spectacular. A panorama stretched out all the way from the lowlands before eventually breaking out into a wide-open plain that was cut through by the lazy river, which wound itself into the mountain's valley in advance of leading up toward the passes above.

It's as good a spot as any, Tarwin thought to himself as he enjoyed feeling the heat from the sun's rays warming his skin for the last time.

Suddenly a voice cut through his quiet revelry. "I see them!" it cried. The sounds of morning birds and rustling leaves were changed to that of men shouting and the snapping of tree branches as their pursuers came closer, threatening to fall upon them.

"What are we going to do, Tarwin?" Korballa alarmed once more as he turned around to look behind him at his long-time accomplice, who was now facing himself over the ledge.

Tarwin tried to drown them all out so that everything was silent. He focused on the sound of his heartbeat instead; it was deep and full. The sound of his breathing seemed much louder than usual as well. He swallowed hard and felt weak in the knees as his mind began to race in those last few moments before stepping off into oblivion.

Korballa saw him disappear over the ledge and ran over to see firsthand his friend of so many campaigning seasons lying dead and broken far down on the rocks below. He stood there in shock as Matrius's man, Rickimer, closed the final distance which ran between them and grabbed Korballa boldly, pulling him back roughly from the edge.

"I've got him!" Rickimer shouted, as the other men began to arrive and pile on top of him, keeping him pinned down and paralyzed under their collective weight.

"Where's the rope?" Finnigan called out, whereupon another of the bunch tossed it promptly over so that they could begin securing their prisoner.

"Eww wee you're in trouble now, son," Finnigan joked down brutally towards his catch as Matrius continued past them, walking to where Tarwin had jumped off. He was most certainly dead.

Turning back with some disappointment, Matrius proceeded to issue orders to his men regarding the one still living.

"Don't tie his feet up," he told them. "We'll have to run him back since both their horses are spent and none of ours can hold the extra weight."

"Aye, Captain," complied Rickimer, who ceased with the feet and instead went to yank up his trophy as was.

"Get up, you," he huffed, as Finnigan and another man helped pull Korballa up on his feet. "It's time to go now."

Korballa said nothing as he was picked up and tied to the back of Rickimer's horse before being trotted away.

Chapter 22

The great army had started traversing itself slowly and full of care up towards the mountain pass since dawn. General Vega, with his cavalry, had already set up an advance screening party and were heading the front of the long column on its downward course leading into an increasingly hot and humid subtropical valley. The surroundings were lush and green, with densely packed plant life that seemed to be teeming out from every direction. It was as if a whole new world had been entered upon when compared to the barren and brown, grass-filled plains from which they had just come. The calls of wild birds and of creatures wholly unknown were all heard in increasing diversity, abundance, and volume the deeper down into the misty white jungles that they descended.

"Bollocks, eye think eye'm dying," complained Grieves up from behind to his new major and proven friend, Yusri. "Ere it is only noon yet and eye've already sweated a whole bucket full," he continued lamenting to all those within close enough proximity to listen. "Eye'm starting to feel dizzy eye am," the big man whined further.

"Here," Yusri reached back with his own jug of diluted wine that was not yet empty. "Drink this and save your spit," he chided. "They'll be no stopping until the new camp is reached somewhere past the bottom." His arm pointed in declination following along the path of the men and pack animals that were preceding them.

"Ah," Grieves refreshed deeply after taking a long pull from out of the container and then wiping his mouth clean. "A thousand thanks, Major." He grinned widely. It still very much gave him a kick to refer to his no longer enlisted comrade by his new and exalted status. Much to his own chagrin, Yusri still often produced a smile from the remark as well.

"Eye'v never seen anything like it," the extra-large companion who enjoyed talking commented after. "Av you, Yusri?" He was referring to the densely packed and colored tropical rainforest that was now surrounding them.

"I have not," he reported back brusquely with his naturally distempered demeanor.

"Is it not strange, then?" Grieves asked him, growing a wee bit concerned. "Ow is it so different ere?"

"I don't know," Yusri answered back, thinking while he spoke, "but I'm sure the mountain has something to do with it."

"So, yew don't think it's the gods playing tricks on us?" Grieves worried over.

"No," Yusri considered the thought. "At least I hope not," he said while making a sign.

Further up the snaking column of bronze-clad warriors rode General Ballista atop his magnificent red stallion, The Red Hare. His attending staff were all present, and seeing as how Captain Matrius had been sent out in pursuit of the two renegades the night before, Pan Shepherd now rode atop Masonista's mount who, even now, was positioned beside his chief.

"Tell me, shepherd," General Ballista made to open a dialogue with the boy whilst swatting away at some flying insect that had buzzed in too closely.

The shepherd boy looked over.

"Why were you left alone to guard so many hundreds of sheep?" His question came equipped with an inquisitive stare. "Especially considering the great importance you said that your people here place upon them." He motioned outward.

"My family were the shepherds of the area, sir," Pan revealed his truth dolefully. "I used to have my father and my two older brothers too," he divulged. "We would all herd the sheep together."

"And so?" Ballista pressed on. "Why were they not found with you two days ago when you were first come upon by my scouts?" His quick eye maintained its glaring focus.

"Because, sir," the shepherd boy described with mourning, "last year there was a flux on this side of the mountain that took my father and my two brothers too." Pan started to tear up. "Only my grandmother and me were left," his sorrowful tale ended more sadly. "But she died a few months back." Pan turned his face away to hide his grief.

The general nodded his acceptance before inquiring deeper. "I am sorry for your troubles," he said dishonestly. "But that still does not explain why a mere boy was left alone to be in charge of so heavy a task," the commander continued to fish for a reason, much to Masonista's satisfaction. "Especially with no one to aid you." His look turned sour.

"A great many people died during the flux, sir," Pan fabricated the truth. "Most all of the villages have been in confusion since then," he carried on. "But eventually the chiefs will assign a new family to be shepherds, and then I will have help again," the boy finished recounting, like how a child reads off a list.

General Ballista looked up from the shepherd and into the face of his equine chaperone, Masonista, who nodded back his approval at him from the apparent unsolicited revelation.

"Very good," he spoke aloud, well pleased by the fine news. "So tell me then, boy," his demeanor changed back to that of an amiable captor, "where is the closest town or settlement where gold is located?"

Pan queried his own mind for a moment's rumination before touching upon the point sought. "The village of Crescony would probably be the closest one, sir," imparted the shepherd boy. "But pretty much all of the places have it," he added on as extra bait.

The general and his companions were mightily encouraged by these fortuitous remarks, so Ballista readily pursued him down the rabbit hole further. "And how far is this village?" He was well curious to know.

"You would reach it on the third day," Pan remembered. "I always pass by on my way home."

Ballista shook his head. "Tell me," he said, "what is it like there?" The shepherd boy's assessment was desired. "Does it have walls of wood or stone?" he sought directly. "And how many people live inside as well?"

Pan replied readily enough. "It's surrounded by a wooden wall, sir, and many people live there."

"How many?" Ballista repeated himself, searching for more clarity.

Pan began to look confused until he came up with a way to answer. "About ten or fifteen flocks, I would say," his rough calculations were used to judge.

The general nodded his head once again, understanding in his mind the place to be small and lightly guarded, especially when compared to the much more massive and well-trained host which was soon to set upon it.

Just then a messenger arrived from General Vega's division. "Sir!" the rider saluted and awaited his command to speak.

"Report," General Ballista directed over to the envoy along with his attention as he awaited the dispatcher's news.

"General," the cavalryman started. "General Vega sends me to report that a suitable spot has been found, sir, to make an encampment for the night," he carried on. "General Vega asks if they should continue farther or begin setting up a perimeter there, sir?" He waited for an answer that was fast incoming.

"How far is the good General from us now?" General Ballista cast over for a response.

"About an hour's march from here, General," replied the equestrian.

"That will be fine," Ballista made to issue out orders. "You tell General Vega to set up a perimeter around his current position and to then have sent out some reconnaissance patrols to see what can be discovered before dark," the general instructed his rider.

"Yes, General," the unidentified soldier threw up another hard salute before being dismissed back to his station with notice.

"What does all that mean?" Pan's boyhood curiosity aroused him to inquire.

"It means that we'll stop soon," General Ballista detailed with a smile.

Chapter 23

Korballa was brought inside of General Ballista's newly reconstructed tabernacle about three hours before dark. He could hardly stand from having been dragged so far so fast. Both his feet were almost completely gnawed to the nub so that you could see the white of bone sticking out in multiple places. Captain Matrius, along with his scout Rickimer, were there to help keep the prisoner standing in his place.

The commandant gazed mercilessly at the returned fugitive for some time until speaking. "Well, Korballa," he began by issuing out in a harsh measure. "You have utterly disgraced yourself," his first cut sliced deep.

"I was informed that Tarwin," Korballa looked up at him, "did the honorable thing and took his own life." He looked away again as General Ballista continued, "Why then did you not do the honorable thing as well?" The general smelled cowardice in his captor.

Korballa neither spoke nor looked up from out of his pitiful expression.

"Not only did you couple my property without permission, but in your foolish and amateurish attempt to cover it up," he added on spitefully, "you also killed my personal physician and a good friend as well."

Korballa stayed silent, casting his eyes down as far as they could go.

"And in addition to those two damnable offenses," General Ballista prepared to close the book on him, "you then attempted to desert camp during the very alarm that you created with the same horses that I had just gifted you." He shook his head in disbelief. "And then you went and lamed them both."

The chamber was deathly quiet as neither man made to speak until many seconds had passed.

"So then," Ballista made to force the issue, "what do you have to say for yourself?"

"General Ballista," Korballa lifted his head, wincing through the pain of his mangled feet's injuries after gathering himself. "I never meant for this to happen."

He choked up before continuing on, "I never meant to." He stopped himself and stared pleadingly. "I humbly ask your pardon, General, and I beg you for my life."

"You ask me for a pardon?" General Ballista was flabbergasted. "And beg me for your life?" he smarted with a laugh. "After all this?" He waved an arm around.

"Yes, General," Korballa managed a whimper as his face dropped back down to the floor.

The army's commander sat back deep into his chair before insulting him. "You are a coward, Korballa," General Ballista grimaced the truth. "And a fool," he tacked on further.

Korballa hung there by his slim margins with all the hopes and dreams of a condemned man standing at the gallows. Anything would be better than the certain death that awaited him currently; or so he thought.

"Very well," Ballista insidiously granted his reprieve, much to the surprise of everyone else there. "Captain Matrius," the general turned to give attention to his cavalryman. "Remove the prisoner outside and wait there," he ordered as the two men made immediately to obey, dragging out the staggered and amazed Korballa, who even made a call of, "Oh, thank you, General!" over his shoulder.

"Masonista," the general then addressed to his chief aide. "Go and find a black-smith to bring me here now with his hammer and a long nail."

"Just one, General?" the confused Masonista sought to clarify before turning and heading off to complete his task.

"Just one," General Ballista confirmed. "And Masonista," his leader stopped him again prior to leaving, causing him once more to turn around. "Bring back with you two axes as well," the mysterious commission was appended on further.

"Yes, General," Masonista again paid homage in advance of moving out to procure the required man and materials.

Ballista stood up from his chair once Masonista had departed. Only his personal oath men remained inside with him now. The brooding lion then skulked heavily across the animal hides and tapestry rich floor which carpeted his inner sanctum to where a rack containing his personal weapons was located. There were bows, spears, swords, knives, daggers, and all other manner of instruments for war. Every blade there had tasted blood on at least one occasion and more than one amongst them had grown drunk off its excess. The general patted a sword fondly.

He took his time, making sure to select the right tool for the job by running his hand over the top of each one until finding what he was looking for. General Ballista then pulled the knife off the rack and carried it with him.

Masonista returned a short time later with the worried blacksmith in tow. He thought himself certainly in some kind of trouble despite Masonista's repeated insistences that it wasn't so. The specified equipment had been brought along as well.

"Man Blacksmith," General Ballista greeted him with a respectful nod which put the man more slightly at ease. "Tell me, what is your name?"

"Vip-Vipsonius, General," he stuttered out, betraying his frayed nerves. "How can I help to please you today, sir?" he ingratiated himself deferentially.

"I need your skill with the hammer, Vipsonius," Ballista ambiguously replied as he made to lead them out of the tabernacle. "Follow me please," he insisted while exiting.

Captain Matrius and his man, Rickimer, were still waiting there as instructed with their prisoner, Korballa, who was near frenzied from both excitement and fear. "What are you going to do with me, General?" the cutthroat supplicated himself beggingly.

Ballista hardly noticed him as he walked past, making clear by his steady step that his men should follow after. "Send a detachment of riders off into that tree line, Masonista," the general directed to his advisor. "Have them set up a perimeter there," he added while leading his company in tow across the encampment to where the jungle started.

The ground was soft and thick with tangled grass that packed black loamy earth beneath it so that at times it felt as though one were walking on sand. Others around the camp stopped their activities and bumped or nudged one another as the silent and quick-moving procession passed them by with General Ballista inexplicably at its head. It was obvious that the man taken with them was in some kind of trouble.

Once the woods had been scouted and they were given the all clear, the general and his party proceeded into the tropical rainforest where he began to walk freely, examining the many different trees around. This continued on for some time. Masonista was making ready to inquire as to just what he was doing when the surveyor spotted a specimen that seemed to meet his fancy.

"This one," he declared aloud as the blacksmith, two horsemen, their prisoner Korballa, Masonista, and the general's four bodyguards all reached him, standing around looking up.

General Ballista turned to the two horsemen next. "I want for each of you to take an ax and chop down this tree," he surprised them both, who were quite confused, but willing, as they picked up their instruments and began to obey.

"Try to make it flat, gentlemen," their observant leader detailed further. "As much like a table as you can."

Chips of wood flew off in chunks and wedges with each blow from the ax so that in a short time the tropical hardwood cracked and split. It fell with a reverberating crash down onto the forest floor below as a myriad of unsettled birds and other creatures cried, cawed, and ran out from their alarm.

Leaves fell all around them as the sun's rays peered through the previously unbroken canopy, shining down a golden light onto the freshly chopped wood. Each man there now looked to their general to see what he would have them to do next.

"Man Blacksmith," he called over, having already forgotten the man's name. "Come and join me, if you will."

Vipsonius immediately hopped to, arriving by his general's side not more than a moment later. "Yes, General," he offered himself eagerly, seeking only to avoid displeasure.

General Ballista motioned him closer whereupon he whispered something into his ear. What was said could not be heard, but judging by the face that it put on the poor blacksmith, Korballa was made extremely nervous. It appeared as though he had become both frightened and repulsed at the same time, as though some repugnant request had been asked of him.

"But General, sir, I—" the blacksmith begged off and started to protest, but General Ballista abruptly cut him off.

"You will do it," he ordered him with his merciless stare, "or I will have them do it to you next." He motioned over to his oath men who were all standing there, attentive and alert.

The unknown threat immediately had its intended effect as the blacksmith nodded his head at the consequence and made no further remonstration.

"Are you ready then?" General Ballista queried him.

"Yes, General," the blacksmith, Vipsonius, answered, downtrodden, the way a man who is clearly forced against his will would be apt to do.

"Good." General Ballista next faced over towards Captain Matrius and his man Rickimer. "Captain Matrius," he began. "I want for you two to carry Korballa over there and hold him up by that tree stump," he directed. "Keep him there."

"Yes, General," Matrius accepted the order without delay and motioned for Rickimer to begin helping move the man forward. Korballa increasingly protested their attempts the closer that he was carried. Whatever was going to happen, he knew that that stump was going to be a part of it.

Once he was positioned, General Ballista signaled for the blacksmith to commence. Everyone there, excepting for those two, was at the height of suspense, especially Korballa, who was now equally terrified as well.

The blacksmith sighed heavily and walked slowly over to where Korballa was being held. He reached the prisoner and then placed the hammer and nail down onto the stump without ever so much as looking up at him. Then Vipsonius began to undo Korballa's trousers, causing him much alarm.

"Hey," he challenged. "Hey, what are you doing there?" he protested more loudly as the blacksmith undid his britches and pulled his pants low, exposing his cauliflower penis to the world. It was nearly covered in large and splitting white warts from base to tip.

"What are you doing?" Korballa cried louder as he tried to close his legs and shy away his manliness from the group of intensely curious and half disgusted on-lookers. A few there who could now see where this was going began to wince themselves.

The blacksmith didn't say a word as he gripped Korballa's wart ridden dick and pulled it outwards, stretching it over the stump.

Korballa became frantic. He tried to squirm and fight harder so that General Ballista was forced to motion for two of his companion swordsmen to go and help hold the man still.

He twisted and yelled as he saw the blacksmith reach down and pick up the long nail before placing it in the center of his meaty cock.

"No!" Korballa screamed. "General, please!" he was almost shrieking already. "General, please I beg of you, have mercy!" he cried ever louder as the blacksmith held his dick in place with the nail and then picked up his hammer.

"This is mercy," General Ballista retorted grimly as he gave the final nod for the punishment to continue.

"No!" Korballa shrilled, twisting and turning violently so that the other two swordsmen were called over to help hold the raging beast still. With six strong men holding him steady, there was nothing that Korballa could do. Ballista eyed him intently and Masonista looked away as the blacksmith made his first swing.

The force of the blow drove the whole nail right through Korballa's cylindrical appendage and into the solid wood below. The high-pitched squeal was so terrible that only General Ballista remained unmoved. It sounded like a pig being slowly slaughtered. Everybody else there felt deeply affected as Korballa's screams became blood curdling. He did everything possible to get away, but he was held too fast. He was unable to look away from the hammer blows that rose and fell, agonizingly steady, to drive the nail in ever deeper.

"Please!" Korballa now pleaded with the blacksmith, who pounded through eyes that were full of tears. "For the love of gods!" he begged as Vipsonius struck harder. "Please stop!"

The blacksmith tried to make quick use of his work, but even still it took half a minute of hammering to drive the nail all the way in. He looked to General Ballista twice to see if he could stop, but on both occasions was made to keep going so that on the last stroke, the blacksmith began to pull the entire busted organ into the freshly split wood.

Korballa's pain was unworldly and his misery impossible to describe. All were touched except for Ballista, who stood there unflinchingly as each strike hit home.

When the blacksmith had finally been given leave to stop, he immediately stumbled away into the tropical brush and fell onto his knees where he began to vomit. Korballa was still being held firmly in place as he jerked and slammed about like a gaffed fish that's just been pulled in the boat, trying desperately to free himself while screaming incoherently.

After the immediate shock had passed him by and the prisoner began to rip a little less violently, Ballista ordered them to, "Let him go."

The six men who had been keeping him in his fixed position until now all made to relieve their grips simultaneously so that Korballa was left completely unsecured except for his mangled penis that was nailed completely to the tree stump.

Korballa continued to bawl and cry pitifully, throwing his hands repeatedly down towards his pulverized cock with both held wide open and at a total loss as to what to do. It was like having one's hand stuck tight inside of an oven that slowly cooked and burnt the flesh all the way to the bone.

"Now then." General Ballista smiled sadistically. "Am I not a man of my word?" he spoke around to those in attendance before addressing Korballa directly. "You see that I have left you alive, Korballa," he addressed him who only continued to bawl and mew. "How much of a man you will be afterwards, however," he was referring to his current predicament, "has yet to be seen." And with that, he made a move to take out his knife.

"Here," the general said as he unsheathed the blade that he had taken with him to carry. He stabbed it down into the tree trunk next to Korballa's busted and broken organ. "I leave this for you, to use as you see fit." He grinned maliciously before breaking free his ire-filled gaze and began to nonchalantly walk back towards the encampment.

"Masonista," he called back over his shoulder without even looking.

"Yes, General?" the shocked and appalled slave called from behind him.

"Call in the detachment," Ballista ordered him as he continued to make his way back into the camp, leaving the rest to follow.

The next day, Korballa's body was discovered lying next to the tree trunk. His throat had been cut, either by himself or someone else from the camp or jungle who grew weary of his constant lamentations. No one ever did try to find out which. The force of his body falling, and the height of the stump, caused the appendage to be ripped away entirely so that only his brutalized remnants remained nailed, split, and splattered on the bloody wood.

Chapter 24

Pan Shepherd was finally able to reunite with his flock. A pronounced limp still existed whenever he walked, but there was no longer any need to carry him. The sixty or so odd sheep that remained baaed pitifully at his arrival, and all ran over to crowd round the pen's enclosure to where their benefactor was first seen. The boy was deeply saddened to see so many of his flock had been culled, but he was also more than a little grateful for what still remained. When Pan climbed inside the fence to be with them again for the first time, he was quickly overwhelmed by their stampede. They brought him down low by sheer numbers alone so that for the first time in days, the youthful shepherd rolled around in open laughter, despite the dirt and the filth.

Pan's reunion wasn't permanent, however, and so while he hated having to leave them there, at least for the present, there was nothing else to be done. The sheep would just have to stay where they were. After the happy assemblage was ended and Pan had himself said his good-byes, the shepherd boy then set his sights upon a hot meal over inside of the kitchens. The journey didn't make it very far, however, before the other soldiers and camp followers who were gathered nearby made such a fuss about his presence there that any further passage became impossible.

"That's the shepherd boy!" a first one shouted, creating quite the stir in that densely packed and populous area.

"Our little hero!" went out the second call from an old and haggardly woman who was busily laundering rags for a pittance. "He's the one that led the third to victory," acclaimed a shopkeeper selling wares close by. "I hear he knows where gold is!" some soldier rumored from out of the crowd that was blocking his path forward, leading to an even bigger increase in both fanfare and volume.

Before Pan could even understand what was happening, he had once again been hefted up to be carried, only this time it was not done by a single hapless soldier but instead by an adoring crowd. The boy was treated as a sort of special mascot or lucky charm that was paraded around to the different parts of the encampment whilst all the while being touched, pinched, or prodded for good luck and good-will.

The inflamed passions of all those people pushing and squeezing to get at him and gawk at the slave boy who'd led an army with the indestructible General Juba and won was intense. His youthful person was kept lifted on high for quite some time, like some religious artifact, while the wild throngs handed and pushed at him every manner of trinket or foodstuffs that they had to offer until within a very short time, he had quite forgotten about his need for an eatery.

Pan was still very much in the midst of enjoying this continuous series of ceaseless adulations when suddenly he heard Beocca's voice call out to him.

"Hi, Pan!" the little enchantress called up happily from back down on earth. She was all full of excitement and smiles as her small hand waved vigorously.

"Hi, Beocca!" Pan radiantly exclaimed with a wide grin from atop his constantly moving caravan of supporters. "What are you doing here?" he called out to her excitedly.

Beocca's response was to laugh and titter as she ran to keep up. "I didn't know you were telling the truth!" she accused him with a sternness that they both knew was false.

The cheerful young Pan made to hulloo all the more freely until eventually the mob swallowed him whole.

The golden rod, Beocca, continued to trail the boisterous group of merry cheer until it reached the point where they'd first started. Only then did Pan Shepherd finally get returned to solid ground. As his many supporters and well-wishers began to slowly disperse and die out, he again saw his most special friend, standing there waiting to greet him.

"Hi, Beocca," Pan repeated once more with a swollen smile that was worn almost completely around his still busted up and blue bruised face.

"Hi, Pan," little Beocca reiterated with a joyous jubilance also.

"I saw your sheep," she told him fondly before adding on, with her eyes opened wide like some gossiper divulging a secret detail. "Everyone knows who you are."

"I used to have a lot more," the boy said sadly, ignoring the last part of her sentence completely. "Do you like it here, Beocca?" He was talking about the jungle,

"Oh yes," she snuggled the remark. "There are lots of pretty flowers here!" Beocca told him with a sparkling exuberance. "And so many nice birds as well!"

"Which one's your favorite?" Pan sincerely wanted to know.

"My favorite what?" Beocca turned her head halfcocked at the question.

Pan blushed without knowing why. "Your favorite flower," he posed specifically.

"Mmm," she hummed through her own thoughts. "I like the yellow ones best." She was sure.

Pan cemented the fact in his mind before delving further. "Where do you work at?" he next inquired of her.

"Work?" The girl restated the word while her mind shifted gears. "In the kitchen mostly," Beocca made clear. "Today they made me peel onions for hours." She stuck out her tongue in dismay and then raised her nose up.

Pan laughed at her expression, causing Beocca to do the same. "Will you be there tomorrow?" He checked to make sure.

The girl paused to think about it briefly. "Yes, yes I think so," she opened up honestly. "But why do you want to know?" Beocca wondered at him curiously, giving off a strange feeling.

"No reason," he reassured her. "I just wanted to know where I could find you is all." And the two both smiled.

"What are you doing now?" Beocca prodded, staring at him with her orbs of emerald.

"Not much," replied Pan. "I was going to go eat but I'm full now." He stuck out his belly and rubbed it like a great fat man, causing his erstwhile companion to giggle.

"Would you like to come play with me?" Little Beocca simpered up to her new friend sweetly, like sugar on the cane.

"Okay," Pan gleefully responded as she reached out to take him by the hand.

Back inside the central tabernacle, General Vega stood ready to give his report in person after having just come back from the front lines.

"It's no good, General," Vega stated as a matter of fact. "None of it, I'm afraid," his expert assessment started out poorly. "There's simply no room to maneuver," he warned. "My men are spending most their time just trying to hack through this endless vegetation, and in some places it grows so thick that you can hardly see past ten men to your front or side."

General Ballista sat there, still and unmoved, but listening attentively as he bid for his man to continue.

"I lost a man today from snakebite, General, gods be damned," the cavalry commander soon commented. "The accursed beast was sat there hanging on a tree branch and he didn't see it," General Vega kept on relating the scene. "Bit the poor bastard right square in the face." He indicated the spot where the fangs went in with his fingers. "Happened right as he and his horse were walking underneath." The leader of the equestrians shook his head in regret. "It was quite a shame really," Vega prepared to close. "Damn fine waste of a good man," he added the thought, "and he was well liked."

"I don't doubt it," Ballista accepted this ominous report with ease. He was well used to dealing with difficulties after a life spent on campaign. "The gods are fickle, General," the commander shrugged his shoulders and turned his hands up, after the fact. "You know that as well as I."

Vega nodded in agreement to this reality of life.

"I appreciate fully how tough the terrain is, General," sympathized his chief. "However, we have received word that there will be a settlement reached soon."

"But General," the commander of the cavalry made to resist. "It is impossible for me to properly scout our path forward, sir," he tried hard to drive his point home. "I cannot know for certain what is out there."

"It will only be for one more day, General," Ballista sought to cool his nerves. "And we have little reason to believe that anything encountered out there would be more than minor anyway."

General Vega did not agree with his commander's assessment, but he accepted the judgment without question. "As you wish, General," he confirmed with a bow.

"Good," it was settled. "Then have your cavalry detachments continue pushing out at dawn, and make due the best you can."

"Yes, General," Vega reiterated his assent.

"That will be all then, General," Ballista nodded respectfully before dismissing him.

The army's chief cavalry officer snapped promptly to attention before turning on heel and taking a polished stride right out of the room.

As soon as he had left, Ballista's chief aide also made a move to protest.

"You're risking too much, General," Masonista chided him crossly, as only he could.

"I risk what I must, Masonista," General Ballista corrected him doggedly. "Our coffers are almost empty and all the men still unpaid."

"I am aware of that sir but—"

"But nothing," Ballista did not let him finish. "Then we must push forward to collect payment," he argued further. "It is much too late to turn back now," the assessment was freely given. "Not empty-handed at least."

"But what if the boy is lying, General?" entreated Masonista, who continued to harangue him. "What if he is wrong?"

"Then we shall just have to wait until tomorrow and find out," General Ballista eyed his man coldly. "And besides," he added cynically, "if we do lose men to fighting then we'll have less gold to pay."

Chapter 25

Bright and early the following day, General Ballista's great army broke out of camp once more and moved back off into the surrounding wilderness. They spooked most of the ground animals well in advance so that not much else was seen beyond the astounding diversity of plant life and flowering vegetation. Up into the trees, however, was an entirely different story as there were all manner of songbirds and small mammals within the upward branching boughs, including some kind of strange, long-tailed creatures that appeared to those beneath as furry dwarfs. Spies, still others thought them, and more than a few men from out of the highly superstitious rank and file took their howling to be an ominous sign.

Nearer to the center of the army's formation, Pan Shepherd continued riding as before; he was sitting atop Masonista's mount, which walked beside the general's. The mid-morning sun burned down brightly, serving as a near constant reminder of their many hours spent moving since dawn.

"What distance remains, boy?" investigated the general in reference to the town.

"We'll get there tomorrow at this pace, sir," Pan's opinion was shared freely.

Ballista nodded. "And what about this damnable jungle?" he sought to discern. "When does it end?"

"It's pretty off and on, sir, mostly," the boy tried explaining. "There's a few big places where the people have cleared it away, but otherwise it's pretty much always like this," he said whilst looking around at the tropical density.

"At the settlement also?" the general checked specifically, betraying a hint of concern.

"Oh no, sir," Pan reassured him, allowing him to breathe a small sigh of relief. "It's all been pretty much opened up around there."

"Right down this road you say?" General Ballista half pointed along with his stare.

"You can't miss it sir," the little shepherd boy confirmed confidently.

Ballista allowed himself to relax slightly.

The jungle grew hot and steamy as the day progressed with frequent rain showers occurring all throughout. The precipitous downpouring of so much water began to mire the carts of oxen and weaken the bow strings as well, but it did make collecting and keeping easy. Progress became slow and arduous. During the many showers, fat raindrops would fall warm and heavy, going steadily through the sunlit canopy that was high above. They slipped and slid down the leaves that were there to make a million shimmering cracks in an otherwise endless sea of vibrant green.

"Eye don't like it ere, Yusri," Grieves bemoaned up to him from behind. "My sweat stays stuck to my body like how a fur traps heat," he complained bitterly.

"Drink some more water," Yusri responded stiffly with a quick glance back. "We've still got plenty of more ground to cover before this day is done."

"Gods alive," Grieves railed against the injustice of it all.

The heat, coupled with the humidity and heavy armor, was almost unbearable. Yusri felt the same as Grieves did, but he tried his best to hide it. By the time the new campsite had finally been reached later that afternoon, however, almost all of the men there were utterly exhausted.

General Ballista, wishing to boost his army's morale after such a tiring day, decided to raise their spirits by allowing an extra ration of wine for his men. However, this had the added and undesired effect of leaving the mostly dehydrated soldiers to become much more inebriated than usual.

Pan had himself been given his leave to roam freely around the busily constructing encampment. He was completely safe there now and hardly watched though always seen. Wherever he went there were hearty cheers and loud adulations. The shepherd boy did what he could to suppress the pity he felt towards their amiable lot and then went off to pick some wildflowers for Beocca instead. The yellow ones were selected most. After his bouquet was completed and properly arranged, he next set off to find her.

He went first to the kitchens where he expected to see her, but she was absent. Unperturbed by this initial thwarting, the determined explorer next checked inside of the cafeterias instead. As he continued to look without success, however, his concern for her began to grow. They needed to be gone soon, otherwise it would become too late.

Pan's search grew more exasperated and desperate the further down the sun sank into the sky. Time was running out fast, and even though he seemed to have checked for her everywhere, she still remained elusively hidden. The shepherd never considered leaving her though. While his mind would have been unable to articulate such a thought, his heart already well knew that where there's love, there's hope. Just when the situation was becoming critical, however, and Pan was about to start shouting her name, she appeared. Her own vision had not yet reached him, but nevertheless, there she was. Pan's chief concern walked busily and with an intense concentration worn about her oval face as she carried back a burden of large sticks in both arms.

Of course, Pan faulted himself for not thinking of it sooner, She was out collecting more wood for the fires!

With not a moment to lose, he ran over to see her. She saw him too before he arrived.

"Beocca!" Pan called out to her.

"Hi, Pan!" she greeted him warmly, quite clearly happy to see him.

"Hi, Beocca." He smiled back, very pleased to see her as well. With great haste and hurry, however, Pan grabbed his young friend by the arm and pulled her expediently over next to a tree.

Beocca whinnied at the unexpected fun before challenging him good naturedly. "What are you doing, silly?" she squeaked out in incredulous laughter. "You almost made me drop all my wood!" she incriminated him light-heartedly.

"Listen, Beocca," Pan tried interrupting her.

"Are those all for me?" The little golden child suddenly brightened like a rose ripened on the vine. She dropped her kindling into a pile and then reached out for the bouquet.

Pan blushed for the second time in his life as he abashedly handed them over. "I picked them for you before I came," he detailed gingerly.

"They're all so pretty!" she excitedly amazed before pushing her face down into the colorful bunch and inhaling deeply. "And they smell really good too!"

Pan simpered awkwardly until regaining his focus.

"Listen, Beocca," he stopped short, making her listen.

"What is it?" she asked him with some growing concern.

"You have to come with me now," he told her seriously.

"Now?" Beocca repeated, not understanding at all. "But to where?" She investigated curiously.

"Into the jungle," Pan explained. "To somewhere that's safe."

Beocca laughed and began to giggle. "But here is safe, silly," she tinkered like a bell. "Not in the jungle!" her voice inflected into a humorous disbelief.

"No, Beocca," Pan warned her most dreadfully. "Soon everybody is going to die here." His words fell like lightning bolts, causing an extreme consternation.

"Die?" Her eyes widened to their fullest. "But why would that happen?" she pleaded for him to tell her.

"They'll kill you, too, if they find you here," he mystified further. "That's why you have to come with me."

Beocca looked scared and unsure. "But what about your sheep?" her child's mind innocently inquired.

Pan smiled at her in appreciation before relieving. "Don't worry," he said knowingly, "they won't hurt those."

Beocca was still grossly unsure about the entire affair.

"I'll tell you everything," Pan promised her, "but right now we just have to go." And with that, he grabbed Beocca by the hand and began to run off with her into the tightly-packed forest, easily bypassing the half-drunken guards with ease.

Later that night, when the shepherd boy was called to be seen by the general, it was returned to him soon after that he was nowhere to be found.

"What do you mean you can't find him?" General Ballista interrogated the messenger angrily. "Go and look for him then!" he nearly shouted.

Once the tabernacle was cleared, Masonista himself began to speak. "General if —"

"I know," Ballista cut him off short as he began consulting his maps attentively.

A short time later, a dispatcher appeared from General Vega's division with even more disturbing news.

"What is it?" General Ballista asked him sharply and short of temper.

"Sir," the rider saluted hard and crisp before delivering his message. "General Vega sends me to report, sir, that enemy soldiers have been sighted in the area."

"How many?" his next question flew out. "And from what direction?"

"It's impossible to tell right now, General," the outrider regretted to inform him. "The immense vegetation prevents us from getting an accurate count, sir, but they appear to be blocking us across the entire path forward."

"Masonista," General Ballista energized himself immediately. "Send word to all division commanders to go on high alert status, effective now," he directed. "And send word to General Juba to fortify the rearguard position there and protect all supplies."

"Yes, General," his well-oiled right hand immediately set out.

Another courier arrived while Vega's was still present, this time from Juba himself. There was apparently an intense skirmishing operation taking place there, which was threatening to cut off supplies if nothing was done.

"General Juba awaits your instructions, General," the envoy stood waiting after having notified his division's predicament to the army's commander and chief.

Before General Ballista had been given any leave to provide an answer to him, the banshees started.

Fierce yips and wild moans started spilling forth from out of the darkness in what seemed to be every direction around them.

Major Yusri and about a dozen other survivors there knew exactly what that sound meant, and they were terrified. Shivers ran down their spines as those all-familiar cries were now being heard for the second time.

The camp became like an ant pile disturbed. Thousands of armed and armored figures began darting about in all directions and haste, trying desperately to take up their defensive positions before the fighting started.

The shrieks and the screams went on unabated for hours, but no attacks ever came. Even worse was that the dog-tired and hungry soldiers were forced to stay inside of their defensive postures all night long with hardly any sleep between them and no proper mess as well.

Inside General Ballista's headquarters, an emergency council of war was being held with all of his division commanders present and on scene. It was a risky move, given the circumstances, but the general assumed, quite rightly it would turn out, that no attack would arrive before dawn, despite all the bluster.

"What's our plan, General?" Juba was the first one to speak once the assembly was completed.

"Our native guide has disappeared," their commander started badly.

Murmurs of surprise and discontent could be heard rising from the crowd, especially from Juba, who could be heard telling his nearest neighbor in choice terms that he hadn't trusted the boy from the start.

"Taking a step back," General Ballista went on, "And giving this a clear view," he looked grimly out to his division leaders, "I believe that our army has been led into a trap."

Masonista stood there behind his chief, firm and unmoved, displaying no appreciable emotion to those around him. The general's last statement was given time to settle around the room so that all could be made fully aware of their clear and present danger.

"We have no credible intelligence to let us know how many of the enemy are out there at this time," Ballista continued on his downward spiral. "Or even where they all may be."

More than one of his officers visibly shook their heads at this inexplicably bad turn of events in which they now found themselves a partner. General Juba was the only one out of them all who did not appear in the least concerned.

"However," the general then quickly changed his tune. "We still have over 25,000 well-trained and heavily armored infantry," their seasoned conqueror reminded them. "We also have more than 5,000 light cavalry as well." A few in the crowd nodded optimistically at that fact. "Added to all those," the general strengthened their cause even further, "we have enough supplies with us for three full days of operations." This reinforcement was added to much effect. "And we are only two days out from the pass."

His cabal began to grow encouraged once more.

"Therefore," the army's undisputed leader got to the meat of it, "it is my intention to wait out their initial attack tomorrow, here." He pointed down to a spread map on the table. "Inside of our current defensive positions." Ballista looked around to the expectant, but not disagreeable, faces of his men. "Once we have taken the brunt of their assault," their general carried on to the finish, "then we will begin a fighting withdrawal back the way we came."

The men stamped their feet in approval as General Ballista began to scan the room, meeting each one of his most trusted and valuable commanders, eye to eye.

"I expect for an attack to commence at dawn, gentleman," he spoke to each and all of them with an equal reverence. "So I suggest that tonight you make your peace with the gods." His smile was defiant and gleaming. "Because tomorrow," their general forewarned, "you may go to meet them in person."

More feet were stomped, and martial noises made.

"Keep the men at their stations for the night," Ballista instructed them. "Double the fire watch, and ensure that provisions are taken around and dispersed well before first light," details were added. "Tomorrow looks to be a bloody day," his last message was brief and stout, "so let's get about it."

His commanders nodded their assent and began shaking hands and clasping each other by the arms and shoulders for what could very well be their last good-byes.

General Ballista watched their congregation for a while longer before dismissing each man with a hardy handshake and sending them back to their post.

"You too, Masonista," he shook hands with him as well before showing his old friend the door. "I'll see you at dawn."

Chapter 26

The marauding enemy's hoots and howls maintained themselves near constantly throughout the night, so by morning most of their own soldiers had still not slept a wink, though no man's belly was empty either. The dawn came and went, but still no attack came. The army remained on high alert however, like a porcupine with all spines bristling, while General Ballista continued waiting for the assault that did not come. Only the endless yowling persisted, growing at times to such an incessant fever pitch that it drove some men into angst and despair.

By mid-morning, General Ballista's overall concern had grown by a great deal. Clearly his enemy was not trying to attack him while inside of their current fortified position. It was therefore becoming more and more evident that this was no leaderless rag-tag confederation of individual tribesmen, but that there was instead someone or some group which was guiding them.

If he lied about that, the commandant considered to himself, remembering Pan and their many conversations together, Then he could have been lying about the flux too. It was a stressful thought, as Ballista realized just how much he didn't know.

He could have been lying about everything, his crown weighed heavily. "There was probably never any gold at all," Ballista stated out loud before returning inwards, But my men picked him up, the general began second-guessing himself as innumerous contradictions started to rattle around in his own head.

"Gods be damned." Ballista smashed down hard with an iron fist upon the wooden table, causing it to nearly split. He and his army could not stay where they were for much longer. His opposition knew as well as he did that supplies there were limited. Furthermore, most of his men were still worn down and tired from yesterday. Even more so now after the near constant harassment coupled by a lack of sleep.

The general and Masonista poured over his maps inside of the tabernacle while outside it started to rain, further sogging both the ground and their archers' bow strings. Calls were put out to try and protect the latter from the moisture, but it was a largely losing fight.

"They're not going to attack us here, General," Masonista's protests were more forceful this time. "Not until we've run out of food and are starving," he well-reasoned further. "Otherwise they would have done it already," his experience kept on dictating to a continuation of silence. "Sir, I implore you," the advisor's resolve was adamant. "We must abandon camp and retreat."

General Ballista remained quietly occupied, carefully studying his untenable position upon the maps. "How has it come to this, Masonista?" he asked more rhetorically than anything else. "I've been outmaneuvered by a child."

"Sir!" Masonista cut in forcefully, ignoring his self-deprecation. "We must break out and retreat," the impetus was now. "They could be moving in more reinforcements as I speak, General, and our supply lines have already been cut off since last night." He was nearly shouting.

Ballista breathed in deeply before slowly sliding his hands off the table as he made to stand up, fully erect.

"Very well," he finally issued forth the order that many, including Masonista, had long been expecting for hours. "Assemble the army."

Immediately, a flurry of activity began as attendants and slaves alike began running around in every direction, trying to pack hurriedly that which was most important while everything else was to be left behind. The general himself paced busily back and forth in calculated rumination while his inner sanctum was quickly put all away about him. Multiple wagons and carts were piled high with his personal effects and belongings so that before long he too was exposed to nature and rain.

Knowing that there was no defeat except death, General Ballista steeled himself for the day that lie ahead and readied himself to go to war. "My horse!" he then roared out most fiercely.

Back inside of the formation's center where Major Yusri's soldiers were now located, he was busily preparing both himself and his men for their immediate evacuation.

"Take only what you can easily carry," he told them forcefully. "Leave everything else behind," his orders were passed down from on high.

"But what about the tent and my cot?" the bewildered Grieves made to inquire. "And we're to leave our cooking pots too?" he padded on there as extra.

"Can you carry it all with you?" Yusri prepared to make an example of him.

"Well, no, not exactly, Yusri, but—" he began to parry.

"Then leave it behind!" the major yelled in exasperation while shaking his head incredulously at the offending party.

"Alright then," Grieves took it upon the chin. "Well a which eye was just askin wadn't eye?" he said under his breath like a younger brother following the rebuking of an elder.

Yusri ignored him. "Helmets, swords, and shields," the major continued calling out to them as he moved amongst his men. "So far as I'm concerned," the hard veteran wizened mercilessly, "everything else is unnecessary."

As soon as was humanly possible, the great army prepared itself to break out of camp. The formation would stay the same as it had before, only the direction of movement would be changed as the lumbering mass of people and animals prepared themselves to go backward instead of forward.

Right on cue, the mighty host began to file out in good order from within their fortified encampment. The indefatigable General Juba was leading their way. Generals Alaric, Lysander, and Ziggurat, with their three divisions, would now make up the rear.

The cavalry had been mostly pulled in tight where it was believed that they could give better support for the infantry columns marching past. Due to everything else involved, however, and with limited space on the main tract they mostly only got in the way of things. This problem forced General Ballista to send them farther afield to make more room for the supply wagons and camp followers who were moving along in the center. Thus, the lines of communication were increased further.

The operation was still progressing smoothly until just after the last soldiers had made off to depart. It was at that time that the enemy decided to strike.

The screaming yips and howls which had until then mostly been constant now once more reached into a deafening pitch that did not die out. The ground began to shake and rumble as so many men came charging out from the dense jungle coverage that surrounded them on all sides. Only the path back into camp remained open. Most of the bowmen's strings were too wet to properly function, and the forest came up so close in many instances that the enemy could not even be seen until they were right up on top of them. This made the archers mostly ineffective from the start.

An overwhelming horde had been sent against their rear, which acted like a pincer directed at the back of their formation. It was designed to break the long column in two and then drive a wedge between them. The two sides clashed together with a thunderous roar as the tribesmen fell upon them. The fighting was savage and intense from the very start as the screams of men began to fill the surrounding air. By the time word of an attack reached General Juba's location, all the way at the front, their rearguard had already been cut off and surrounded.

The violent blows suffered on both sides were ferocious as each grappled desperately in an all-out attempt to combat the other. The sheer number of enemy fighters that were continuously funneled into the ever-expanding gap, however, soon made it clear that theirs was a lost cause.

It didn't take long for General Alaric to sound the alarm and have his ninth division begin an organized retreat back into camp. Generals Ziggurat and Lysander, seeing his men giving up on the fight, made the fateful decision to follow suit with their own troops as well and so went with him in, despite the fact that the encampment had just been stripped bare of most supplies. Their wooden bastion was then immediately surrounded on every side and placed under siege, just out of bow shot.

General Ballista, upon hearing word of the attack, immediately turned his magnificent red stallion into the direction of the fray and galloped off. His many attending officers and oath men who were with him tried their best to keep up with the horse that almost flew.

When the general arrived at the scene of bedlam, he could no longer even see his rear divisions' standards. They were nowhere to be found. All he saw was a teeming mass of murderous barbarians with their hackles raised who had filled the roadway and who were now trying desperately to breach through on three sides to attack him.

General Ballista took one more practiced look around and then began issuing out orders.

"General Augustine!" he yelled over to first.

"Yes, General!" the recipient of his shout snapped to in an instant.

"Take first division and move them up to reform our left flank," the supreme commander delegated with vigor and strength. "Inform Thymistocles when you arrive there that he and his eighth division should move immediately back to make and reform our rear."

"Understood, General," Augustine saluted hard and rode off with his staff officers pursuant.

"General Phocus." Ballista next turned to face his other man who was also in the center column with him.

"Sir!" Phocus reacted sharply, raising his voice high enough to be heard through the din of open battle.

"Take your second division and move'm up on the right flank." He wasn't done. "You tell General Uddica when you get there to slide his sixth division backward to help form up the new rearguard with General Thymistocles's men," the commandant finished, putting General Phocus to flight.

"Masonista!" He then looked towards his most trusted advisor.

"Tell me what to do, General," the bespoken lieutenant zealously sought his duty.

"I need you to find out where in the seven furies Generals Lysander, Ziggurat, and Alaric's divisions are located," he pressured him further. "I must know where they are."

As Masonista paid homage to his chief and then made to set out in hot pursuit of his goal, General Ballista stopped him once more before leaving. "I ride to General Juba and General Vega's position to see how things go there," he spirited. "You tell those three bastards I said to reform themselves back up into the center whenever they are found!"

"Yes, General!" Masoinsta dutifully complied as he turned to make haste towards where the fighting was fiercest.

General Ballista turned his own seething mount around and proceeded to charge forward towards the front of his long army. Major Yusri and infantryman Grieves saw him tearing by enroute to some unknown destination while they themselves were moving on the double quick over to the left flank. Since fourth division had been slaughtered, Major Yusri and his detachment had been reassigned into first under the command of General Augastine, who was now busily rearranging his men.

"Say," Grieve's startled out, "wasn't that the general riding past just now, Yusri?" The big man checked with his best friend and ranking officer after Ballista blew past atop The Red Hare with his retinue trailing a full ten seconds after.

"Looked like it," the major answered, as laconic as ever.

"Where do you think he was running to so fast?" Grieves wondered aloud what others were thinking.

"How should I know?" Yusri defended himself and their commander too. "My job is to lead you fools, not the whole bloody army," his fire branded. "But seeing as how General Ballista has never lost a battle," their major reminded them, "then I feel confident that he knows what he's doing."

This truth brought back some much-needed confidence to the men following close by.

"But what about what happened to us, and the fourth?" Grieves soured the mood by his outspoken ineptitude.

"We weren't with the general!" Yusri fired back piercingly so that no further comment was given from that quarter. The immediate issue now it seemed was that a part of their army was under heavy attack, and no one seemed to know from where or if they'd be next.

Within a few minutes of Grieves and Yusri arriving at their new positions, however, the wonderment ceased. Projectiles began to rain down upon them in droves. Sharpened sticks of wood and sling-thrown stones pelted and pierced men randomly up and down the line. Due to the thickness of the forest foliage, it was incredibly difficult to see from where the shots were coming until they'd already struck.

"Shields!" Yusri shouted to his men, who hefted them on high to keep their vitals covered.

The dings and thuds of the impacts were accompanied by the far too often screams of another victim saying that they'd been hit.

The worn-out soldiers of first division continued to hold the same stance until their arms ached from the effort. Eventually, however, the intense barrage slowly weakened and then stopped. A short interlude next followed where the weary and sweat-sodden warriors of the first tried hard to regain their stamina before the rush came, guzzling and devouring whatever they had around them.

They did not have to wait long.

"Calm," Yusri anchored his troops against the incoming assault.

The intense shrieking only grew louder as its reverberations began to be felt like a pressure wave coming forward. Any moment now, men would come bursting out from amongst the deep greenery to seek death and destruction upon the many bronzed invaders.

"Spears!" Yusri shouted as the first combatants broke out from amongst the tree line at full sprint, leaping with every step. All up and down the line, the men inside the second and third ranks threw hard their spears, catching many of the incoming and lightly armed fighters directly in the chest, nailing them down instantly.

It was not enough by far, however. Within seconds, the initial flood had become a raging torrent that brought with it an avalanche of violent humanity in its wake.

"Brace yourselves!" Yusri shouted as he and his men dug deep, preparing for the explosive impact that was fast approaching. Grieves was standing on his right side, protecting him there.

"Yusri, I don't know what to do!" his neighbor bawled, overcome once again by fear and terror. The need to go shit was unbearable.

"Just do what you did last time!" his wildly alert companion shouted back with an encouraging grin.

The collision was incredible. The banging clash produced by the two competing juggernauts created such a titanic thunder that all the jungle's inhabitants within leagues were scared witless and sent into a terrified flight. All along the line, men of first division were pushed back so that even the third rank and farther were moved to the rear. Those back ranks recovered quickly, however, and began to shove forward mightily so that even though the dam had swelled to swollen, it didn't break.

Yusri could hardly see through the ravenous blows and wildly swinging limbs that were trying desperately to burst through his shield and armor.

With the initial inertia absorbed and the men of the front line no longer being actively slid to the rear, attack calls began to ring out from the officers present, like Yusri, whose job it was to direct the slaughter.

"Tolo! Tolo!" Yusri roared to his men from behind his pressing shield. They responded in the same way that their countless hours of rigorous training had taught them to. The first line lowered themselves almost to a knee while at the same time arching their shields into a slant so that the immediate attackers were pushed forward to falling on them. The second row behind then chopped, stabbed, and pierced down onto the off-balance fighters, leaving a trail of dead bodies lying twisted and bloody in their wake.

Grieves swung and stabbed mightily next to Yusri, his strength and size being both weapons of their own against the innumerable horde. He and his companion stoutly held the line firm, along with the rest of their first division, during that initial invasion.

"Back one! Back one!" their major next shouted after a few more minutes spent in desperate fighting. The first line retired through the ranks to the rear. The others all moved up one, taking their new places and leaving the second row to be actively engaged in the armed conflict.

Further ahead of their struggle, General Ballista caught sight of General Vega's cavalry while enroute towards Juba up at the front.

"General Vega!" The commander and chief pulled up The Red Hare harshly. Behind him his trailing entourage struggled to catch up.

"Yes, General?" The cavalryman readily offered his assistance in any way that he was able.

"There is an attack happening on our rear," Ballista spoke fast but orderly. "I want you to send half of your force to the back to act as support for the infantry," he dictated. "You lead them."

"As you wish, General," Vega graciously accepted the charge. "But what about my other half, sir?" he requested to know before leaving.

"Keep them up here in support of General Juba's division," Ballista said to him. "We must not lose control of this path."

"Understood, General," Vega bowed from his horse's front before setting off. Ballista, meanwhile, turned with his own retinue and made the last dash up to the army's head.

All appeared quiet there on the southern front, and the road to the pass was still clearly open though no supplies were getting through. General Juba had put a halt to any further marching once word of the attack had spread, but even so, they were still being pushed steadily forward from the sheer force of arms that was taking place in their rear.

"We haven't seen them today, sir," Juba gave his report in person. "The bastards are still blocking the road somewhere farther up, though," he growled. "There's still no supplies getting through."

The general shook his head. "They've probably taken the previous depot," he thought out loud while morosely considering the possibility of a hostile camp that was now blocking his retreat.

"What are your orders, sir?" General Juba inquired.

"Keep forward momentum to a minimum, General," Ballista made clear as his other officers and attendants finally reached him, their own horses sucking up air. "Once I've received word from the rear guard then we'll keep pushing forward."

"As you wish, General," acquiesced the indomitable Juba towards his commander and chief. General Ballista then immediately whirled The Red Hare back around and began cascading headlong in the same direction that he'd come, leaving everyone else in his dust.

Chapter 27

"Why don't you fight?" Yusri challenged Grieves in a growing exasperation while they both stood standing inside of the second line, awaiting more combat.

"Well ear it is that eye'v been fightin right now then ain't eye?" His target of reproach deflected with good reason.

"Enaut! Enaut!" The current officer of the line called out from in front, causing both Yusri and Grieves to take part in the maneuver. Each man ripped up his sword hard from underneath, just as the first rank hooked over. Warm metal plunged deep into the flesh of their enemies as both weapons' blades sliced meat.

"You see ere?" Grieves pointed down with his shield hand towards the reddened example of his work.

"No, you big oaf," Yusri corrected him like an impatient teacher. "I mean why don't you fight like last time?" He grunted the query through gritted teeth while continuing to push the front trooper forward. Weapons banged and clattered violently all around them as grown men trying to hold their own guts in screamed for their mothers.

"Wasn't it that eye told yew eye can't remember it?" Grieves testily reminded him while shoving hard on the back of his own man as well.

"Gods damned useless bloke you are then," Yusri spat hot from distemper, just as the foremost soldier went down. "Sons of Hades!" he shouted angrily before immediately stepping in to take his place.

Blows rained down heavily like a summer monsoon upon his already dinged up and dented in bronze shield. It was all Major Yusri could do to simply try and deflect while staying upright. He uppercut with his short sword over and over again, stabbing relentlessly into the soft underbelly of whoever's body happened to be there at the time. His left hand held the shield up high while his right carried death incarnate.

"Back one! Back one!" Major Yusri heard the first line officer start to bellow. He maintained his position in the formation, however, while the rest of that rank filed back into the rear to have their spots retaken. Grieves stepped up once again beside him and did his best to try and stem the tide.

Side by side, the two warriors fought valiantly. Yusri with his well-practiced and lethal strokes while Grieves used mostly brute strength and enormity. Together they felled many opponents while also losing men themselves. Grieves was no God of War that day, but he did hold his own until the call to retire came.

"Back one, back one!" Yusri shouted vehemently as the second rank mechanically stepped forward, ready to fill the void.

After filing through to the rear, Yusri slapped his friend Grieves on the shoulder and said, "Look! You see there?" He was pointing over to General Ballista, who was now seen flying back atop The Red Hare in the opposite direction than what they'd seen him going earlier. "I told you he knows what he's about," the major spoke confidently as the sounds of deadly mayhem filled the air.

"I sure hope you're right." Grieves lacked the same enthusiasm.

General Ballista came across Masonista while he was still on his way back to meet him.

"General!" His adviser made to report immediately on what he knew. "Generals Lysander, Alaric and Ziggurats divisions have returned into camp," the news was very grave. "They retreated inside during the initial attack." His briefing ended with, "They are currently trapped there."

"They're not trapped, Masonista," General Ballista bristled defiantly at his slave's talk. "They're only cut off and surrounded."

"As you say, General," his chief attendant was forced to agree with him. "But those three divisions make up over six thousand men and their officers," he noted regrettably. "Their sudden loss will bode terribly for the army's morale."

"I know it." Ballista eyed him with a keen annoyance. "Have you received any word directly?"

"None, sir," came the uncomforting reply. "The enemy massed their forces precisely, General," he continued on explaining. "They drove a wedge right between the back of our formation and funneled in over ten thousand men." The situation grew severe, "They've blocked the path back completely."

It was a heavy blow. One in which General Ballista would not give in to easily. "We must mass our cavalry there and attack," he forced the issue, "to force a way through."

"We could try, General," Masonista was not immune to the idea, "but the day's fast advancing."

"Then there's not another moment to lose." Ballista grinned assuredly before bidding his posse to follow.

They found General Vega outside of the rearguard headquarters, still directing actions there.

"General Vega," Ballista made to address him as soon as he'd arrived.

The signified officer saluted his general grandly and with great respect as a war raged on all around them. Men gave up their lives in savage brutality just to acquire and hold mere patches of bloodied jungle grass. "How goes it here?" the commander openly inquired.

Vega pursed his lips slightly. "It's growing pretty warm down here, sir," he observed from on horseback, "but it's nothing that we can't handle."

"I'm happy to hear you say that, General," congratulated his chief. "Because I have a mission for you."

General Vega listened attentively while Ballista informed him of the dire circumstances regarding the three cutoff divisions. "And so I want you to smash your way through to the old encampment there so that our boys can get a chance to join us," he finished his stratagem.

General Vega was no coward, but he was at only half strength, and those crowds outside of their shield wall were both deep as well as numerous.

"I believe we can do it, General," he was cautiously optimistic, "but I will need some infantry as support."

Ballista readily agreed. "You tell General Phocus that I said to give you 800 men from his second division to accompany you as you see fit."

"Very well, sir," the elegantly dressed cavalryman saluted and moved with purpose to prepare his strike.

"Masonista," Ballista looked around to find him.

"Yes, General," the aforementioned responded from behind.

"Inform the division commanders to begin making camp here for the day," his decree went out after turning to face him.

"Here?" the chief steward challenged openly. "But we've hardly made any forward progress at all, General." He was clearly opposed to the idea. "And need I remind you further that our supply lines continue to be cut off as well?"

"What you say is true, Masonista," General Ballista had to agree. "However we cannot simply run away and leave 6,000 men to the slaughter." He considered the situation carefully. "Especially not after what's happened in the pass." His head shook at the fourth's misfortune. "It would not sit right with the men."

"The men are exhausted general, and—"

"Exactly," the chief justice interjected himself. "The men are exhausted and in a few hours' time it will grow dark, so for today," the general glared over towards his main attendant, "we have gone on far enough." He put his foot down.

"And our supplies?" Masonista responded with yet another act of willful disobedience, the only one who was able to do so. "What are we to tell the men when we have no more food to give them?"

"Do not trouble yourself on that account, Masonista," his general answered him back knowingly. "There will be many less mouths to feed by the time that this battle is done."

Back in the rearguard, General Vega was finished preparing with his men and officers on the ground. The procured troops out of General Phocus's second division had all been given their instructions and made ready to fight. All that was needed now was to open the back ranks and salvo out through the gap.

It was reasoned that they would only actually need to make it within sight of the camp. Presumably once there, those cut off divisions would then see their rescue attempt being made and flood out in order to help them. It was certainly felt by the men involved to be worth the effort.

"Any questions then, gentlemen?" The leader of their expedition looked to his officers' faces.

"No sir," came the chorus in unison.

Their warriors' hearts were unquestionably all fierce and brave, but after so many days of arduous marching, near constant harassment, and little to no low sleep, the exhaustion factor was beginning to set in.

For now, however, the soldiers involved with the operation had adrenaline as their master. None there would have been able to sleep a wink if they'd tried as they each lined up inside of their own lines and made ready for the command to rush forward.

Directly outside of their still formidable shield wall that had been rotating ranks for hours seemed an endless horde of scantily clad but heavily determined barbarians with every manner of weapon that could be found. They had been constantly crowding in and pushing back the great army for hours so that by now, their previous day's encampment could no longer be seen down the throng and hate-filled roadway.

The horses snorted and dug in their hooves nervously. Riders reached out to grip hard old friends and say their last goodbyes with martial poise and vigor. The soldiers on the ground took their places within the inside of the cavalry's formation, which would soon be leading their way. All along the back lines, men were informed to clear out of the path whenever the drums were rolled.

When everything was made ready and the sun still burned with a few hours of life left, General Vega took his position in the vanguard. He looked around to his chief officers and lieutenants. Each reached out to him to receive his touch of courage before facing forward with the resolve of hungry lions who've missed too many meals.

The din of battle was ceaseless and overwhelming as the regular cycling of their bronze warriors continued like a sundial's shadow in morning. General Ballista's army continued to hold its own against such formidable odds, but their casualties were mounting as losses became harder to replace and their lines more shallow.

General Vega raised his sword high into the air so that it glimmered in the sunlight. "Make ready!" He stood up on his mount as tall as he could go with both eyes kept dead ahead, following the sword's point. "Charge!" He dropped his arm low whilst kicking the haunches of his mount to launch his war horse out into an erstwhile run.

With the indication given, the war drums beat methodically a chant so that the center portion of their back lines opened like a double door, causing the enemy to flood inside. They were met head-on, however, by close to 2,500 charging horsemen and another 800 hand-picked warriors that were held as reserve inside. The flood in quickly reversed its course to flow outward as the equestrians jumped and trampled over the lightly armed combatants who were piling in.

"Heeah!" Vega glowered as he lopped off a part of a man's skull before twisting on his equine's back and raining down another lethal blow to some unfortunate bastard on his opposite side.

The cavalry kept moving, pushing forward and spilling out of the great army's rear in an incessant tide that seemed to be cutting through the horde like a winter breeze through thin fabric.

The fighting was raucous and raw as men trained from childhood to fight on horseback experienced the ultimate contest inside of that narrow jungle roadway. Some horsemen were simply jumped on and pulled off their mounts by sheer numbers alone before being torn to pieces on the ground. The men on foot pushed forward also, moving as fast as they could in a vain attempt to keep up. Eventually, however, the horsemen began to break away from their depleted counterparts whose energy reserves now fast began to fail them.

"General Vega sir!" One of his most experienced officers fought up next to him in the fray, swinging and slicing as he went. "Sir," he cried, "we're losing the rear!"

Swiping and slashing constantly, the unflinching Vega was able to look back and take account of the quickly deteriorating situation there. Without the infantrymen's support, he reasoned in a flash, our cavalry will be exposed on all sides and surrounded.

General Vega returned a desperate look again to the front. We haven't even made it around the bend, he despaired. There's no way we'd make it.

With no time left to spare, General Vega made the split-second decision. "Turn back!" his voice hailed the cry. "Go back!" he sounded the alarm once more as his hornsmen began their blaring.

Whether the men inside the camp could hear their efforts or not was irrelevant; the breakthrough had failed. They would be left to their own devices from now.

The battle back into their formation was terrible. The hordes of tribesmen had begun to recover from the initial surprise and were now becoming much more efficient at taking down the armored riders. General Vega began to lose men by the hundreds in the frantic panic that followed. The frightened horses and riders came crashing through their own front lines killing and maiming scores while the enemy began to pour in through the gaps. A desperate melee ensued there that was only just prevented from becoming a route by the onset of darkness. It was almost dusk when General Ballista first heard the news.

"Six thousand men," he kept repeating to himself, and that was not even accounting for the 2,200 or so dead or lost in the effort to save them. It was a major blow, almost critical.

Inside first division, Major Yusri and his lower ranking compatriots were still struggling to hold on. Every muscle in their bodies ached and groaned as they remorselessly swung and stabbed at their enemies. The time spent away from the front line was now hardly enough for them to even catch their breaths before they were again called back into the melee.

"Yusri, eye'm scared," Grieves heaved up and down over to him between his billowing breaths. "Eye'm not sure ow much longer eye can keep going."

"Don't talk like that, you blustering fool," Yusri barked back peevishly. "Those bastards are as tired as we are!"

Blows began falling with less velocity and force as the sun fell further. Eventually, at mid dusk, there was a moment when both sides seemed to accept that the day's fighting was over. The tribesmen pulled off slowly, backstepping into the jungles with their shields and weapons still facing outward. In a few more moments, they were gone.

A collective sigh of exhaustive relief seemed to go up from the leftover survivors as they looked around themselves and began taking stock of their many dead.

"Gods be praised," Grieves gave thanks towards the heavens. "Eye didn't think we'd make it, Yusri," he emotionally disclosed, his eyes growing moist with tears.

"I told you we would," his short friend reassured him, rubbing the giant man on the back for comfort as he did so.

Back inside of the general's tabernacle, another emergency council was arranged.

Before their discussions were opened, however, General Ballista called for the butcher's bill.

The results were not pretty.

"Sixth division lost 233 killed and another 680 wounded, General," General Uddica reported first. He was just over half strength with all his remaining men being both sleep-deprived and exhausted.

General Ballista nodded his head and bid for the next man to continue. "Eighth division has lost 390, General, and another 849 wounded." His division's strength was even less than half.

General Phocus's accounting followed. "Second division lost 911 men, General." He winced at the number. His had been the division selected to give men for the failed breakout attempt. "Another 715 are wounded, sir." That meant second division's combat readiness was now under a quarter strength.

Ballista grimly requested for the count to continue. General Augustine went next. "Sir," he delivered the details, "first division reports 267 dead or unaccounted for and another 458 as injured, General." His force was still at around 60 percent.

Juba's turn then followed. "We experienced no fighting today, General," he said disapprovingly.

General Vega announced his figures last. "One thousand, six hundred, fifty-six killed and 766 wounded, General." He was down to half capacity too.

It was a sobering moment as the full total was calculated. Almost 3,500 were dead and as many injured along with the 6,000 poor and cutoff souls lost in the camp. In only one day of fighting, General Ballista had lost use of almost half his force with all those who remained being dehydrated, hungry, sore, sleep deprived, and exhausted with more than a few feeling very scared as well. It was a recipe for disaster.

"What are we going to do, General?" Augastine spoke up in order to ask what the others were thinking.

General Ballista's face remained unmoved and steady as he stood up to address them.

"Things have not gone the way they should've." It was almost an apology. "We have no choice now," he poignantly addressed his innermost cabal, "but to push back toward the pass at all cost." Ballista's stare was grave and piercing. "Beginning at dawn."

The other generals voiced their approval by tone or through the stamping of feet.

"General Juba," his commander and chief spoke over to the man who looked back expectantly. "I want you and your third division to take rearguard tomorrow," he declared. "It seems like most of the enemy's assaults have been focused there."

"We will give them death, General," the fearsome tiger growled.

"I have no doubt," Ballista commented before turning towards his other two generals, Uddica and Clymistocles, who were standing nearby. "I want your two divisions to lead at the front tomorrow, and General Vega," he looked over to him as well, "I want you and the remainder of our cavalry to clear the path forward."

"Consider it done, General," Vega complied willingly.

"It's a two-day march before we reach the pass, gentlemen," he told them all with a sober-minded stare. "They will most likely be far from easy."

Chapter 28

Throughout that long night, the remaining men of General Ballista's beleaguered army were forced to stay inside of their own hastily constructed perimeter. They listened in horror while innumerous comrades who'd been captured during that day's fighting were slowly tortured and killed just inside the tree line. The sounds produced by their own side's bloodcurdling screams of horror and death, coupled with the near endless yips and howls of the enemy combatants, left more than one soldier to run off into the no man's land surrounding and hurl obscenities towards the darkness.

By the third day's dawning, General Ballista's army was nearly broken. Most of the troops within hadn't slept for days, and if they did piss at all anymore, then it was a deep brown and rusty color. Hunger was not yet a concern, but the bronzed warriors were totally unused to the intense humidity there, and despite drinking more than they were used to, it still wasn't close to enough. Many of the army's soldiers began to experience symptoms of severe dehydration as a result.

As the sun increased its zenith on that death-filled morning, there was found to be a heavy fog covering the jungle floor. The strange phenomenon was thought to resemble some type of ominous snow which had covered and kept hidden the many thousands of dead underneath it. The bodies that were left lying there were already starting to turn and fester from the tropical heat. The survivors soon watched with disgust as black flies and other crawling insects started to lay eggs inside of the quickly bloating and putrefying corpses.

Morale was becoming abysmal as the increasingly fragile individuals who were left tried their best to patch up any injuries and wounds, in whatever way possible, before dragging themselves back into standing. Things did not bode well inside of the general's tabernacle either, as he and his officers prepared to flee.

"Keep the wounded and supplies inside of the center," stipulated Ballista. "And Vega," he considered next, "you and your cavalry are to keep the road clear."

General Vega was ready.

"Everyone else," he proclaimed, "keep moving at all cost." The point was well taken. "We must make it back to the pass."

The gathered assembly all murmured their approval.

"Alright then, gentleman," the supreme leader checked from left to right for the last time. "Let's get about it."

Outside of General Ballista's enclosure, the early fog had mostly lifted. The dissipation showed clearly enemy troops massed upon the homebound roadway, blocking their path forward just out of bow shot. The tribesmen all stood staring, menacingly grim and silent, still partially enveloped by the billowing white mist.

As the general's staff were hurriedly concluding their preparations for moving out with the army, it once again started to rain. The downpour quickly turned thick and heavy, causing the surrounding area to transform into a muddy morass as puddles became shallow ponds that soaked everything, man and beast alike.

It was a bad omen as the army finally received the order to creep forward. Horns blew and war drums commenced their steady cadence while worn-down troops started marching out in a line.

Contact was immediate. Stones, spears, and arrows were all attempted to be used against them in a lethal manner from both flanks simultaneously. Soldiers continued getting picked off in ones and twos as the rain fell harder, making it even more difficult to see the incoming missiles before they'd struck. Water ran down the inside of men's eyes and helmets too, making their vision blurry. Still, they pushed onward.

"Fine mornin this is then!" Grieves shouted over to his major and friend while deflecting the incoming strays.

"Aye," Yusri answered back jokingly. "Strenuous day it is," he laughed out his reply.

"Cack!" Grieves happened to catch upon his joke's witticism, throwing a chuckle back into the storm as well.

The army continued to progress slowly towards the scowling enemy with General Vega's cavalry kept close out in front. Only once the supporting infantry was near enough behind to charge with them did he then give the order to do so.

"Attack!" Vega cried as he reared back his chestnut stallion on two legs prior to pushing it into a run. The rest of his equestrians followed suit and galloped right into the enemy's center with the infantry coming up from the rear.

General Ballista had been counting on the bulk of his foe's strikes to be directed at the largely fresh division of Juba's third that was stationed in the rearguard. Instead, it was Generals Clymistacles and Uddica's men that were once again bearing the brunt of their vicious assaults.

"Keep pushing!" the overall commander roared from atop his crimson stallion, The Red Hare. "Masonista!" he yelled to his most trusted confidant who was close by.

"Yes, General?" The called upon waited for word.

"Send to the rear for Juba's division," he instructed him. "Have 500 of his infantry brought up here immediately."

"Yes, General," Masonista snapped to before throwing his horse into reverse and heading off at a clip.

It was still not yet mid-morning when the rain stopped, and by then everything and everyone had been soaked. The howling from inside the jungle on both sides of the road became intensely uproarious as well. The enemy commander was clearly rallying his men in preparation to force the issue.

"Send word to Generals Augustine and Phocus' divisions," Ballista passed with angst. "Tell them that they must brace and hold."

Some unnamed staff officer saluted his understanding of the directive and left right away to act as an envoy.

General Ballista could see the situation was dangerous.

"You two!" He turned to a pair of his oath men.

"Sir!" "General!" Each of them shouted in turn.

"Go now and find every able-bodied person who is fit to hold a blade," he commanded them. "And see that one gets placed into their hands," his orders grew desperate and severe. "Then send them out as small groups to fill the gaps."

Their complicity was swift and immediate as they then each set out to begin organizing the militia of civilians and wounded for combat.

Yusri was therefore positively surprised to look over and see the heavily bandaged Quiminax limping up with a sword in his hand. "What in the seven furies are you doing here?" the major inquired incredulously. "You should still be in bed, not waddling about on the battlefield!"

"They told us you sissies couldn't handle things by yourself," he blackballed with humor as Grieves remained anxious and jittery nearby, unlike his usual person.

Finally, the attack came. It was devastating, and from both sides. "Get ready!" Major Yusri and the other surviving officers of first division shouted out as their worn down and exhausted men clanged shields together and prepared for another engagement.

Grieves and Yusri, along with all the injured and civilians, were set up in the last rank to start with and prepared themselves to push and heave with all their might to prevent their line from buckling inward.

"Brace yourselves!" The shouts went out as the tumbling tribesman spilled forward like a raging river. They screamed incoherent madness and promised only violence and death as they closed the last gap between their two sides, crashing through the jungle's woodwork.

They careened into the shield wall of first division with a terrible and sudden velocity that pushed the entire column backward before they could get their feet reset and begin the excruciating work of combat.

Back inside of General Vega's division, the fighting was as fierce and intense as any he had ever seen. Everywhere around him blades rose and fell with such force and ferocity that at any one time the whole mass appeared to be constantly teeming. Spurts of red or pink mist exploded out into the crowd at random spots and locations as particularly hard hits or lethal blows found their marks and sprayed blood. Vega just managed to catch sight of Clymistocles as he was killed while on horseback.

The 500 new arrivals from General Juba's third division arrived just in time and came pouring into the melee at a run so that together, with the rest of their front formation, they were slowly turning the tide, despite the heavy losses.

"Send word to General Juba and ask for news there!" Ballista singled out a waiting horseman, who immediately flew away on his special assignment.

All around the interior, small groups of freshly armed cripples and noncombatants could be seen being corralled by the soldiers to plug in gaps at different parts of the line. Ballista knew it was only a temporary stop-gap at best.

General Uddica fell next, and with it came word that his sixth division was in danger of being overwhelmed.

"Gods be damned!" Ballista yelled his frustration directly to the ones above. "Masonista," he charged severely, "go and sort out the sixth." Further decree followed, "And keep them moving!" His addition was clear.

"Yes, General," Masonista obeyed dutifully whilst paying his commander homage.

"You must drive them forward, Masonista!" his general called after him. It was an easier thing said than done when under such direct assault. It was only his professional army's extensive training that made such maneuvers feasible at all.

Word came up from the rear that Juba's sector was all clear. "The bastards want us to retreat," he spat out disdainfully. "So they can then surround and annihilate us too."

General Ballista began to grow angry. "Sons of whores," he steamed, hot. "Gods damned vipers," his hatred bellowed while his eyes began darting around the battlefield quickly.

The front was a mass of confused fighting, but slowly, they were cutting their way through while on both sides his, flanks were being pushed in closer, making his entire base of operations that more narrow and confined.

"You there, scout!" he stopped a passing horseman who turned out to be the captain. "Captain Matrius," Ballista briefly brightened. "I'm glad to find you still swinging a sword."

"Still going strong, sir!" he lied and waited to see why he'd been halted.

"Captain Matrius," the general informed him, "I want you to fly back to General Juba's third division as quick as you can, and tell him to break off another 500 men." He paused. "You tell him to split those 500 into two detachments of 250 each and then send one each to General Augustine's first division and the other over to sixth." He flashed his eyes sharply at him. "Did you get all that, soldier?"

"Clear as crystal, sir," confirmed Matrius, who then turned to go and find Juba.

Inside of General Augustine's first division, Major Yusri fought alongside his two friends like it was old times again. Quiminax had a severe leg wound that prevented him from fighting in the front line, but he stayed right behind Yusri and Grieves both and helped them kill tribesmen.

Yusri stayed firm with a low center of gravity as he pushed from behind his bronze shield and continued to hook the sharpness of his blade into the bodies of his enemies. Even still, he could feel his energy starting to wane. As the fighting went on, eventually some unknown assailant's ax managed to find its way through a gap in the shield wall and land itself into Yusri's shoulder, causing moderate injury.

"Juno's cunt!" he blasted as a result of the piercing pain while beginning to fight all the harder. Grieves, who saw his best friend almost go down, began to grow more afraid.

"Ah that's just a scratch," Quiminax shouted up from behind them. "You should see the one I've got!" he laughed out loud while continuing to swing, smiling in the face of death.

The tribesman's attack continued pouring on from three sides with the front slowly clearing. The bulk of enemy reinforcements were being sent into the flanks to try and collide the whole army inward. Juba's reinforcements arrived there at a critical juncture.

The fighting was mad and haphazard, but they were holding their own. Men were dying all around them, irreplaceable men whose absences all began to be felt up and down the column. Still, they moved forward.

If I ever get my hands on that gods forsaken shepherd, Ballista's mind made time to threaten as all of his lies became painfully obvious. The enemy was being killed at a rate of four or five to one, and yet ceaselessly they poured on with never a let up in sight. Flux indeed!

The fighting raged on like that for another hour before the front finally pushed free. "Go forward, men!" the commander shouted to all of his troops within hearing. "Keep moving!" he hullooed out to them from on horseback.

The quickly dissipating force began to try and slide through faster, but the fighting on the flanks was dragging both sides back like liquid through a pipe. The center was advancing quicker than the rest, and if things continued on like that, then the outside would break in and they would all be overrun.

"Fuck the furies," Ballista raged aloud as mass became critical. The front and back were now clear, but both sides continued to be hammered.

"Send word to General Vega to slow his advance!" Ballista roared. "Tell him that he must not push forward too quickly!"

When the racing dispatcher reached General Vega's still warm position with the news, he duly complied, allowing for the army to catch up with itself. It was now already past noon, and the heat of the day, coupled with the steam that had been created from that morning's heavy downpours, threatened to turn the whole area into a nightmarish sauna.

Soldiers began to cramp up or stroke out from the heat and lack of water so injuries and losses now occurred from more than just the enemy alone. The edifice was cracking.

Looking around from on horseback, General Ballista once more surveyed the scene. His flanks were both heavily engaged in severe fighting while to his front and rear the—Wait a minute, his mind thought as he stared down the expanse of open jungle roadway leading back toward the passes. "What in the ..." his voice trailed away as his brain tried to process what was happening.

Suddenly, horns sounded from the enigma, unlike any he had ever heard before. Long and loud cries poured out from the snake-like snouts of a great and many gray beasts who appeared in the way-off distance, charging down the roadway.

The men who were not directly engaged in the fighting turned to try and see from whence the sound came, but only those on horseback were high enough to have a view of what was coming.

Unknown and massive creatures they were. Great spikes were worn around their ankles, and atop their tree-high backs were carried singular pagodas which overflowed with tribesmen carrying slings, bows, and spears.

General Ballista, nor any of his men, beasts, or horses, had ever seen such animals before. The effect was immediate and severe. The horses in the front began to grow skittish and bucked or tried to bolt with their riders as the strange terrors came bearing down upon them. The infantry could feel their approach before they ever saw them as their weight and number shook the very earth beneath.

The road was packed tight with the lumbering giants that squeezed and rumbled past one another straight towards them. With their flanks both busily engaged and only the roadway left open, there was nowhere for Ballista's troops to go.

When the infantry finally saw the war elephants advancing, unit cohesion began to break down. General Vega tried his best to rally a group of his horsemen, bravely attempting to make a stand. When the wall of gray inertia arrived, however, there was nowhere left for Vega or his men to go. The giant beasts simply crashed through the valiant general, trampling him and his cavalry underneath. The last that Ballista saw of his dauntless commander was when his head was being crushed, screaming, under a massive foot, pink brains popping out the top of his skull.

The huge and violent monstrosities crashed into Ballista's front, driving deep into his ranks and throwing the men there into utter confusion so that they almost routed.

General Ballista gazed once more around the battlefield. His flanks still held, but only barely, and his front was being driven in on top of him by creatures bigger than any he'd ever seen before. Only General Juba with his 1,000 men of the third remained largely unscathed.

"Gracus!" Ballista turned to another of his oath men who remained by his side.

"Yes, General." The bespoken kept his nerve despite the chaos surrounding. "Send word to Juba," Ballista told him. "Tell him that he is needed here."

A crisp and quick salute flew topside before the dispatcher spun around and bolted off.

"Well then," the general turned to all those who were still close enough to hear him speak. "It seems as though you'd best to get your swords ready." He smiled fatefully at their impending doom.

A messenger arrived from first division, stating that General Augastine was dead. It would fall on their own officers to lead them now as Ballista had no one left to send.

The tribesman on that side of the battle hacked and cut desperately with a second wind, which had begun to arrive as they could sense just how close they were to breaking through. Yusri and Grieves, along with the rest of the first, were giving it all they could, but even still, their hope was fading. Even Quiminax could only grimace and swing on in silence as his humor had by now failed him also.

In the corner of his eye, Grieves could see the bronze men falling. It was like being in a school of sardines that were being schooled up and eaten. As men fought on for their lives and an increasing amount became butchered to pieces, the panic of the last few days finally overflowed and drove the giant mad.

Yusri became startled, despite the unbelievable noise that was there already. Grieves suddenly shrieked out a berserker's cry right next to him, erupting like a long dormant volcano that had finally blown its top. He bellowed out an unintelligible hatred and anger that built up every vein on his face into bulging so that under his helmet of bronze it appeared as though a demon lie beneath.

Their army was starting to disintegrate all around them, but Grieves knew none of it. The tyrant of rage had no other thought other than to murderously dominate.

He burst out of formation, pulling Quiminax, who'd been with him, up involuntarily to take his place on the front line. Grieves was now surrounded by fighters, but his speed and strength were uncanny. He turned with a heaving strike that laid down two men in a single stroke before exploding back the other direction and sending another corpse flying.

He roared again, bossing another pair of tribesmen with his shield, and causing them both to tumble downward before swinging around 180 degrees to kill a man who was behind him. Four adversaries now lay dead from the giant, screaming fanatic who had begun to actively chase down and pursue the same ones who'd just been attacking him before. Had it not been such a brutal performance it may have almost been comical.

Over where Ballista was located, he could see General Juba jogging up with his battle ax held firm across his prow.

"It's been a pleasure to lead you all these many years," Ballista spoke to all those who were present. "Remember, the gods are watching." He eyed them boldly and with a pirate's pride.

The stunned onlookers did not know what to make of this unheard-of speech, and so said nothing, waiting out the pause for their general to speak further.

"Safety only lies within the pass now," their leader told them. "You'll have to try and make it there the best way you can."

Their sky was falling. Everything was chaos and mayhem. Tribesmen were beginning to break through their flanks in spots that could no longer be plugged or held, and the giant beasts who'd come crashing through his cavalry in front were now being joined by a fresh wave of fighters.

Chapter 29

Grieves continued fighting on like an angry hornet, being both endlessly tenacious and utterly unafraid. Yusri, in the brief respite that followed from his friends' insane madness, thoughtfully searched the battlefield around them. His vision could find no set lines, just disorganized masses of mingling warriors fighting desperately on all sides. For the first time as well, he discovered the great gray giants that were running amok inside of their imperiled formation, tearing apart gaping holes. It was a shocking sight to behold. Adding to the inherent breakdown were the dozens of tribesmen who had already broken through the ranks, and who were now roaming freely inside of their perimeter at will. Soon they would get behind them too, and then the massacre would start. The battle was almost done.

Yusri's life flashed in front of him. He saw the smiling faces of his two daughters first with their little laughs that tricked both ears into almost hearing them. The mother of their three children, to whom even life itself came in distant second, next whispered on longingly, begging for a return to home. With these thoughts of family arrived an overwhelming desire to live that shook Yusri to the very core. It was only the wrath of a charging foe which prevented any further meditations from ongoing at the time.

He took his man square on the shield boss, slamming together like two bull rams competing for mating rights. Before the second collision occurred, however, Yusri turned inward so that his opponent came stumbling forward into the second rank where another man felled him with a single strike while he was still off balance.

Comprehending the present situation clearly meant coming to terms with the disintegration that was fast underway. The major himself realized this fact whereupon he took up his own command, turning to what men remained standing and issuing them out orders.

"Let's go!" he resolutely shouted to his wounded friend, Quiminax, and all the rest there who were still close enough by to hear him. "On me!" Major Yusri began to lead.

He raised his sword arm up high, forming their rallying point like a beacon's light before advancing. "Forward!" The call rang deeply as Yusri and his followers burst free from within their quickly collapsing flank, which was in the process of being rolled up like an old carpet.

Yusri's detachment made straight towards the raging Grieves, who was slowly and indiscriminately killing his way towards the jungle like a warrior deity.

"Gods below!" Quiminax seized on the amazement. "Grieves fights like the fury himself!" he cried out, loudly.

The major's other soldiers did too marvel at the death-defying spectacle that was Grieves, who continuously murdered their enemies in such close proximity. It could hardly be called anything else considering the ease with which it was done and the lack of any mercy shown. The attention could not yet be absolute, however, because the attack on themselves was still constant and from every side, like how a nut surrounds its kernel. Nevertheless, whenever they were not fully engaged, all eyes were stuck upon the deranged berserker, who continued to hack uncontrollably at anything and everything that moved that wasn't bronze clad. His bloodlust was insatiable.

Many of the enemy soldiers, by this point, seeing readily the advantage, had already begun stripping bare the corpses of dead comrades and then taking over their armor. One such mimic managed to get close enough onto Grieves that a blow was landed. A cut sliced deep into his bulging thigh before the great bear turned with such a savage ferocity and intent that the offending party regretted instantly his mistake before being sliced in two, directly between the neck and collar.

The tribal army continued pouring on from all sides now, hooting and hollering without any end as they began breaking through in multiple places, enveloping the entire perimeter.

"Grieves, we have to go!" Yusri tried reaching through to the reaper of men.

Grieves himself heard none of it except for the high-pitched ringing sounds that filled each of his ears. He swung so hard, so fast, that his blade sliced clear through another man's neck enroute to shattering itself against the nearby tree. The instantly decapitated body stood there, unsure of itself for a full few seconds, until falling down with blood spurting out of its top like an over-boiled teapot.

The cohort following behind Yusri, in the meantime, was of decent size. It currently stood between about twenty-five to thirty warriors who were still there, fighting frantically to survive, falling by the ones and twos periodically. Sometimes from the enemy, and other times from heatstroke or exhaustion.

As more incoming tribesmen approached the battle, they began to take notice. There was the main army, with its many supplies which were now up mostly for grabs, and then there was the cloud of moving death that was floating swiftly off into the jungle with an enormously vicious killer mounted at its head. Most of the enemy, unsurprisingly, therefore chose to take the path of least resistance and headed off towards the plunder and profit instead.

"Move faster, gods damn you!" Yusri pushed the ranting Grieves onward insultingly until they reached the far tree line. Enemy soldiers still came at them now, but it was very few and far between. Soon after, there were none at all as the small roving band of fugitives moved off briskly into the tropical terrain to try and achieve their escape.

Back within the collapsing center, Juba arrived with his 1000 leftover warriors from third division. "Can we salvage it, sir?" the grim-faced general asked his supreme commander whilst peering around at the chaos during their last few moments of calm before the storm.

"If we could knock them out of the fight," Ballista pointed towards the stampede of careening juggernauts being reinforced by more tribesmen, "then we might well have a chance." "But it doesn't seem very likely." He smiled in spite of the reckoning.

Juba nodded his understanding. "Then it will be like old times again," the fearsome tiger growled maliciously before peering up.

Ballista laughed. "How's that?" he joked through the warzone. "Because the odds are overwhelming?" The death-defying general grinned widely.

"You've hit the nail square, sir." Juba's eyes gleamed like frost on a new morning.

His reference caused the general's mind to glance at Korballa's penis being hammered on the tree stump. "Why, my dear Juba," Ballista then allowed himself to become sentimental. "I will certainly toast your name tonight in the great hall," he spoke of death.

"It's been an honor to serve under you, sir," the indefatigable Juba saluted his leader.

Ballista returned his homage. "I thank you, General" he told him truthfully. "My apologies for all… this." He cast an arm outward after a second's delay.

"It's no matter," Juba spat unconcernedly.

Both men then signified to the other. Ballista, from atop his most magnificent red stallion, and Juba, who was clutching tightly at his battle ax whilst standing down on the ground below.

During this meeting, Juba's men had no need for orders. It was fight or die now, and they all knew it. There was nowhere else for them to go. With that knowledge well known, the last somewhat fresh portion of third division made a large difference in the ongoing herculean efforts still being made. They immediately spread out into large groups upon arrival to begin clearing out the second half of their perimeter from invaders. The three sides were now holding, albeit barely, while the front ranks continued to be smashed in and destroyed by the living siege engines that were continuously crashing through towards his rear. General Ballista could now see the faces of their riders clearly.

"Fight fiercely, Juba!" he called down to his most daunting of companions. "Remember," General Ballista addressed him audaciously in advance of turning to go and fight, "the gods are watching!"

With that final hoorah, the great general reared The Red Hare on high, and without further ado, began racing it towards the left side of the fray to where the fighting was fiercest. As Ballista, with his oath men, pointed themselves towards those terrifically large creatures therein, Masonista himself came bounding out from an angle to intercept them.

"General!" alarmed his most trusted of confidants, who was all blood covered and bruised when he stopped them. "Sixth division has been overrun, sir," he gasped out the terrible news. "Our lines there are broken!"

"I know our lines are broken!" Ballista yelled at him impatiently. "The whole damn army's being destroyed." He swept an arm around to show his man the obvious.

"Then what are your orders, General?" Masonista didn't know what to do.

"Do as you wish," Ballista awarded him his freedom with a solemn calmness that was brought on by the impromptu occasion. "I give you your liberty now to choose."

Masonista became bereft at this unexpected release and was almost overcome by emotion. "But what about you, General?" He managed to make himself heard through the din of slaughter.

"I will stay with the army," Ballista committed himself totally. "Goodbye old friend." He patted his freedman on the shoulder before inhaling deeply and pulling out his long sword.

Everywhere in sight, there was now only combat and violence as the Great Army floundered and whittled away to nothingness due to the innumerable forces that were being stacked against it. The encirclement had by then been completed. Their only way out now was through the densely packed walls of angry tribesmen and elephants as the army closed tightly in on itself, forming a defensive circle.

General Ballista kept his whinnying mount corralled next to the undecided Masonista until he locked eyes with the driver of an enormous monster. Waiting no more, the fearless horseman bellowed out a thundering war cry before pushing The Red Hare off into a run and leaving his freedman behind to do and decide as he pleased.

Juba had himself turned after their last meeting and began to trot over closer toward the right, having no one to stop him along the way. As he grew nearer to the melee, his inner war drums increased tenfold with every step. Hate, disdain, and contempt on a genocidal scale burst up from the blackened soul that laid within to prepare his limbs and mind for a cataclysm of coming violence and bloodshed.

Juba started to yell loudly; the distance itself was not that far away now. He saw two crippling giants there, thrashing amongst the groups of soldiers, both friend and foe alike with their deadly mayhem.

The terror-inducing cry built up to an alpine peak just as Juba reached the shield wall and bulldozed himself through. He thus appeared thick as thieves amongst their many enemies who were now almost surrounding him on every side.

His weight was heavy on the lead foot as he twisted from the forward inertia and bum-rushed into the side of an opposing combatant to still himself and send the other man flying. Juba then immediately shoved the butt of his ax directly across from where he stood and into the sternum of an opposing tribesman, crushing it inward by the devastating impact of its heavy point.

With a short grip near the ax head, the attacking general then turned behind himself and slashed his heavy blade into the unprotected gullet of a charging victim which split open and sprayed the surrounding air nearby like an erupting geyser. The gurgling and spurting casualty fell with their head leaned back and both hands held fast to the gaping wound.

While still in close quarters, the axman maintained his shortened grip and this time swung hard, chopping through a wicker shield and arm bone. Juba screamed defiantly as blood began draining from his hair and beard like an oversaturated mop.

He checked two men who were rushing him with his ax pole held horizontally across his chest. The brutal clothesline bruised or broke many ribs in the process before Juba then came up and over the top of his head to chop down into one of the fallen men's ribcages, opening it up like a bird's nest with the solid blow. The other laid-low tribesman rolled out of the way and stumbled off backwards onto his heels, falling down repeatedly as he tried to scurry away with both arms clutching at his battered breast.

A massive gray beast came close to him now, still trampling and bringing on death. Juba charged the great creature without question. It could not see him coming because of its attack to the front and Juba's arriving from the oblique. He reached the back left leg just as it was rearing up onto its hindquarters in preparation for a new assault. The general planted both feet firmly prior to giving the first full swing of the day. It connected clean and flush, plunging deep into the back of the wrinkled and tree-like leg as though he were a lumberjack driving through wood.

The effect was immediate and severe as the lumbering animal, which had already been standing on only two legs, suddenly began to topple over backward instead of forward. It poured forth a trumpeting cry from within its long trunk as it gave way to gravity and collapsed behind itself, squashing both their own men and all the soldiers from the parapet.

That's one, Juba smiled to himself as the great beast rolled about on its backside, crushing more underneath, while their own soldiers drove forward to plunge spears into its unprotected belly, opening it up and spilling its immense innards right out into a pile on the earth. It tooted its horn horribly as it thrashed around in the throes of death.

General Ballista, for his part, made to attack them as well. He had already made eye contact with a leviathan from his quarter and so set off The Red Hare into a gallop directly towards the colossal brute. Watching those two head off into battle was an unforgettable moment to anyone who saw it. The commander rode like his horse was a part of him, as though they formed the minotaur itself.

When Ballista reached the back of his own men, who were three ranks deep at the time, he did not slow down or trample through them, but he leaped over the top of their entire line instead. The general crash landed into the enemy soldiers, causing instant havoc within their squeezing mob. The Red Hare then turned its rear in half a circle, knocking over a dozen men in the process before kicking backward to shatter another person's jaw.

The horseman was already swinging as well, his long sword reaching far and wide into the masses of lightly armored tribesmen who were still reeling from the immediate shock of what was going on. Ballista gave them no time to recover, however, as he and his bronco continued to buck, kick, turn, and charge with the sword falling ceaselessly to both sides, driving deep into the flesh of men.

The driver of the titan that he'd seen earlier could see this commotion and himself began to rumble towards the pair, killing or injuring their own who were not aware or simply too unhurried to move out of the way. As the clumsy beast drove closer still, General Ballista smiled at its slowness and kicked his own horse off into a canter.

The two opposing sides careened towards each other through the crowds, treading and squashing many underfoot during the occasion. When they were nearly right on top of each other, the horse, bred of fire, twitched right in an instant to clear out of the way with its rider ducking to avoid thrown spears. The other driver carried forward, trying to set about his heavy-footed animal into a turn. The nimble red stallion, in the meantime, had already run past and chopped hard into a back knee as it did so. The pain of the blow sped up the creature's reaction time significantly so that it whipped itself about in a lethal fury to try and catch them, spilling over its own men as it did so.

General Ballista and his hare kept running around the wounded behemoth as it turned, exposing the crook of a different leg, which was immediately driven into by the general's sword deep enough to kill any man. The elephant reared in pain, shouting through its trumpet as its controller tried desperately to bring it to heel. As it stood up, Ballista reached its front once more so that the two sides could once again lock faces.

When the animal started to fall back down onto the earth, looking to crush both horse and rider under a forefoot, the extravagant duo dug in and peeled off dead ahead, darting beneath it. With his sword held high and firm, General Ballista punctured the vulnerable stomach halfway down its midline when it landed back on all fours, and then he dragged the blade back with him all the way to its rear. The poor beast buckled inward straight away, collapsing to the ground in advance of rolling over on its side to crush, maim, and injure all those unfortunates who were caught underneath it before dying miserably.

"Did you see that up there?" Ballista challenged defiantly towards the clear blue sky before resuming his blood work.

Juba was fighting mightily on his own behalf as well. He continued to gash open a corpse-laden trail throughout the enemy formation, swinging and chopping with deadly effect. After the fearsome general had brought down yet another war elephant single-handedly, however, along with the many scores of tribesmen, he was set aside and targeted by the elites. The other groups of leading warriors who rode atop of the surviving siege towers hollered out in their strange dialect to communicate and coordinate between themselves before directing their ground troops into action.

The fearless Juba fought on heroically and without hesitation, vanquishing every single foe that he encountered, regardless of their size or weapon. After killing another pair of tribesmen, the incessant general made to continue moving forward until he looked up and saw that there was no one left in front of him to fight. A gap had been formed. The caged tiger then turned around immediately and saw that a ring of space was now surrounding him there too. After having gone so far into the enemy's lines, he was all alone now.

Suddenly, a spear was thrown. He dodged it easily, but then another came, and still another after that. Juba then realized that his time was up.

In the short pause that followed, as the many tribesmen surrounding prepared their throws to be both well aimed and simultaneous, General Juba gripped his battle ax firmly across his chest and planted both feet solid as rocks onto the ground before unleashing out with a death-defying roar. It was still ongoing when the spears were thrown from all sides and angles so that his outburst was cut short by the sounds of being punctured.

The legendary warrior did not cry out, however. He only grimaced and growled while the spears tore into him, so that he was rendered dead well before his body ever hit the earth.

With less than a few thousand troops remaining, the surviving horsemen decided to take their chances and make a run for it. Matrius and Masonista, along with a few hundred others, gathered themselves up and made deliberately to where Juba had just been. The two dead elephants, coupled with the distracted tribesmen, meant that it was their best option for taking flight, and they hightailed it out of there at full speed. The fleeing riders did not even slow down to move their own men out of the way as they instead simply ran over from the rear.

The wedge of riders hopped and kicked into the mass of surprised tribesmen, chopping and hacking down furiously as they drove through in their mad dash to freedom. Some of the runaways didn't make it, but most, Matrius and Masonista included, were able to escape through the narrow corridor and rush onto the open jungle roadway where they proceeded to race away without ever looking back.

The valley of death closed in on itself like a parted sea just as soon as the last cavalryman made his successful exodus, leaving all the remaining bronze warriors trapped inside by the conquering waves.

General Ballista watched the breakout with resignation. Despite the hopelessness, however, he fought on bravely and was so far unscathed. The famous Red Hare, however, was not so fortunate. Eventually, the legendary stallion's many culminating wounds caused it to grow weak and weary from the blood loss, forcing their retreat back inside of his own lines.

Once they were within the relative safety of their inner perimeter, General Ballista dismounted and attended to his dying friend.

"Shh now," he comforted the magnificent animal and long-time friend, petting its nose gently as he did so. "That's a good boy, Red," the general whispered softly as it knelt down on its front two legs before falling over to its side and lying there in a labored breathing. "You just stay here and rest now, okay?" Ballista continued rubbing him with a genuine love and affection. "I'll take care of things from here," he smiled at his old friend once more before standing up and resolutely turning.

"Soldiers of the Great Army!" the supreme commander erupted out to all those who could still listen. "No defeat! No surrender!" General Ballista screamed.

"There is no hope but a glorious death!" he rallied to the heavens. "Remember!" their zealous leader added with fire and brimstone. "The gods are watching!"

After this last stirring speech, General Ballista looked up to the sky, then over to his now dead horse, and finally towards the fast-coming end. The circle was quickly shrinking around them. There were fewer and fewer remaining men left to hold them all back.

General Ballista searched for his opening and waited with gritted teeth. When he saw his spot appear, he went for it. The indomitable warrior ran forward to a freshly opened gap in the ranks with both hands held firmly around his sword's handle. The first incoming enemy through the hole was dealt with by an upward blow that came swinging from underneath and the second from the downwards slice that followed it. The break in the lines was thus cleared, but Ballista made no attempt to either stand fast or try to plug it. Instead, he took in a deep breath and hurled it out like a Silverback Gorilla on the charge before bounding off alone into the breach. He was never seen or heard from after.

The battle finally ended before nightfall. The last few hundred survivors who were left collectively threw down their arms and begged to be allowed to surrender. This request was denied by the enemy, however, and so the tribesmen started to massacre. The remaining warriors of the Great Army were cut into pieces with some men holding their hands up pitifully in a vain last attempt at self-defense. The bravest amongst them resisted little and so were killed swiftly while those who attempted to repel and block the blows only prolonged their agony and suffering greatly as limbs and appendages were cut and hacked off until the head and trunk were finally left exposed enough to be struck and chopped with ease.

Chapter 30

Back inside of their besieged camp, the three division commanders debated in a fog of war.

"We have no supplies," Alaric doubled down vehemently during their second day of discussions. "My men have checked everywhere," he told them. "There's no food to be found."

"Well, a breakout would be suicide," General Ziggurat warned against any such notion. "We're completely outnumbered and surrounded."

"Then we must try to negotiate," Lysander sounded a tune that the others could hum to. "We should prepare a peace delegation to seek terms."

The trio were in agreement with this plan, so it was decided by volunteers that General Ziggurat would ride out under a white flag of truce with four other men of consequence.

When the time came for the emissaries to leave the fort, all of its walls and vantage points were chock full of men who were watching intently. Together, they stared with hope-filled eyes as the five horsemen departed their camp. General Ziggurat himself was personally carrying the banner of parley.

They rode a little bit past bow shot and then waited. Soon enough, the jungle started to come alive as tribesmen began to appear out from the woodwork in front of them, approaching slowly. By the time they heard the warning shouts of their comrades behind them, however, it was too late. A war party had snuck out from the tree line and quietly approached their rear so that when the first horseman finally turned around to see them coming, they were already being set upon. Each of the party was subsequently butchered in full sight of the camp. Their disregarded pleas for mercy which preceded death carried easily across the space dividing them. The five horses were also taken as well, so now the leftover survivors had even less food to eat.

The situation within the palisade became dire as men openly began agitating and expressing their doubts. No one had any idea about the rest of the engagements going on or what had befallen their companions in the main army. Isolated days passed by inside of the foodless camp with increasing despondency and despair. All of the horses and what little pack animals they still possessed were quickly eaten. Eventually, when there was nothing left but hunger, it was decided that another peace offering should be made, this time containing much value.

The soldiers had by this time very little left to give, but between the 6,000 or so who were still alive they were able to produce a significant horde. Their remaining wealth was then piled onto one of the animal's wagons that was leftover, and afterwards they had some of their soldiers help to pull it out with them as General Lysander led the way. This time, all of the men walked on foot carrying and waving around white flags with another person given the role of repeating over and over again that, "We surrender!"

The cartload of treasures was once more carried out into the open space and placed like before. The deputation then hungrily awaited close by for some response.

On this attempt, however, the group were much more wary and on guard against treachery, desperate as they were to make a deal. They therefore noticed immediately when some marauding raiders tried to get into a position to cut off their retreat back towards camp.

The delegates protested loudly and wailed for peace as they started to retire. Once the tribesmen saw that their ruse was up, however, they charged them. This forced General Lysander and the others to ignominiously sprint back behind the gate, leaving behind their wealth of so many years on the field to be taken and carted away right in front of them.

No more food of any kind existed inside of the camp. It was now also made abundantly clear to all that they would not be allowed to leave there peacefully either. The tribesmen, it seemed, were intent on making them starve. The two generals then, and with what high ranking officers remained, decided to hold a public council. Together they clearly explained the situation and its choices to the men. None were pleasant, and though success was deemed very dim indeed, the decision was eventually made to try and fight their way out, come what may. It was thought a better choice by most than just simply waiting around to die.

The problem was that by now the surviving men were all extremely weak and hungry. They were tired with fatigue and had very little energy left to fall back on. Each knew and agreed that if the army were to open the gates now and make a run for it, they would all soon be caught and slaughtered. The soldiers, therefore, had to get their strength back somehow and the only way to do that was to eat.

"And so it's been decided," General Lysander informed the assembled troops a short time later, "that lots will be drawn." The announcement sent an immediate chill down every man's spine. "One out of every forty soldiers will be selected." He looked around dolefully. "So please fall into your division's line and may the gods protect you." Lysander made a sign before stepping away.

Men long known to each other, sometimes even family and kin, were made to select lots against themselves. All in all, 150 men drew up short and were selected to be killed and eaten. It was a heinous affair. The condemned men lined up, quiet and dejected, to have their throats slit in groups. The men who cut cried piteous tears while those they sliced clutched helplessly at their torn open gullets as friends and supporters held and hugged them, weeping into death. Their collective tears and lamentations reached up to the very heavens above.

After the selected unfortunates had been sacrificed, they were then butchered out of sight. Following that, a thick soup was prepared and served out in hearty portions to all of the men who were still breathing. Nobody said a word during the meal that followed, but many were heard crying or sobbing between bites and swallows. A funeral service was held later that night where the leftover remains were dutifully buried with full honors.

With their bellies thus full of dead brethren, the dejected remnants of the Great Army prepared to wait out one more long night before breaking free at dawn.

When that new day's gray period of morning finally came into being, the men were ready. Everyone there knew his duty, and none intended to allow the previous day's atrocity to have been paid in vain. Prior to starting, General Alaric stepped in front of his men and said a few words.

"Soldiers," he started bleakly. "We exist now only in blackness." His countenance was morose and severe. "The only light," the general pointed to that of which he spoke, "exists back there, on the other side of that mountain." A short pause next followed where he searched around at the forlorn faces. "When we leave here," General Alaric carried on, "there will be no mercy." They were not beaten around the bush. "You will not be allowed to surrender your arms," their commander reminded them once more of what they themselves had seen already. "If you give up the fight," the point was crystalized, "then you give up living." His eyes flashed determinedly through the crowd.

The attending infantry murmured their tacit approval and understanding.

"Stay together and keep moving," their general next commanded them. "Remember," Alaric detailed further, "you've just got to keep by this route," He was again pointing back towards the way they'd come. "And the mountains will be there in two days' time."

His men felt a glimmer of hope.

"So, it's every hand to his sword, spear, or bow," their general concluded. "And don't forget our dear brothers' sacrifices!"

A few hardy cheers with as many shouts went up from the surrounding mass of sobered troops who were then dismissed and ordered to make themselves ready with as little gear as possible. They were assembled soon after at the staging area with the divisions in line for an attack column. When the all-ready call was given and received, the gates were thrown open and the army started to move out on the double.

Generals Lysander and Alaric, along with their three split divisions, managed to make it almost an entire league outside the camp without any incident. When they came around the bend to where General Vega's charge had reached previously, however, they saw the carnage and grew more afraid. The dead were lying everywhere, as thick as carpet in some places. All of their men were stripped bare with the armor removed.

The entire roadway was filled with corpses, and though they had been there for less than a week, the stench was unbearable. Black buzzing clouds of horrid flies flew incessantly all around them as they continued to move forward. The forest was silent. After managing to pass through these scenes of devastation, however, the roadway eventually cleared, and the sun started shining. Birds could be heard in the trees again, and for just a little while, some men started to whisper of life. It was still early in the afternoon when the two generals discovered that an army was blocking their path in the roadway.

For a split second, the two leaders became intoxicatingly excited as they saw the bronze metal shimmering in the sunlight. All too soon it became obvious, however, that the armor being worn by the tribesmen had been pilfered from their own dead.

"We must push forward, men." This time it was Lysander who rallied the troops, refusing to give in. "We must break through or die!" he screamed before readying himself for the plunge. The generals both raised their swords up high and pointed them forward at the enemy before shouting, "Exsultay!" at the top of their lungs. Their exhortation continued with strength and vigor. "Exsultay!" The other soldiers began to take up the call of martial prowess as well.

The hungry, desolate and worn-down men of the three lost divisions dug deep to find their last reserves of strength and courage. Every man steeled himself for this final effort as they cried out, "Exsultay!" along with their chiefs.

When the fervor was judged ripe, General Lysander let the hounds off their leashes and bellowed out an, "Attack!" call while he and Alaric began to charge. Their soldiers behind them started to follow while letting loose their own desperate shouts of war. The tribesman in the roadway, meanwhile, made no moves at all as they watched the incautious runaways sprint nearer.

While General Alaric and Lysander's men were beginning to close the gap between them, they both saw only too late the flood of fighters who were suddenly pouring out from their flanks. There was no time to halt the attack, however, as their two sides were slammed together and another violent melee ensued.

Seeing their own men now on the attack and the two generals with an exposed vanguard continuing to push forward, the mass of tribesmen in the roadway began to scream and yowl. At some unseen order that followed, the previously stationary force launched itself into a full broadside, colliding together with the generals' troops like two waves on an opposing track.

Again, the fighting was savage and fierce. Only this time the hand-to-hand combat was against well-armored soldiers using the same weapons that they had. Casualties were therefore much higher as the three divisions were encircled on all sides and battered remorselessly like a lee shore. Hours passed with thousands dying before news came that General Lysander was dead as well. By then there were just hundreds left anyway. It was only the onset of darkness that stopped any further fighting as the contestants could no longer see where their blows struck or from whence others came.

General Alaric did his men proud that day by fighting valiantly throughout the battle, receiving many injuries both slight and moderate in the affair. He and the last remaining four hundred or so beat-up and spent survivors endured a wretched night in the road amongst the dead. Some lucky few managed to fall asleep, and those who did slept soundly atop the bodies, such was the level of their own exhaustion. For the rest, however, the incessant yips, howls, and impending doom were all too great to ignore, so as tired as they felt, sleep still did not come.

"What are we going to do, General?" some of his men asked him in gloomy desolation as the night grew thicker, hoping for some kind of miracle.

Alaric knew that he had little left to offer them now except for hard truth, so the issue was laid out plainly. "We have tried to surrender ourselves numerous times," the general struck straight to the point, "and they have only killed us for it." The reality was very discouraging.

"Perhaps, now that we are so few, they may let us live?" one of his few remaining officers conjectured.

"It's possible," Alaric agreed, "but nothing that we've seen so far makes it seem likely."

"Maybe they will take us as slaves?" a petrified young lieutenant tried to think optimistically.

"Let us wait until tomorrow comes and see what the gods decide," their general calmed them, despite his own misgivings. "For now, you all should try to get some rest."

The remaining night passed hot and sticky but without further incident. Hours passed by slowly until the first light of dawn brought with it a dim radiance that slowly grew brighter as the sun rose into the sky. The last remaining soldiers slowly gathered up their things and milled about, checking for any food or water amongst the enemy dead. As soon as it was light enough to see clearly, however, the men discovered that they were completely surrounded. A ring of thousands was standing guard around them, watching silently.

The survivors all gathered close together into a group facing outward with General Alaric still leading them, searching for a way out. Eventually, the back ranks of the tribesmen started to open and move out of the way to allow for a group of importantly dressed figures to come forward. Only one of the men spoke, however, once they'd arrived about a stone's throw away from the unchained captives.

"You came here seeking death and plunder," the elder tribesman accused them with a grainy voice and clear conscience. "So tell us now," he tilted his head like a philosopher might, "have you not found everything you wanted?"

"These men here are defeated," Alaric ignored the question and beckoned behind himself to the hundreds of soldiers that were still under his command. Not a single one left there was unhurt or uninjured, many seriously. "Please allow us to surrender," the general negotiated. "Even slavery is better than a certain death," he entreated further on behalf of his rabble.

"We do not keep slaves here," the elder replied, a little discordantly. "Nor do we suffer any to be kept." His grey eyes were thoughtful but severe.

"So, then what is to become of us?" The general asked the all-important question. He and the others awaited his response with a breathless trepidation.

"You shall all die here." The blow was brutal.

The general made to protest along with the others, but it was no use. Without another word, the mysterious group turned away and began walking back through their own ranks toward the forest. Upon their exiting the ring of warriors, those left surrounding the last stand lowered their spears and began to slowly close in for the kill.

Men despaired, cursed, and begged. Still a few others fought, including the general, but were quickly dispatched by the overwhelming wall of blades. Those who remained quickly became terrified and pitiful as they climbed and clamored over top of one another to try and get away into the fast-disappearing center. Victims cried out in agonizing pain and suffering as they were stabbed repeatedly through by the shrinking box. Not a single soldier was left alive as each and all were stripped and made bare with their bloodied corpses left behind for the beasts and the carrion to feed on.

Chapter 31

It was mid-morning when Pan finally arrived with Beocca in tow to a small wooden door that was built into the grassy knoll of an earthen hovel. He knocked excitedly.

"Who lives here?" Beocca tried to ask him as the entranceway flew open.

"Pan!" the shocked and amazed voice cried out in felicity, quickly sweeping him off his feet and into a hug that was held suffocatingly tight. This made Beocca feel more at ease. "Well now," the old woman started to question after finishing his greeting. "Who's this then?" she inquired while placing him down.

"This is my friend, Nana." Pan looked between them with a happy grin.

"How lovely," the old woman spoke warmly. "And does your friend have a name?" she gently pushed for Beocca to tell her by speaking in her direction.

The small girl dragged one of her toes on the ground in pointed circles as she squeaked out shyly and without peeping up, "My name's Beocca."

The grandmother smiled. "It's a mighty fine pleasure to meet you, Miss Beocca," said Nana while reaching out to give a light squeeze on the cheek, causing her face to rise. "Why, what beautiful green eyes you have." the old woman complimented, taken aback after first seeing them, causing their owner's face to brighten. After this charm was given, their hostess then guessed expectantly, "I bet you two must be hungry?"

"Oh yes ma'am." Beocca and Pan's eyes each widened like saucers. "My stomach's been talking for hours!" she exclaimed with giggles, quickly regaining her confidence.

"We haven't eaten since yesterday, Nana," the shepherd boy emphasized, trying to impress her.

"Bless your sweet souls," she sympathized sincerely. "You're probably starving then." Nana pointed them over to the table in the next room. "You all go and sit down there," she directed kindly, "and I'll bring you over something shortly."

With their mouths now watering, Pan took Beocca by the hand and led her to the wooden surface that had a workbench underneath. "What is this place?" Beocca again asked him after sitting.

Pan looked around at the cozy dwelling which now spilled in light from around the windows that invited the new day inside. "Okay," he told her. "I can tell you now."

"Tell me what, silly?" Beocca wondered humorously.

"Everything," the shepherd boy earnestly revealed.

Beocca's countenance changed capriciously into seriousness, the same way that a child's does before hearing some whispered secret. "What is it?" She was nearly lost by captivation.

Pan began to share his story with her. "The whole army is dead now," he divulged first, leaving her crestfallen.

"Everybody?" she repeated painfully, waiting for more clarity.

"Everybody," the shepherd boy confirmed back what he'd been told.

Beocca started to cry.

"What's wrong?" Pan asked her worriedly, not understanding why. "I thought you hated the army?"

"I do!" she despaired openly, causing the grandmother to glance into the room. "But some of the people there were nice," Beocca kicked around the statement bashfully.

Pan sank his head in a dejected manner. "I know," he agreed with her while remembering Matrius, who was assumed dead. "But that's why I saved you," the shepherd boy explained endearingly, returning his gaze on to level. "I knew that you were a good person."

Beocca sniffed and snorted as she grieved for the many fine people lost. "But how did you know what would happen?" she hit upon curiously once her mind had broached the subject.

"Our chief took me," he noted heavily and with a pause, "after my family died."

"But how did they die?" interrupted Beocca with an innocent's candor.

"I was with my daa and two brothers," Pan remembered darkly. "On the other side of the mountain," he informed. "They sent me to find one of our sheep that was up on the ridgeline," the boy explained. "It had gone astray, you see."

Beocca nodded.

After hesitating for a moment, the shepherd continued. "While I was there, horsemen came." Pan began to grit his teeth as he relived the scene. "I could see them," Beocca found out, "but they didn't see me."

"How come?" His companion was looking increasingly sad as the tale unwound further.

"Because I hid behind some rocks." He looked at her, shame-faced and distraught. "They killed my daa first." The shepherd boy winced from the memory's pain. "Then when my two brothers tried to run away," he sniffled and wiped away some forming tears, "they were chased down and killed too." Pan became upset. "I saw them laughing while they did it," his embittered voice announced coldly.

Beocca felt scared from this accounting, but she patted him anyway, and before he had time to finish, his Nana interrupted them.

"It's ready," she introduced herself from across the room as their hot food was carried over. The scent was tantalizing. "This here is rabbit stew," notified their chef while placing the bowls down. "And a fresh piece of bread to go with it," the old woman added as extra. "I just baked it yesterday!" his grandmother delighted.

"Thank you, Nana," Pan politely accepted, remembering back to that first dinner with Tarwin and Korballa inside the camp. It seemed so long ago now.

"Thank you, Nana," Beocca copied him sweetly before picking up her spoon and starting to dig in with zeal.

Pan's caretaker smiled at the pair. "If you want anymore, don't be afraid to say so," she instructed them while their mouths were full. "I've got plenty more." His Nana chuckled while leaving the room. The chickens needed feeding also.

After a few minutes were spent satiating their gnawing stomachs, Beocca redirected to her opening concerns. "But how did you know about the army?" she was still trying to figure it out.

"The chief told me," Pan explained, leaving his family behind, "after I brought back the sheep and told everyone what had happened."

"What did they say when they heard?" Beocca leaned in.

"There was a great meeting of the elders," Pan gossiped freely. "And when it was done, they sent me to live with them; me and all my sheep," recollected the shepherd.

"Why?" Beocca still did not understand him.

"So they could teach me what to say when the army came," Pan enlightened her.

"But how did they know it was coming?" The young girl was becoming adorably exasperated.

"Others told us," Pan rethreaded their past. "Survivors and refugees from the lowlands warned our elders that those first horsemen were just the eyes," Pan pronounced confidently his people's history while he continued to eat. "And that the body would eventually arrive to follow." The prediction had proved accurate.

Such abstract notions didn't make much sense to Beocca at her age. "So they're the ones who told you what to do?" She was more interested in learning.

"Mostly." Pan nodded his head in the affirmative. "They didn't tell me everything though," he contemplated his rape furtively.

"Couldn't they have chosen someone else?" Beocca tinkered with reason. "How come they picked you?"

"I volunteered," Pan narrowed the shadow.

"But why?" she wanted to grasp.

"Because only vengeance can wash away hatred," he imparted a cold stare into the void before quickly cracking open a smile. "And besides," he joked, "I was the only shepherd left in the tribe."

Beocca flashed her teeth. "Do you think the general knew it was you?" she posited.

"It doesn't matter," Pan responded flippantly.

"Why not?" The girl was perplexed.

"Because I do," he stated with all the ferocity of a young lion just as his docile Nana entered the room.

In the days that followed, Pan took Beocca all around his and the neighboring villages. He showed her many trails and cut throughs which led from one town to the next along with lots of hidden gems and treasures along the way. She especially loved swimming at the waterfall.

Within a fortnight there was a huge parade and celebration, the biggest one that either of them had ever seen. Weapons, armor, and wealth were all marched past to great fanfare In the nearby towns as the waving throngs threw kisses and blessings toward their high-born leaders riding atop the great war elephants rumbling by. Many thousands of horses were also seen being ridden as well where before they had possessed none. They were now an incredible force to be reckoned with despite the huge losses in manpower. Their casualties had been enormous.

A few months later when all the celebrations had ended and the remembrances were done, Pan and Beocca found themselves playing beside a pond that was rimmed by shade trees with their growing herd of sheep grazing close by. During a rest from their latest exertions, while laying on their backs and looking up at the sky, Beocca pondered randomly the thought.

"Pan," the girl talked over, catching his attention.

"Yea," he inflected back, waiting to hear what she would have to say.

"Why did they have to kill them all?" She was speaking about the army that had held her captive. "Why couldn't they have just talked to them instead?"

"Because you can't reason with a tiger, Beocca," Pan lessoned her. "You can either kill it," he meted out, "or risk having it kill you."

The girl only nodded and said nothing with her head lost up in the clouds.

Epilogue

The fire turned to embers and cooled with short bursts of flames erupting out of it periodically. It had at one time burned brightly, backlighting the story's illumination. Now it only served as charred remains, a sort of burnt clock that was all but out of time. The audience stayed there still and silent, waiting to see if any more words would be spoken as the crickets and toads sang songs in the near distance.

"But what about Yusri and Grieves, Grandpa?" a little one shouted, overcome with curiosity.

"Yea!" came the concurrence of many voices from amongst the crowd who now wondered the same.

The village patriarch chuckled softly before speaking. "As to what happened to those two," the old elder eluded. "I think that their adventure is a story best left for another night," he disappointed them mightily.

A collective chorus of light-hearted complaints could be heard coming from the children in attendance. Their fomenting wave of rebellion, however, was stopped short as the parents, who had only recently come down to retrieve them, stepped forward to intercede.

"Alright, alright," the adults butt in on the storyteller's behalf. "That's enough tales for one night," they said as the moms and dads began to scout for their little ones.

Ralla and Agarus's mother commented to her husband directly, "I swear he adds more blood and guts every time he tells that story." She shook her head disapprovingly, causing the father's laughter. "They'll probably have nightmares for a week!"

"I'm sure he wasn't trying to scare them, love," the husband offered as he gave a kiss to his honeypot on the cheek, leading her to smile. "It just makes for a better story is all," the father tried to be forgiving.

"Look, Agarus!" Ralla pushed onto her younger brother's shoulder to get his attention ahead of pointing. "Mom and Daa are here to get us."

Bodi started to stand up with the others while Agarus began waving in their direction. "We're over here!" he yelled, causing his mother's eyes to find them.

"Bye, Ralla," Bodi made to go. "I'll be at the river tomorrow if you feel like joining us," he blushed while inviting her.

Ralla grinned mischievously. "Okay," she accepted the offer. "See you tomorrow then." Their plan was cemented just as her parents reached them.

"So did you two like the story?" their father wanted to know as they headed for the trail leading back home.

"Yea, I did!" Agarus shouted with glee before he began to relive some of the many furious scenes of combat, punching and kicking off into the night air beside them.

"I liked it too," Ralla admitted. "But I also thought it was very sad."

"So did I," her mother chimed in. "War is such a dreadful thing."

After a few more minutes spent walking beneath those towering trees, the familial bunch returned to their warm-lit dwelling. The same fireflies, or perhaps they were new ones now, sometimes flashed within the darkness to give off a sudden glow of light.

"Straight to bed now, you two!" their mother called upon entering the house and closing the front door.

The brother and sister duo joked and played enroute to their final destination, throwing on night garments as they did in preparation for sleeping. Their parents came to tuck them in a short time later.

"What happened to Yusri and Grieves?" Agarus asked his mother while she was pulling up the covers.

"You'll have to wait and hear for yourself," she left him in doubt.

"But did they live?" he wondered worriedly, causing both his parents to smile.

"Yes, son," his father relieved him. "They lived."

"I'm glad," Ralla added. "I liked them."

"So did we," their parents agreed prior to kissing them both goodnight. On the way out, their mother stopped just short of the door and took one last look into the room before gently clicking it closed right behind her.

The End

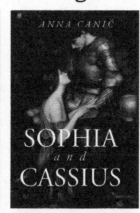
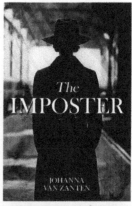
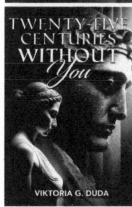
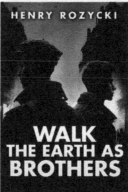